THE
FATED BORN SERIES
BOOK ONE

FATED BORN

D1452959

Kristin L. Hamblin

FATED BORN

Kristin L Hamblin – kristinlhamblin.com

Copyright © 2022 by Crown of Laurel Press

© Cover design: Franziska Stern - www.coverdungeon.com - Instagram: @coverdungeonrabbit

Editing by Kelley Lynn of Cookie Lynn Publishing Services

Map by Angel Perez

ISBN: 978-1-959230-00-7

Library of Congress Control Number: 2022916159

For my daughters. Never stop working for your dreams.

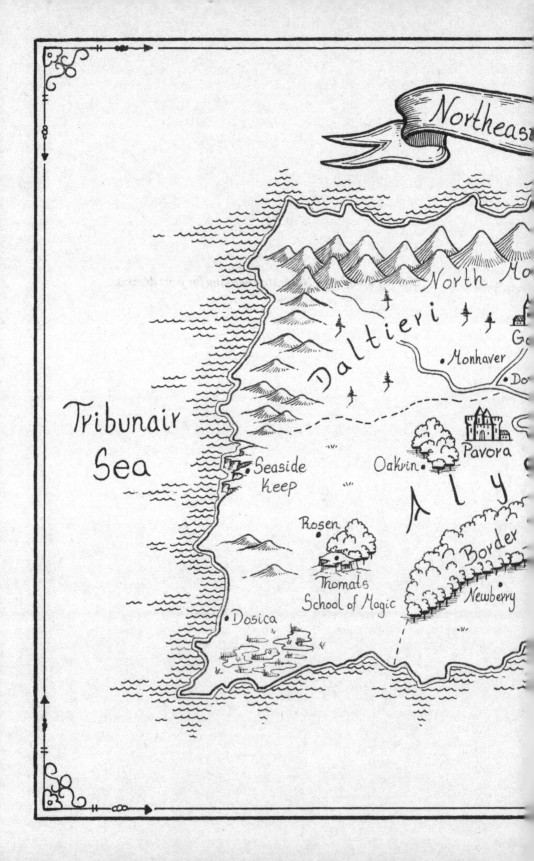

CHAPTER
ONE

Centuries of habit plastered the smile on Ardenis's face. It was what humans did, or at least what everyone here thought humans did, so it was what he did too. In fact, as Ardenis crossed through the stone courtyard, sandals slipping over smooth rock, everyone he met wore various versions of the same smile. Their matching blue robes smattered the otherwise clean, sunny space.

"Good morning, Amalia," Ardenis said, spotting her. She was a watcher of mortals, like him.

Amalia locked eyes, but frowned in his direction. He tilted his head, studying her as she made to pass him by.

Had Amalia been emotionally altered? It wasn't his calling to enforce the rules, though if she'd been altered—

But then her smile appeared. It looked as forced as his felt.

Ardenis watched her over his shoulder as he left the courtyard behind. He shrugged, swishing past rows of sweet-smelling roses in constant bloom in this world where rain didn't exist, the weather always perfect. The watchtower loomed ahead, where he worked observing the world below and its inhabitants in order to pass along information to the council. The stacked stone towered several stories high, the tallest structure in Acantha.

Inside the white-domed space, morning light from the tall windows cast over the motionless forms of the night watchers, still deep within the thrall of observing the mortal world of Thera.

The watch window, an elevated pool of white marble filled with pristine water, beckoned, and Ardenis took his seat before it. Though they didn't have magic like Thera, he liked to think of the window as their own form of it, allowing them to see another world.

He rested his arms on the hard ledge and breathed a quiet sigh. Mortal humans would call it contentment, if such emotions existed here in Acantha. Even after countless millennia, the devotion to his calling hadn't diminished.

More people filed inside, smiling and nodding hello. The council dictated that everyone in Acantha wear the same blue robes, but gave allowances for hairstyles, so long as they kept with the current trends on Thera. Ardenis preferred his jaw-length and disheveled.

He focused on the smooth water, so white in its marble casing it almost glowed. A soft, round light appeared on the surface of the pool, and then an image formed of the world below—the earthen realm. Someday, when it was his turn, he'd go there and be born to a mortal body.

Ardenis stared until the image seemed to surround him, until he seemed to actually be there, floating in the sky. From this vantage, the forests of Thera were puffy shapes of green hugging the contours of the land below, broken only by the expansive blue of the Tribunair Sea, the deep red of the Sengi Desert, and the grey of North Mountain jutting toward where he sat in premortal Acantha. The names of the landscape changed over time, depending on who ruled and the language.

Floating above the land, yet still rooted in his chair in the watchtower, he waited patiently for the Fates to guide him. Soon, a gentle tug to his middle directed him where to go.

Like a diving eagle, Ardenis's vision soared past dense forests and sprawling fields, through small towns of humble homes and bigger cities clogged with merchants and stone buildings, until he viewed a family farm in the heart of the kingdom of Alysies.

The slow trickle of a lazy creek flowed nearby, dividing a cow pasture from grain crops. The wind gusted and whipped the trees surrounding the sizable plot of land, sending the green summer foliage to crackle and flutter.

Ardenis closed his eyes, listening to the rustling and imagining how the kiss of a warm summer wind might feel on his cheek. It was the same with snow, or a spring rain—sensations he'd never experienced, only seen. He longed for them, in truth, but those thoughts were dangerous.

He squeezed his eyes tighter. No one should want for more than this existence, lest an enforcer learn of it and report them for being emotionally altered.

His time to be born to Thera would come. One day, when his instincts aligned with his desire to leave. He hadn't felt the nudge to make that choice yet.

Not far from a modest farmhouse, a young man propped his axe against a chopping block and wiped sweat from his brow. His billowy ivory shirt clung to him over simple, dirt-stained trousers. He stacked wood in neat lines, sun-blond hair hanging loose over brown eyes, framing a strong jawline. He was lean in the way most farmers were in this region, working as long as the sun would let them, to produce just enough not to go hungry.

A reassuring tug pulled at Ardenis's middle. He nodded to himself. While the boy and his humble circumstances appeared inconsequential, all events in the history of Thera started with a simple moment. Perhaps he'd have a Fating of the future to share with the council.

Ardenis kept his gaze trained on the boy, trusting the Fates put him here for a reason. A force even higher than the council, which governed everyone's instincts, the Fates were unpredictable. There was an importance surrounding the young man—an awareness

Ardenis had developed over the years. He only needed to watch long enough to find out what it was.

Toward the end of the day, the farm boy joined an older, grayer version of himself—likely his father—inside a slightly leaning, faded barn. They pitched fresh hay together into four small stalls. An old mare watched them, occasionally lipping at the bucket of water on a stool.

The father stuck his pitchfork upright in the ground, causing the horse to flick its ears. "Tomorrow I want to get an early start on those fields." He dipped a ladle into the bucket and took a drink. "You've done good today."

The boy accepted the praise with a hint of a smile, sticking his pitchfork next to his father's. He took the ladle and drank as well, wiping his mouth of stray drips with the back of his hand. "The coyotes have been at the chickens again, Pa. I was thinking of staying up late and seeing if I could trap one, or maybe kill it with my bow." He looked at his shoes, scuffing the toe of one in the loose hay and dirt.

His father watched him beneath bushy eyebrows, taking the ladle and another slow sip of water. "Sure, Damian," he said, though it sounded almost like a question. "That's a fine idea. Can I tell your mother to expect a new pelt?"

"Of course." Damian's smile lit up, and Ardenis leaned closer to the watch window. He'd had too much time viewing mortals not to be able to read them. The boy was hiding something. Could this be why Ardenis's instincts had brought him here?

With a shake of his head, Damian's father trudged up the dusty trail to the farmhouse. The sun slid to the horizon, as would the sun in Acantha. Ardenis's watch was ending and his friends would be expecting him. The daily routine of a thousand millennia took over, pulling his brief excitement over the simple farm boy to a close. He focused, shifting his vision out of Thera and back to Acantha, the vibrant green world fading to the white of the watchtower.

His instincts slammed into him, and his eyes widened. *So strong!*

He'd never felt his instincts so strong. They forced him back to the boy.

Patience replaced shock as Ardenis waited, steady with the knowledge he was meant to be here. His friends would understand the delay, maybe even expect it after all the times he'd kept them waiting when he'd stayed longer in the watchtower.

Damian sat on an overturned feed bucket, alternating his gaze between the road that led from his property and a piece of wood he whittled, shavings piling between his shoes. When the only light left in the farmhouse was a candle in the front window, Damian stood and walked toward the woods, abandoning a set of bow and arrows.

Someone laughed from within the trees bordering the road. A girl, though Ardenis couldn't see more than the shadow of her. Even with the ability to be anywhere and everywhere, watchers could not see in the dark.

"Eva," Damian called out in a loud whisper. His whole countenance had lit up upon hearing that laugh.

The leaves crunched as she moved.

Damian chuckled and jogged toward the sound, glancing once back at his house. He took a step into the dark tree line. The mature oaks with their full canopy of summer foliage blocked the disappearing twilight. Damian paused.

"Eva," he said a little louder.

No sound.

"Please, I'm begging you, don't make me wait a moment longer." He absently broke a twig off a branch.

Eva laughed and stepped from behind a nearby tree into the moonlight.

Ardenis inhaled.

She was beautiful. No more than seventeen, with fine brown hair piled high in a loose bun on her head, pieces cascading around her face. Her skin was flawless, like smooth satin, and flushed with excitement. Her elegant green dress hugged her body from neck to waist, then flowed loose and shiny down to her ankles. The fine attire was a stark contrast to Damian's dingy farmer's garb.

Damian approached with a slow smile and placed a hand gently against her cheek.

Ardenis blinked. He'd lingered too long. He needed to end his watch *now*. Before a rule was broken.

Eva raised her face to Damian. Ardenis locked onto her and stopped. Her green eyes were stunning—but not because of the color. Because of what they said as she gazed upon Damian and he pulled her in close. A thousand words poured from her silent gaze, a conversation more meaningful than the voices of the greatest kings or most powerful mages.

Ardenis felt like an intruder on their stolen moment, which was ridiculous. It was his duty to watch Thera and report the findings to the council.

Except he couldn't report this moment to the council, could he? He wasn't supposed to be here.

Ardenis swallowed hard. He always reported anything of note to the council. Always.

Eva searched Damian with a scorching intensity, barely blinking so as to not miss a second of him. Her eyes held the look of—

No.

Ardenis wrenched himself out of Thera, his vision blurring with the struggle. He blinked hard and focused on the white walls of the watch room. Quiet. Familiar. The other watchers, mostly night watch now, sat around the marble pool. No one looked his way. They didn't suspect he'd almost made a mistake. The council and their enforcers couldn't know how close he'd come to breaking the most important rule a watcher had.

Do not observe mortal love.

In all his years, he'd never observed a private moment between lovers. It was forbidden. Romantic love did not exist in Acantha. Acanthians were souls awaiting their time to leave this world and be born in the mortal world. They didn't have children or family—that's what Thera was for.

His instincts ratcheted, nearly pulling him back to Thera against his will. His gaze shot to the water, clean and clear. Fate wanted him to watch this moment.

What would happen if he did?

What would happen if he didn't?

Ardenis closed his eyes against the strain, like strong hands shoving his chest, the way humans sometimes did to each other on Thera, only harder, and over and over in time with his beating heart.

Go back, go back, go back!

But if he trusted the Fates, he'd break the council's rules.

Unease pooled in Ardenis's stomach. It was too much. He relented, turning his focus back onto the couple.

Damian pressed a kiss to Eva's fingertips. Pulling her in closer, he slowly leaned forward. With a soft smile, Eva lifted her mouth to his. Their lips met in the sweetest kiss never seen by a watcher of Thera.

Their kiss was gentle, and tender, and full of...

Ardenis gripped his chair.

It was love. Ardenis was watching true love. The kind forbidden to him and anyone in Acantha. The kind they had been warned not to watch.

Why did the Fates want him to witness this?

A stirring within his soul sent Ardenis's heart fluttering. These two mortals loved each other. And it was beautiful, so much more than he'd imagined it could be every time he'd looked away.

It could only just be this once. He'd be okay if it was just this once. Sweat coated his palms. He'd seen what happened to those whose human emotions awoke prematurely, marking them emotionally altered.

Exile to the Dark Unknown.

"Damian!" the young man's father shouted from the front porch.

The couple jumped and broke apart, laughing. Damian pulled Eva into a careful jog, dodging branches and tree roots, fleeing deeper into the thick woods. The moon had risen enough to shine in slanted beams through the trees, lighting their way. Damian looked over his shoulder, and Ardenis saw what he saw—Eva, a picture of happiness and young beauty. Wisps of her hair blew loose in the wind, and fireflies danced in the trees around them, reflecting into her eyes so full of love.

Ardenis's breathing sped. It was madness. Through all the history he'd witnessed over the millennia, he'd taken every step to remain neutral—to maintain the emotional veil and serve in his duty as a watcher. Acantha couldn't function without the vital information watchers provided, allowing everyone to learn of humans and prepare their souls for the life that awaited. If watchers were to learn of love and brought that dangerous emotion back into Acantha, Ardenis didn't even want to contemplate the far-reaching consequences. But the consequence to his eternal life should he become emotionally altered and was caught? He shuddered.

And still, he couldn't make himself stop. Didn't want to stop.

Damian dodged behind a thick oak tree, pulling Eva with him. They held each other, muffling their laughter against one another. They kissed again, not so gently this time. Passionately, hungrily, their breathing turning ragged.

Ardenis's lips parted.

Damian's father's voice, muffled by the trees, sounded again from a distance.

"I must go," Damian said between kisses.

"No, not yet. Just a little longer," Eva pleaded as he pulled away. "We have so little time." She tried to tug him to her for another kiss.

Ardenis leaned forward, enthralled.

"I'll walk you back to your aunt's." His lips moved against hers as he spoke. "But first I have to say something. Your father is lord of these lands, and I'm nobody—"

Eva scoffed and pushed away from him. He caught her wrists on his chest and pulled her back.

"Let me finish." He spoke with patience, rubbing his thumb over her hand, pure adoration in his tender gaze. "Your father's lord of these lands, and I'm nobody, but I would crawl on hands and knees to the ends of Thera for you."

Her eyes twinkled, and she wrapped both arms around his neck, pulling him closer and claiming his lips in a deep kiss.

Like a fist unclenching, the pull of his instincts eased. The demand to view the couple was gone.

Ardenis ended his watch, coming back to himself in the tower. His instincts didn't protest this time. The familiarity of the white-domed room wasn't enough to help his heart resume its normal pace or gain control of his breathing.

Romantic love, they'd been warned, could change his very soul, and he'd witnessed it anyway. A power beyond any magic on Thera, more potent than any mages' spell.

His breath shook. What had he done?

CHAPTER

TWO

Ardenis sat at the watch window, elbows propped on the marble ledge. He squeezed his palms into his eyes, trying to push the image of Eva and her tender gaze from his mind. Shame and satisfaction filled him simultaneously, competing for attention he didn't know how to give.

When he dropped his hands, Hector's gaze bore into him from across the room.

Ardenis stopped cold. As a rule enforcer working directly for the council, Hector was bound to report anything he deemed as rule breaking.

Hector's blank expression gave nothing away. Motionless at the side of the room in his pressed robe, his stiff black hair framed a face that always appeared clenched and sour. He'd turned watchers over to the council if they failed to distance themselves, became too emotionally involved. Some had been from Ardenis's own recommendation.

Ardenis nodded to the rule enforcer, willing his heart to slow.

Hector looked away.

Ardenis stood slowly, quietly, hoping not to portray his guilt.

Guilt. Something he'd never experienced before. He'd never had to hide anything. Was he already affected?

Hector followed him outside into the temperate night air. Ardenis kept his gaze ahead. He made for the council hall, forcing his steps to slow and ignoring Hector behind him.

As on Thera, it was dark outside the watchtower with time running congruently between the worlds. Moonlight brushed the stone walkway and bathed the distant buildings in shades of blue, but offered no comfort from Hector's looming presence.

Ardenis wished it would rain. Rain would wash over him and he'd forget the way Eva's lips had brushed against Damian's. Rain would hide him from what he'd done. But it never rained in Acantha.

Hector's pace increased until he finally fell into step beside him.

"A word, Ardenis Watcher Fater," Hector said, pleasantly enough.

Ardenis didn't slow. "How may I assist you, Enforcer?"

"You seemed to be in a state when you ended your watch." Hector's tone almost sounded accusatory. "Is there anything you need to report?"

Ardenis's shoulders tightened. The questioning wasn't unusual —it was their duty, after all—but still. Watchers could ill afford to cross wills with an enforcer. Or have the wrong kind of attention on them.

Ardenis didn't look at him. "Yes, at times watching isn't as pleasant as the council likes the people of Acantha to believe," he said. "I worked past my watch today, and need rest." Not a lie, never a lie. Acanthians didn't know what it meant to lie. Only watchers did.

Hector continued to trail him, so Ardenis stopped outside of the council hall beside the regional bulletin board, a normal, unsuspecting place to stand. Rose petals drifted on the slight breeze. Torchlight flickered, causing shadows to dance and sway.

Hector cleared his throat. "I expect the council to receive a full report, then."

"Of course, Enforcer. Goodnight." Ardenis faced the bulletin board, pretending to read the latest news from the council.

Everything the watchers observed, they passed on to the council. If deemed worthy to share, they posted it here. All so they could mimic mortals, but without mortal emotions, preparing for their future lives. The smiling and waving. Everyone was polite to everyone in Acantha. They didn't know how else to be—how else it would be when they became mortal.

He didn't breathe until Hector nodded and walked out of sight.

Hector didn't suspect. Everything would be okay.

Ardenis blinked, finally noticing what he'd been pretending to read. Not the latest happenings on Thera, but the list of rules that governed each branch of Acantha. The rules, words ingrained in his every action, seemed to scream at him.

Watchers' Edict

- Attend the watchtower daily
- Observe mortal evolution
- Report observations only to the council in session
- Do not become partial or display partiality to any individual mortal or evolutionary event
- Do not observe mortal love
- Report any unusual emotions within yourself or others to the council or a rule enforcer

The pride he usually felt at those words and his long-standing service—over three-hundred thousand years—was chased away by that new, foreign sensation.

Guilt.

Acanthians appreciated what watchers did for them, bringing

news of the earthen realm. It was only through this news that they knew how to conduct their daily lives—what to eat and when, how to act, what to do in between work and sleep. And it was only through this news and their instincts that they knew when the time was right to be born, to leave premortal Acantha and begin their mortal lives on Thera.

Ardenis continued across the courtyard, mostly empty but for the looming council hall. He stared up at it. His feet had taken him where they always did at the end of a watch—directly to the people he now had to omit the truth from.

The council.

Tall marble columns lit with blazing torches wrapped around the building, their smoothness reflecting the orange glow of another beautiful night. A thick, tall grove of trees extended from either side like a fence, blocking him and every non-council member from seeing beyond. Council members, rarely seen outside their building, lived separately from the rest of Acantha, using rule enforcers to do their bidding.

Up a short set of stairs, Ardenis walked through the thick wooden doors, engraved with a map of the northeastern hemisphere of the mortal world. The picture represented the part of Thera this section of Acantha supplied souls to, and the part Ardenis spent his days watching. The gavel above it represented the council's rule and right to govern Acantha's strict laws.

In the foyer, dim with dark wood and sparse wall sconces, Sarafina Enforcer sat behind the desk, scrawling inside the record book. Ardenis nodded hello as she looked up.

He opened his mouth to speak, but the door to the council room burst open. Gharum Head Councilman stepped through, shoving a hand through his short black hair and adjusting his robe, stitched with the same emblem as on the council hall door.

Behind Gharum, two rule enforcers held a councilwoman up by her arms, gripping hard. The councilwoman's eyes were wide, like the mortals Ardenis had seen in distress when watching Thera.

"Ardenis Watcher Fater, do you come to report to the council?" Sarafina asked, her pleasant tone drawing Ardenis's gaze. She stared at him, even when the detained councilwoman kicked and thrashed. They dragged her out of the council hall, her screeching echoing back into the building.

Acanthians didn't act that way. The councilwoman was obviously emotionally altered. But how? The council didn't have access to view the mortal world and become subject to their emotions as watchers did.

Gharum remained by the door, watching Ardenis with a neutral expression highlighted by his pointy chin.

Ardenis turned back to Sarafina and smiled. "I do, thank you."

"Come in, Ardenis. We just finished." Gharum gestured him forward, though two others waited before him. They always sent Ardenis ahead of the line because of his gift.

Putting the unusual scene from his mind, Ardenis followed him through a short hall and into the chamber, where a murmur of conversations greeted him. A long, curtained window let in scant light from the torches outside, the light quickly absorbed by the dark wood lining the room. The council now sat silent, men and women smiling and waiting from their tiered benches. A few more trickled in from a side bring their number to around twenty.

Usually, ten members attended a session, but for Ardenis there was often double. They placed his findings in high regard. Though everyone in Acantha was the same age, he was the longest serving watcher—most couldn't handle the emotional influence for long. It was also his gift that drew everyone to him. The gift of Fating.

Ardenis took his place behind a podium in the center of a low platform and faced the room. His mind raced. What could he say about his watch today? Maybe it didn't matter. Maybe Damian and Eva's love wouldn't mean anything in the grandness of time.

Gharum Head Councilman stood at the front of the council members. "Ardenis Watcher Fater," he said. "What news do you bring the council?" His tone was calm, and the questions were familiar. He seemed completely unfazed by whatever had taken place in the room before.

Ardenis welcomed the comforting routine he'd repeated since the beginning of the human race, easing some of the tightness in his chest. "Today I watched Damian perform chores at his farm. Their techniques are rudimentary, offering nothing we haven't already seen." The technology in Acantha mirrored only the most advanced in Thera.

"Were you following your instincts?"

Ardenis nodded. "Yes. I haven't yet discovered why I'm meant to watch this mortal, but there's an importance surrounding him. The answer will come in time."

Gharum scanned the council, a pleasant smile on his face. "It's good to trust your instincts. Tell me more about this farm boy."

Ardenis's heart thumped in his chest. "Damian lives on humble land with his parents near the town of Oakrin. He's a hard worker, helping his father with the chores, but nothing of note to mention to the council." His voice shook on the last sentence—almost a lie. Ardenis tapped his finger against the podium. The truth, the words that would surely send him kicking and thrashing like the council member, didn't come.

Ardenis waited, hoping Gharum wouldn't question him further about Damian, or the interesting ways Damian spent his free time.

Gharum took a slow seat, crossing his ankles beneath his robe. "And what of Prince Isaac of Alysies?"

Ardenis released his pent-up breath. Prince Isaac, heir to the throne of Alysies, was a safe topic. Ardenis had observed him several times. "My instincts didn't compel me to watch Prince Isaac today. As of the last time I watched him, the prince has advanced in his sword training. He will make a fine king one day, if he survives into adulthood." Mortals were always inventing new ways to destroy each other, especially where kingdoms were concerned.

Ardenis couldn't deny he felt strongly for this particular mortal. Prince Isaac proved honest and trustworthy as Ardenis had watched him, and the kingdom of Alysies needed a strong leader to keep them from being overrun by their rival kingdoms. However, these feelings of impartiality were why he no longer watched the prince.

"Good." Gharum smiled, showing his teeth. "And has your gift revealed anything new?"

Many council members glanced up.

Ardenis blinked. His gift was unreliable and unpredictable, and of course he'd report it if he'd seen anything, but still the council asked each time. They wanted him to reveal the Fates.

Since the creation of Acantha, when all souls who were ever meant to be born were placed here, Ardenis had the gift of seeing Fatings or glimpses of the future—a blessing no one else possessed. Watchers only saw what happened in the present, but sometimes Ardenis saw events fated to happen.

His Fatings gave Acanthians a rare glimpse into the future of the mortal world they would all eventually be born into. They used their knowledge of Thera and the promptings of the Fates to choose when to be born. The Fates guided them with silent whispers in their ears or a gentle nudge they called instincts. Depending on what he saw—war and famine, peace and abundance—and how individual instincts reacted to it, the number of people who chose to be born usually changed, decreasing or increasing, making his Fatings big events.

Everything he'd ever Fated came to pass.

"Nothing today, Head Councilman."

Gharum watched him for a moment, and then nodded. "Thank you, Ardenis Watcher Fater. We appreciate the news of the mortal world that watchers provide."

Ardenis smiled, relieved. "I will keep watch and report." He nodded his head in the semblance of a bow and left the council hall a little more quickly than usual.

Outside, he sucked in air by the lungful. He'd made it through the council's questioning without having to lie, and without revealing what he'd done. He'd never omitted details of his watching before.

But, it was done. His lie was safe and the rule breaking could come to a stop.

They didn't suspect him.

Night insects chirped in the distance, and light flickered from the lampposts, bathing the cobbled pathways as his steps carried him toward home. It was much too late to meet his friends.

Row after row of identical white stucco houses lined both sides of the path. Azalea bushes of pink and white decorated the thick green grass lawns that never needed tending. Various community buildings rose above the homes in the distance, the soft yellows of candlelight peeking out the windows.

Ardenis knew Acantha was beautiful because of his time watching Thera—so clean and pure—but it lacked the diversity he enjoyed from the watch window. The people of Acantha had no need of diversity. They were here to do their duty until they chose to be born on Thera, and that was it.

That's enough, he reminded himself. He must remain neutral until his instincts and knowledge told him it was time to be born. Emotionless. Safe.

To violate council edict was to risk irreversible exile to the Dark Unknown.

He breathed deeply, inhaling the scent of cloying pollen.

A familiar glow began in front of his eyes—like the glow at the watch window when he viewed Thera. It startled him to a stop.

A Fating!

His heart thumped. He focused hard on the bright haze before him. The light became a blurred picture, and he stared into it, eager and unblinking. The Fates would show him what they wanted.

The blurriness shifted into an image—a mortal man. There was something familiar about him, though he'd never seen the man before. The mortal seemed to lock eyes with him, and Ardenis's breath caught in his throat. The man in the Fating was himself. They didn't resemble each other—Acanthians looked different when they were born, only retaining their gender. Yet, without a doubt it was him, he recognized his soul in that future body.

The man had blue eyes, striking in their pale shade, and long sandy hair—a sharp and welcome contrast to his current black, jaw-length style. He wore unusual clothing—trousers made of a material not yet invented, and a shirt in a style he had not seen. He stood on a street, but instead of stones or dirt, it had concrete—not a widely used material in Thera. Enormous buildings towered on either side of the street, taller than any yet in existence, with panes of glass lining top to bottom. It was similar to the Thera Museum in Acantha, but on a grandiose scale. Crowds of people walked beside the build-ings, slipping between and around one another in a great hurry. Self-propelled vehicles similar to carriages without horses clogged up the streets.

Though the weather didn't appear cold, and there were no clouds in the sky, snow fell around him, melting before it reached the ground. The man's eyebrows creased in puzzlement, and he stared at his reflection in the window. He wasn't alone. He beckoned to someone and called out a name, but Ardenis could not hear. His brow rose, eyes glinting with pure happiness. There was a ring on his finger, which could mean he was married.

The man's mouth curved up into an easy smile as a woman's right hand, smooth and youthful, wearing a silver ring of sapphires and diamonds entered the image. He took it and began to pull her into Ardenis's field of vision. The slenderness of her arm gave way to a narrow shoulder.

"Ardenis."

Ardenis jumped as someone grabbed his hand. The Fating vanished. The dark of night and the chirp of insects rushed in. His eyes widened and found Laida Transfer Leader, his longtime friend.

Her polite smile waited behind gray-blue eyes for his reply. "Why are you standing in the walkway?"

Ardenis shook his head slowly, mind muddled. He'd seen himself in the future, centuries from now—the furthest thing he'd ever fated.

He was fated to be born in the faraway future, in a much more advanced technological age.

"Ardenis?" Laida placed her hands on his shoulders and peered up at him, ever the concerned friend.

He cleared his throat. "I had a Fating."

"Just now? Outside the tower?" Practiced surprise colored her tone, and he nodded. She dropped her arms. "And I interrupted! I apologize."

He shook his head, swallowing. "No. It's as it was meant to be."

Laida leaned closer. "What did you see?"

Ardenis smiled, but pressed his lips together.

"I know. You can't tell me," she said, her tone conveying no sign of disappointment or exasperation, simply stating a fact. She took his arm and pulled him into a walk.

The quiet, peaceful night encircled them as she led him to her home, stars twinkling overhead. Why had the Fates shown him this? What would the council do with this Fating? What did it mean? He became keenly aware of the warmth of her arm as he walked her home in silence.

The images of Eva's kiss and the slender hand from his Fating competed for attention. He needed a distraction.

"Laida, I witnessed a councilwoman being escorted from the hall today. Was she born?" There weren't many options for someone who became emotionally altered like the councilwoman—a forced born or exile.

Laida would know. As the leader of the transfer hall for their region, which housed the gateways between Acantha and Thera, Laida oversaw them, including controlling how many could transfer to the mortal realm on any day.

Her golden braid slipped over her shoulder as she turned toward him, catching his eye. Not even the council could explain why she had golden hair when everyone else had black. But it suited her.

"Yes," she said. "Mevette Councilwoman."

She said this casually, as if someone losing their right to choose when to be born wasn't important—as if being forced to be born was of no consequence to her. Indeed, it wasn't, as it shouldn't be to him.

"Was she exiled?" he asked as they reached her door.

Laida tipped her oval face to him. "No, not exiled."

Good. It would take a truly serious crime to warrant that punishment. To be exiled to the Dark Unknown, never to experience the beauty and pain of a mortal life? Nothing could be worse.

Would that happen to him if he became emotionally altered?

Laida still watched him, waiting politely for the response he was supposed to offer. 'Goodnight,' or 'see you tomorrow.' But the way she looked up at him, head tilted, eyes intent on his next move, it was more than familiar. Endearing. As if staring into her eyes for the first time.

"Laida..." He trailed off. Suddenly whatever he was going to say seemed trivial.

She smiled and raised an eyebrow. The light from the lampposts reflected on her unguarded face.

"Um." He rubbed the back of his neck. "Goodnight."

"Goodnight, Ardenis." Laida's pleasant voice followed her as she turned away and went into her quaint house.

He blinked, like waking from a dream. What was he doing?

He made it to his own home a few lanes over. All the homes were basically the same. Like Laida's, his had a big pale-blue door with a small window, one bedroom, a living area, and a back terrace with a private bathing pool—a privilege because of his gift. There was no need for a kitchen. Acanthians ate all their meals at the public dining hall, and only recreationally. As with most everything else, they did it to mimic the lives that awaited them on Thera. Premortals had no need to eat to survive.

The arrangement was much better than it used to be. When the first humans slept in caves or makeshift shelters, so, too, did the premortals.

After lighting a lamp, Ardenis removed his robe and hung it in the wardrobe next to his spares. Bypassing the drawer of neatly folded nightclothes, he grabbed his journal, lit a candle, and crawled into his single bed. The movements were methodical, automatic. If he hadn't done them a million times, he might have skipped them entirely. He'd had a Fating—of himself.

Ardenis flipped to a blank page and paused. What could he say? That he'd witnessed love and was already planning on lying about it? The mere fact he was hesitant to put it on paper spoke volumes. But he could write about his Fating. At least that was safe. His mind wandered as the words flowed to the page.

What would he have seen if Laida hadn't interrupted? Why had the Fates wanted him to see himself, and in the future, no less? At least he knew he wouldn't be born anytime soon. Couldn't be, if his Fating came true, which it always did.

His quill slowed as realization dawned. His choice, the only true choice he had in this existence, was now taken from him. He was no longer free to be born when he wanted.

Ardenis gripped the quill to near breaking. He hadn't realized how deeply he'd relied on the hope it gave him, knowing he could be born if he wanted. When he couldn't stand one more second of this rainless, perfect existence, if the rigor of watching Theran history became too much, he could have left before. But not anymore. His time to be born was fated for the future.

An unfamiliar feeling of emptiness came over him. This would differentiate him; separate him from the rest of Acantha more than ever before, when the council heard his Fating.

The flickering candle cast light over the small room and the words he'd written describing himself in the future. Fire caused such destruction on Thera, but it couldn't hurt him—Acanthians couldn't get injured or die. He lifted his arm and let his hand drift closer to the flames. With a breath, he plunged his fingertips into the fire.

He felt nothing.

CHAPTER
THREE

A rdenis overslept—the first time that had ever happened. He stepped out his door, into the perfect weather, and frowned. He walked down the same stone pathway and couldn't stand the sight of it.

What was wrong with him?

At the dining hall, he collected his favorites of eggs and sausage, and then sat hunched over his breakfast and ate without enjoyment. It wasn't too late. He could still go on as if no rule had been broken.

He fixed a smile on his face, peering down the rows of his fellow Acanthians. They sat at the long tables and enjoyed a favorite mortal pastime. He caught several pairs of eyes. They watched him, and the other watchers, looking for examples of how mortals truly did things.

Conversations carried to him, relaying the latest gossip. The night watch had reported their mortal observations to the council, and what was deemed relevant had been posted. Prince Isaac was under threat of attack again, this time by a band of brigands led by a man called Warin.

Ardenis's smile turned tentatively genuine. Perhaps today his instincts would show him what the brigands were up to, keeping him far away from scenes of love and adoration.

He arrived on time for his watch at the tower, perturbed he wasn't early like usual. Aside from a forced polite "hello," he ignored the other watchers and their glances as they filed in *with* him instead of after him. A rule enforcer—not Hector—observed silently from the side of the room.

Ardenis avoided him and sat at the watch window, focusing on the pool of water in the center. It glowed and then opened to the world of Thera. His instincts were there, waiting for him. Ardenis's heart skipped a beat when they nudged him toward Damian's farm. He squeezed his hands into a fist and instead turned his gaze toward Prince Isaac. His instincts shoved against him, but he ignored them.

Past fields and streams, his vision soared, until he came upon a great castle at the edge of a large lake. It boasted battlements of stone with banners of blue and silver, embroidered with the most recent monarchy's crest, flapping in the wind. In one of the many towers, Prince Isaac lay safe and sound on his four-poster bed in his expansive bedchamber. He slept peacefully in the late morning, dark hair disheveled and his circlet of choice discarded on the table beside him.

There was still hope of a prosperous future for Alysies, so long as no harm befell Prince Isaac. His mother had died giving birth to his stillborn sister, and his father, King Tristan, had no plans to remarry.

Ardenis's instincts shoved again, making him grunt with the pressure. He gave into them with a grimace, allowing his gaze to go to the humble farm. His fingernails dug painlessly into his palms. Damian sat on the splintering back porch of the farmhouse, skinning a coyote. His father watched on with a bemused smile he kept wiping away when Damian looked up.

"I thought for sure that coyote had eaten you. I called you from the porch, and you didn't answer. Then I found your bow next to the chicken coop, and didn't know what to think." His father paused from sharpening the blade of his axe on a grinder.

"I got bored, so I hunted him down. He'll not be bothering our chickens again." Damian didn't look up from his work.

"No, I suspect not. Which is good. Now you can get to bed on time and get some proper sleep. You've been rundown the past couple of days." He put the axe back to the grinder.

Damian's movements slowed as he sliced his blade across the animal. "Pa, we really don't need this hide. I was thinking I could sell it at market." He didn't meet his father's eyes.

"Not many folks would buy a coyote hide." His father put down the axe and moved to sharpening his knife with a whetting stone. "But if you want to try, I'd be all right with that, so long as your chores are done."

"Thanks, Pa." Damian smiled and continued his practiced pace, scraping skin from muscle.

Damian's father turned away to hide the grin on his face.

After several hours of pleasant, harmless watching, Ardenis's instincts nudged him a different direction. He blinked, noticing the day grew short, and shifted his gaze until he beheld a rundown tavern near the small town of Oakrin, a few hours ride from Damian's farm.

Inside the run-down tavern, a band of brigands sat at warped wooden tables, nursing their drinks. Even with late-afternoon light filtering through the grimy windows, the neglected interior was dark and dirty, with dried ale caked on the floor. They were the only souls in the place, aside from the barkeep, who washed mugs with a filthy rag behind a counter, ignoring his patrons.

Ardenis recognized their leader, Warin—the night watchers had reported his plot against Prince Isaac—by his toothy snarl.

"Come on, men. We've been over this." Warin slammed his hand on the table, jarring the metal mugs. Some of his men jumped, one of them spat, and the rest leered at their half empty drinks. "It's tonight or not at all." He sneered at his cronies.

Several of the men spoke out at once. One of them, Lenard,

shifted in his seat and spoke over the rest. "We're here, ain't we? You dragged us here at this odd hour."

"We want our money," another man said, raising his mug in the air.

Not one of them looked to have bathed in a month. An older townsman walked in, took one look at the baleful glares greeting him, and walked right back out. A wise decision.

Lenard glared at Warin, a look too intense for his skinny frame. "No one's saying we ain't in. We just wanna be sure the plan's solid." He looked at the other men, and they nodded.

"Oh, it's solid." Warin flapped his brown vest, sending dirt and food crumbs flying. "There's no way we'll fail. I've paid a guard on the inside good coin for this information."

"We all know your coin's no good, Warin Foolhardy," a lanky man said from the corner.

Some of the men cringed. Ardenis watched on, eager for more information, something concrete to take to the council.

Warin drew his knife so fast the lanky man didn't have time to flinch before the blade sunk into his chest. His eyes went wide, and he clutched at the bleeding wound. He slumped over, knocking his mug across the table, spilling its contents as he fell dead. No one came to his aid.

"That will be the last person who calls me foolhardy," Warin Folhard said, drawing another knife and pointing it around the room.

The men became preoccupied with their ales and didn't look up, except Lenard. They locked eyes, and Warin threw another knife. It spun end over end and sunk into the table next to Lenard's hand.

Lenard jumped and yelped, then glared at Warin. His sudden paleness made a long scar stand out on his face. Some of the men smirked behind their drinks. The barkeep rolled his eyes.

"Dammit Lenard," Warin said. "Now, we go way back, but I made this deal, and I won't stand anyone double-crossing me." He narrowed his eyes at the rest of the men. "Prove yer worth, and I'll pay ya a bonus."

Lenard yanked the knife out of the table, tossing it once in the air and catching it by the worn leather hilt. He looked hard around the room. "What are we waiting for, then?"

Warin smiled, revealing his missing teeth.

"Let's go kill us a prince!" another man said.

Warin frowned. "Kidnap, not kill. He's worth more to us alive."

Lenard scratched his greasy head. "Lord Ferran said kill."

Ardenis blinked. Interesting. Lord Ferran was Eva's father and ruled in the king's name over these lands, including Damian's. He took part in court politics, and the king trusted him. Why risk it all for such a scheme? Was he in league with the enemy kingdom of Daltieri?

"Shut up and get!" Warin glared and pointed to the door.

The men stood, howling and hollering, bumping into tables and knocking over half-empty pints as they rushed out the door. Warin tossed the barkeep a small sack of coin and a terse nod. The barkeep watched them leave, then spat into the mug and continued washing. He glanced at the dead body and scooped up the coins with a sigh.

Ardenis ended his watch, his vision blurring back to the watch room.

Death didn't faze Ardenis. People came and went, souls born to Thera from Acantha, only to play their part in the great mix of history, then die and go to the Hereafter. Ardenis had seen many friends leave Acantha. Where their journey took them, only time would tell. It was impossible to know who someone became once they reached Thera. Sometimes he wondered if he recognized any of them.

It would take hours for Warin to reach Prince Isaac—plenty of time to report to the council and be back for the rest of the day watch. They'd be interested to know exactly who had hired Warin in this most recent threat against Prince Isaac.

His thoughts stopped short when Amalia Watcher sat in the

chair next to his. She locked eyes with him and tossed her long black hair behind her shoulders.

"Anything interesting happen in Thera yesterday, Ardenis?" she purred. "Anything of import I should focus on?"

He blinked. Amalia had asked an innocent question, one that had much relevance, but the way she'd asked it—it was too full of emotion. He knew Amalia well from their time as watchers together, though she wasn't a close friend—no watcher was. Was Thera getting to her?

"Are you well, Amalia?" Ardenis whispered back—a requirement, so as not to disturb the other watchers. "You seem excitable today. Do you need to spend some time distancing yourself?"

Amalia narrowed her eyes. "You're quick to assume, Ardenis. Perhaps it's you who needs some distance."

Ardenis raised an eyebrow.

She looked away, her features softening. "Forgive me, Watcher Fater. Perhaps you're right."

"Don't be afraid to recognize the signs, Watcher. It's better to distance yourself now than end up forced to be born before your time."

Amalia gave a quick nod, staring at the watch window.

Ardenis straightened his sleeves and stood. He took his own advice and left the tower. When he reached the courtyard outside the council hall, Acanthians filled the space with their blue robes and black hair. Many of them called out greetings, and Ardenis smiled and nodded, not pausing on his way to the council hall.

Outside, the sun set low over the council courtyard. The last of its warmth soaked into his dark robe as he headed back to the tower. His instincts beat like a drum between his ears urging him to get back. That odd sense of unease warred for attention.

Guilt again, he realized with a stumbled step. Not guilt for the rule he'd broken, but guilt for ignoring his instincts, the Fates.

He kept his visit to the council brief, reporting on what little he'd seen of Damian and Warin, and hurried back to the watchtower.

Night had just fallen by the time he focused on Thera.

Damian wasn't on the farm. He jogged down a narrow dirt road lit only by the moon. Ardenis knew whom Damian was going to see. Anticipation mingled with fear and coiled in his gut. Minutes later, Damian gasped. A grin erupted on his face, and he broke into a sprint. Ahead of him, lantern light bathing her ivory dress, Eva covered a laugh with her hand. She set down the light and opened her arms wide.

Damian swept her up, spinning her around by her narrow waist, cotton dress and unbound hair flying. When they stopped, she wrapped her arms tight around him, laughing.

Ardenis sat on the edge of his chair. Eva and Damian's moment singed through the atmosphere, reaching him across the vast distance between the mortal and immortal worlds. The emotion between the two young lovers was a sweet tang in the air. It coated his tongue, and he licked his lips, eager for more. He shared their excitement and hope, and though he had promised himself he wouldn't watch their love again, that promise went ignored.

"I don't want to go back to Oakrin," Eva said. "I can't bear to say goodbye. Can we spend tonight pretending I'm not Lady Eva?" She pressed her cheek against his chest.

Damian smiled warmly down at her, stroking her hair. "Of course, Eva."

"We should both become mages, then we'd be too powerful for them to keep apart."

He chuckled. "You have to be born with magic, love."

"And that's happening less and less these days." She raised a smile to him. "So tell me it will always be this way. That we'll find a way around our parents' expectations."

"And be together, my love. We will."

"Ardenis." The rough tone grated against the pure moment.

Ardenis jumped, his smile disappearing. He broke his gaze from the watch window and focused back to his surroundings.

Hector stood beside him, head tilted. His eyes looked almost stern enough to pass as irritated.

Ardenis blinked and crossed his arms—could Hector see his heart pounding through his robe? Hector's eyes followed the movement.

"How may I help you, Enforcer?" It was unusual to interrupt a watcher in the middle of a watch, even for a rule enforcer. He'd seen it happen to other watchers when they became too affected by their watch. It had never happened to Ardenis.

"You were winded," Hector said, his constant frown in place.

Ardenis's jaw unhinged, but he snapped it closed before his lips parted. What could he say? Watchers didn't get winded. His mind whirled for an explanation.

"I apologize, Enforcer. I did not realize."

Hector nodded slowly, as if not sure what to make of the half-formed response. "And what were you watching?"

Ardenis kept silent. Watchers weren't to speak of Thera except to the council. They knew too much.

"Yes, you can't elaborate on the matter." Hector sniffed. "I'm sure we'll learn the outcome of Warin the Brigand's efforts soon."

Ardenis looked around the room at the multiple watchers—some watching, some looking at them—then back at Hector. The thought of watching Prince Isaac hadn't even entered his mind. Would Warin have arrived at the castle by now?

He willed calm into his voice, something he'd never had to do before. "Thank you for your visit, Enforcer. We are watching according to the Fates' design." His usual response when Hector tried to meddle in watcher business, but even more apt now.

Hector's face remained impassive, his voice inflectionless. "Very good, Ardenis Watcher Fater."

Ardenis nodded. The use of his full title was not enough to distract him from Hector's behavior.

He didn't look up as the door closed behind Hector, but he let a small sigh escape him. It was half frustration—he'd missed part of

Damian and Eva's meeting, and she would leave soon—and half relief. His annoyance was overridden by the fact his second foray into watching Theran love hadn't been discovered.

Though his instincts tried to pull him back to Damian, Ardenis reluctantly moved his gaze across the countryside to the castle of Prince Isaac in Pavora, the capital city of the kingdom of Alysies.

He found Isaac and his swordmaster, Dego, sparring in the center of the training room in the castle. Weapon racks lined the stone walls, and open archways led out to an airy balcony. Servants holding towels and bejeweled cups of water and wine watched from the sides of the room.

Isaac flipped his ear-length light-brown hair off his face and continued trading blows with his swordmaster. His eyes narrowed, intent and focused while he moved. The sharp whack of their wooden swords filled the expansive room.

Isaac shuffled forward, his feet moving with his strikes, maintaining their balanced position. Dego backed up against Isaac's advance, and frowned. Isaac glanced at the frown and switched his strategy, blocking and parrying with little movement, conserving his strength.

"Good, Prince Isaac," Dego said between breaths.

Isaac smiled and lunged for an opening in his swordmaster's defense. Dego blocked, but Isaac's wooden sword grazed his hand.

Ardenis wondered, not for the first time, if Isaac's natural ability could be attributed to any magic still lingering in this royal family. There had been several mages generations back. He'd once thought the prince might possess magic and be sent to Thomats School of Magic, but nothing manifested except for his skill with a blade. Nor was it likely to at his age.

Perhaps that was a good thing for Isaac. When the mages failed to heal Isaac's mother, King Tristan banished them from the castle. The kingdom was lucky he didn't disband the famous school, but he wasn't a complete fool. He still needed mages to fight his wars and defend his borders. But if his son had turned out to have magic, it wouldn't have gone well for the prince.

Magic seemed to ebb and flow on Thera, coming and going over time. New mages were at the lowest point he'd ever seen. This world was past due for something incredible.

"Enough." Dego held up his sword and shook out his hand. He'd slowed in the decade since Ardenis had watched him train Isaac's father, King Tristan.

"I apologize, Swordmaster. Are you alright?" Isaac stood in place, his brows wrinkling.

"Of course." Dego narrowed his eyes and dropped his hand to his side. He loosed a long breath. "Our time is up, my prince."

Isaac nodded, passing his sword to a servant. "Good day, Swordmaster," he called out as he left the room. He popped his head back in, smiling. "Thank you for the lesson."

During Ardenis's millennia as a watcher, he'd learned to recognize the signs of a leader with potential. History followed predictable patterns. At only twelve years of age, Prince Isaac had the capacity to be a great ruler. He was smart and hardworking, and had shown the compassion lacking in his father's rule.

And why did that matter in the grandness of time? Because, he'd grown fond of the kingdom, though he wasn't supposed to. He didn't want to see it fall like every kingdom did eventually. They took care of their people, and more Acanthians chose to be born during times of peace and prosperity. Though, of course, they had no control over where they would end up when they left Acantha.

Ardenis followed as Isaac and a pair of guards made their way to his suite, but a forceful nudge to Ardenis's middle made him pause. Isaac stepped out of sight through his chamber door carved with swirling vines while his guards took their places on either side beneath burning sconces.

Ardenis concentrated and followed his instincts to just beyond the castle. Warin stood in an alley, dark with the moonless night. Several men acted lookout at end of the street, heads swiveling at every sound. Lenard and the rest of the crew surrounded Warin, panting from their journey.

"You men wait here," Warin said, looking each man in the eye. "I'll find my man. He's on guard duty tonight at the eastern wall. He's got a backway in. Once it's secure and the castle is asleep, I'll come get you."

Lenard bent down to scratch his knee. "Good idea, boss."

Warin cracked a toothy grin. "Don't let these fools wander off. Once we have the prince, we'll have our riches."

The men cheered and Warin and Lenard shushed them, punching those closest. Warin scowled their sheepish looks and took off, slinking through the alley and around a corner toward the east side of the castle.

Ardenis rubbed his hands over his knees. Was Isaac in true danger this time? He raced his gaze ahead, beating Warin to the castle. Long stretches of grass spread from the steep stone wall, lit up by torches lining the battlements. The lap of the lake's waves to the north accompanied the high-pitched keening of night insects in the nearby woods. One guard stood closer to the northeast side of the castle wearing Alysian leathers and a sword sheathed at his side. Sweat beaded his forehead through his open helm as his eyes darted around his surroundings.

He looked nervous. He looked like he was up to no good, as if he was indeed waiting for Warin. He also looked very young, barely out of training. How had he got caught up with someone like Warin, a thief and a thorn to society?

The young guard reached for his sword when Warin appeared. The thief edged around the light of the torches, keeping close to the wall and out of view of the guards along the battlements above. Warin watched the young guard as warily as the guard did him until he was halfway down the eastern side and Warin took a yellow square of fabric from his vest pocket and waved it in the air. The guard sheathed his sword, shoulders relaxing as he withdrew a similar square of fabric and waved it back.

Warin jogged the rest of the way, glancing up toward the battlements now and then. The guard met him in the shadow of the wall.

"Warin?" The young guard's voice cracked. He used the yellow square to wipe his damp forehead.

"Yeah," Warin panted. "You the one they sent to get me in?"

"I am," the guard said with more conviction. "There's a secret door this way." He waved Warin forward, and they quickly walked the rest of the length of the wall until they did indeed reach a door in the thick, seamless stone.

There was no handle, no way to open it from the outside. The guard took a knife from his belt and rapped the hilt on the door.

"Wait, wait," Warin said, backing up. "I'm not ready to go in yet. I gotta get the rest of my crew."

The door began to open, stone scraping against stone.

"You don't have to go in all the way," the guard said. He averted his eyes down to his steel foot coverings. "Just step in and get a feel for what you're up against. I'll close the door when you're done."

Warin watched as the door opened the rest of the way, leaning as if he might bolt any second. A guard on the inside nodded to both of them, and then disappeared into the shadows of the castle keep, leaving the door wide open.

The young guard watched Warin, and then gestured toward the door. "I can't leave my post or they'll know something's up. Go in. Just don't let anyone see you."

Warin nodded slowly. "All right then. Makes sense, to get a feel for the place first." He stepped toward the door, alternating his gaze from the young man to the shadowy keep.

Ardenis kept his gaze following close behind. Warin may actually succeed with his kidnapping if he was careful enough. Ardenis had never expected him to get this far.

Warin stepped through the door. It led to a tunnel through the thick wall, tall and wide enough for a single rider. He crept through the darkness, boots crunching over gravely dirt. Torchlight flickered on the other side of the tunnel, but all was silent. At the other side, Warin paused before carefully leaning to peer around the wall.

He shrieked and hopped back into the tunnel. Guards rushed at him from both sides, swords drawn. Warin tripped backwards, landing hard on his back. The guards tackled him, throwing punches as Warin pitifully held his arms over his face.

"To the dungeon," a guard called above the other's yells and punches.

They hauled a half-unconscious Warin to his feet and dragged him further into the keep.

The young guard had watched the whole thing without a hint of surprise on his youthful face. He closed the stone door and marched, chin held high, back to his place on the eastern wall.

Prince Isaac was safe another night.

Ardenis ended his watch, coming back to the soft glow of the white watch room. He sighed in contentment, happy for things to be back to normal. This was the kind of thing he was supposed to watch. He left the watchtower without a word, as the others were well into their own watching and he didn't desire to disturb them. Reporting to the council was blissfully uneventful.

When he approached his house, a light was already lit from within. He entered, peeking slowly around the door, and found Laida asleep on the lounge chair. Her one-of-a-kind golden hair spread in waves over her shoulder and down her back, with her journal tucked under her arm. Ardenis had rarely seen her sleeping. She looked peaceful. His eyes drifted from her hair to her pink lips, slightly parted in the depths of sleep. He shook his head to clear it.

"Laida," he said without touching her. She didn't stir. "Laida," he said a little louder.

"Hmm?" She awoke and stretched. She blinked a few times, focusing on his face. "What time is it?"

"It's late."

"I fell asleep." She sat up. "I came to tell you about the kickball match you missed, but now I'm too tired." She yawned and stretched again.

Ardenis chuckled, hardly caring he'd missed another scheduled recreational kickball match. A pleasant feeling spread through him, chasing away his lingering anxiety. He glanced at Laida's eyes, so different from Eva's, no hint of warmth or passion.

"I know you worked more than your shift at the transfers today. How are things going?" he asked.

Laida laughed. "How did you know?"

He smiled. "Because you're you. You wouldn't trust anyone else to lead in your stead." She also had a competitive side she, and everyone else in Acantha, wasn't aware of.

Laida laughed and stood, tucking her journal into her pocket. "Well," she said, smiling again, "you're right. And it's going smoothly with no delays in people being born."

"Of course not." He laughed, and it felt freeing, not forced.

"I did take a break to play kickball." She nudged his shoulder. He was often her partner when they played.

He met her eyes. "I apologize for missing it, Laida." The words burned a bit in his chest, as if he actually meant them. They weren't just filler for things they were supposed to say to each other.

"What were you doing today?" Her tone was joyful, chasing his guilt away.

He followed her to his door. "Actually, I've been watching a new subject, and I have high hopes for this one." If he could remain emotionally uninvolved.

"Well, I'm sure you'll tell me nothing about it later."

"You never know, maybe it will be big council news in a few years."

She laughed, and they lapsed into companionable silence.

He opened his door, and Laida gave him a hug—a friendly hug, between two good friends—and Ardenis couldn't help but picture Damian and Eva in their loving embrace. The way Eva looked at him.

She left with a parting smile and a wave, leaving him in the doorway, watching as she walked away.

Afterwards, he ignored his journal duties and retrieved his drawing supplies. The motion should have eased his mind, but Ardenis stayed awake well into the night, sketching the eyes that may very well become his downfall.

CHAPTER
FOUR

Ardenis's instincts took him to Damian regularly, and though there was nothing he wasn't supposed to see—certainly no more love—each time he closed his eyes, images of Laida asleep on his lounge chair swarmed him. He pushed them away, but they just came back.

Damian went about his farm chores with his usual diligence, but always at the end of the day, he'd spare a moment and run to check on the coyote hide he'd stretched to tan. He practically bounced with eagerness when he deemed it finally ready to sell. Ardenis looked forward to viewing a trip to town, a break from the monotony of the farm.

The very next morning, he watched as Damian stood beside the leaning barn, packing their one mule with various provisions. The mule accepted the weight of the bags without protest except for the occasional tug at his lead and flick of his ears.

The bright summer sun had risen by the time Damian's mother came to send him off. Slender, with an apron over her simple dress and a scarf over her hair, she carried two linen sacks. She handed him the first, and his arms drooped with its weight. Damian opened it. Sunlight caught the jars of strawberry preserves, casting golden red hues onto the linen.

"Be sure to sell these for a fair price this time." Damian's mother had a thick country accent and a skeptical look on her face. She stuck out the other bag. "I packed you a lunch."

Damian nodded sheepishly and added both bags to the mule's burdens. "I will, Mama. Thank you."

She gave him a quick embrace and a kiss on the cheek. "Be careful." Her tone implied that she worried more than a simple trip to market warranted.

Damian mounted the mule, grinned at his mother, and then they were off. His father waved, hand high over his head, from a distant field. Ardenis watched the rolling farmland and trickle of the occasional stream as Damian plodded on. After a few hours, the sparse houses became more numerous, bunching closer together until he reached the outskirts of Oakrin.

Ardenis had watched the small town grow from nothing but a lush, empty forest—unclaimed land ruled by none but the animals. As more Acanthians were born and more land needed, expansion and war ensued. It currently belonged within Prince Isaac's father, King Tristan's kingdom of Alysies.

Wiping sweat off his brow with the back of his hand, Damian led the mule down the main dirt road through the center of town. The sun sat fat and high overhead, beating its rays straight down. It painted a sweltering picture while Ardenis rested comfortably in his chair, smiling at the rush of sounds reaching out from the market. Damian closed his eyes as a breeze swept past. The wind kicked up dust in the market, which was already abundant with activity.

Carts and wagons lined the lively road. Revelers munched on roasted nuts. Shopkeepers beckoned to customers, while traveling salesmen hocked tonics and cheap jewelry. All manner of food was displayed, available for purchase if one had the coin. Fruits, vegetables, spices, and dried fish decorated tables and carts. Smoke rose from meat roasting on spits, and Ardenis's mouth watered. He inhaled, but of course, couldn't smell anything. Regardless, he loved a good market day. Acantha certainly didn't have such things.

Bards played a lively tune while jugglers entertained the townspeople. The poorest children ran about, snatching items from street carts and pockets. Someone posing as a mage performed cheap magic tricks as copper coins filled his hat—real mages wouldn't be seen at such events. Young women traveled in groups, dust coating the hems of their dresses, giggling as they passed young men.

Damian dismounted and unbound the twine around the coyote hide. A young woman lingered behind her group, one hand to her blushing cheek, and watched him, but he didn't notice. He took his mule by its lead and wandered down the street, leaving the girl pouting and hurrying to catch up to her friends.

He quickly sold the hide and the strawberries to the first bidder, collecting less than what he could have made, and then moved on from the market—the opposite direction of his farm.

Ardenis scooted to the edge of his seat.

Much further on, where the trees grew thicker, Damian stopped at a fork in the road at the base of a steep hill. At the top of the hill sat Lord Ferran's large keep—Eva's home. Though small, high stone walls fortified the imposing castle, and two towers flanked a portcullis gate. Damian stared up at the looming structure, eyes forlorn, and a quiet sigh escaped him.

He led his mule down a short trail through the trees and into a little clearing hidden from the road. The grass was trampled short and removed of branches and debris. Damian unrolled a worn blanket from his pack and spread it on the patch of flattened grass. Next, he unpacked the lunch his mother had prepared, a thick block of white cheese, salted meat, and a crisp loaf of fresh-baked bread, which he slathered with honey.

Damian stared at the trail, eyes alight with the eagerness plain on his face. He didn't touch the food.

A short time later, Ardenis's heart skipped a beat as Eva appeared in the clearing. Her dress—expensive layers of mauve with silver embroidered in swirling patterns down the front—flowed with her movements as she picked her way over exposed tree roots. A white lace scarf adorned her hair, which cascaded in loose chocolate ringlets down her back.

Damian stood quick to his feet and brushed himself off. He wore a huge grin above his travel-stained farm clothes.

Eva broke into a run. She flew into his arms, and he caught her and held her tight, kissing her urgently along the length of her jaw to her lips. She ran her fingers through his wavy hair, and he groaned against her. He touched her face, trailing his hand down to her neck. His fingers brushed along the length of her skin and down her collarbone. Her breath caught. They stopped kissing, but she didn't pull away.

Damian's arm grazed her breast, and she shivered.

Ardenis watched, heart racing and hands gripping the watch window, unable to look away. He'd been safe, he'd stayed away from breaking the rules, why couldn't he just stop now before more came of it?

"We have to be quick, Damian," Eva breathed. She pulled at his shirt. "I snuck away from Mary, but she'll worry soon."

"So eager, love." Damian smiled. "Don't you want to see what I brought you?"

Eva's eyes lit up, and she paused in her efforts to remove his shirt. Her eyelashes fluttered. "You brought me a present?"

Damian reached into his pocket and pulled something out wrapped in cloth. He held his hand in front of her, but didn't open his fist. Eva narrowed her eyes and grabbed, trying to pry his fingers loose, but he just laughed and pulled away.

With a cry of frustration, she pushed him. He tripped over the edge of the blanket, eyes going wide as he grabbed her, hauling her backward with him. They landed together in a heap, laughing, Eva on top. She pushed her dark curls out of the way and leaned down to give him a sweet, lingering kiss. When she pulled back, he held his open fist before her, the cloth wrapping discarded. On his palm was an intricately carved wooden hair comb. The floral design was inlaid with a perfectly round piece of polished turquoise.

Eva gasped. "Oh, Damian. Did you buy this at market? It must have cost a fortune." She touched the comb with delicate fingers.

He laughed, the movement shaking Eva where she still lay on top of him. "I made it, my love. For you."

Eva's eyes widened, long lashes nearly sweeping her eyebrows. "You made this?" She hit him on the chest. "Why did you let me wrestle for it, you oaf? You could have broken it, and I never would have forgiven you."

His mouth formed a pleased smile, adoring eyes gazing up at her. Ardenis found he was smiling too.

Damian tucked the comb into her hair beneath her scarf. "I'm glad you like it."

She rested her head on his chest, ear above his beating heart. "It's beautiful. I didn't realize you were so talented."

"Well," he said, flexing his bicep, "that's just one of my many talents. Care to see some others?" He winked.

"I thought you'd never ask, my dear." Eva reached up and kissed him again.

Damian grabbed her hips and rolled her over on the blanket. She smiled up at him, and he slowly pulled her dress up. She wore no underclothes.

Ardenis ended his watch. The room blurred in patches of white walls as he forced his wide eyes to return to normal. His heart raced in his ears, drowning out the emptiness of the quiet tower and the soft breathing of those around him. He'd watched too long, too much, become too emotionally involved. Again. He should report his findings to the council and have a new watcher take over—let someone else discover the reason behind the need to watch Damian.

But he wouldn't. He squeezed his eyes closed tight. Something was missing from his existence that he'd never noticed until viewing these mortals and their love. Nothing seemed as interesting or exciting as the passion he'd beheld between them.

He sat still, looking down and pretending to view Thera while taking quiet measured breaths until his heart resumed a normal pace. He'd seen nudity, of course, but never intimacy. Never.

And why not? He took a breath. Because it went against the Watcher's Edict. His chair scraped over the marble, the noise echoing in the silence as he got up and walked in what he hoped was a calm manner, out of the tower.

No one followed.

He'd seen mortals display such emotions, and they called it paranoia. Had watching forbidden love caused him to learn new emotions? Was he being paranoid? Or did the enforcers suspect? He'd have to be very careful.

The peaceful mid-afternoon sun blanketed his skin, and he blinked at the brightness. He needed a distraction, to distance himself. He needed a non-watcher. Laida.

The watchtower was quite a distance from the transfer hall, but the walk did little to help him. Instead of clearing his head, confusion plagued him. Images of Eva swarmed with his memory of Laida asleep in his home, so unguarded and without her usual flourish.

He passed many rows of homes and the occasional ever-growing fruit orchard that appeared to replace houses whenever enough of them became empty because of souls being born. Finally, he approached the transfer hall. The large whitewashed wood and stone building boasted a second story, which arched over a front terrace supported by thick columns. Sometimes, during more peaceful and prosperous days on Thera, the line to be born extended outside the building and into the terrace.

Ardenis passed a man being bid goodbye—Yertz, who often played the violin at their evening recreational concerts. The terrace was a popular location to send off friends before their fated journey to the earthen realm, much as mortals sent off friends or family before a voyage. Ardenis smiled his own farewell before passing through the terrace's cool shade and entering the transfer hall.

The building supplied the souls for the northeastern hemisphere of Thera, just as Ardenis's tower watched them live their lives once they left Acantha. There was always a steady stream of people ready to go, following their instincts even in times of earthen turmoil. They entered the transfer hall Laida ran so efficiently, and roughly nine months later, they opened their eyes in Thera, ready to start a new journey, completely unaware of their premortal existence.

Ardenis walked past the line of people. They paused their conversations to nod or smile at him, and he patted those on the back he knew and wished them a good journey.

It was a massive decision—when to be born—which was why watchers were so important. The information he provided to the Acanthians, and their instincts, were all they had to make their decision.

Within the antechamber, crisp-white and echoing with chatter from the front of the line, his friend Vinia stood behind a podium, quill in hand, admitting people into the main room.

She recorded who entered the transfer gateways, tallying up the daily amounts to stay within the limit Laida set. Only so many people could enter the gateways per day. They kept careful track of the quota, but they'd never had to turn someone away. Even when the council bulletins led to an increase in the number of people being born, Laida counteracted with ingenuity and efficiency to maintain order in what Ardenis viewed as chaos.

"Vinia," Ardenis said, smiling at her.

She looked up from the record book and gave him a one-sided grin. "Ardenis, have you decided to be born?" She took down the name of the next person in line.

"Not today." Not for a long time. "I came to spend time with Laida." His smile faltered as he realized he liked the sound of those words.

"Taking a break from the watchtower?" Her tone was friendly, distracted even as she was working, but also curious.

Though emulating curiosity was normal among Acanthians, it

meant she'd noticed he was doing things unusual for him. He hardly ever took breaks from the tower. It was his calling, his duty.

He looked past her, into the main room. "I just needed some distance."

Vinia nodded. All close friends of watchers knew what it meant when they needed distance, even if they didn't understand it.

"Laida's monitoring the transfers, but I'm sure she'd be glad for a visit." Vinia waved him ahead of the line, and he re-formed his smile as he left the antechamber. The voices of those living their last hours in Acantha faded away.

The open space greeted him inside the main room where future citizens of Thera lined up, awaiting their turn. Smooth wooden railings separated each line, keeping up the organization Vinia set in motion with her perfect pacing of letting people through. The railings marked paths that wound around and led to one of many gateways to Thera, where a mother would be blessed with new life in her womb. The gateways themselves were small spaces raised on platforms of black stone and enclosed by white marble except for the open front.

The only exception was the gateway at the far end of the room. The one all in black. The one reserved for the worst law-breakers. With the presence of a full council, the person placed in this gateway did not go to Thera. They did not go to the promised Hereafter. They were sent straight to a dark, black place, destined to be alone for all eternity. Maybe even worse. There were no texts or knowledge to confirm such things.

Ardenis fought back a shudder and moved his gaze along until he spotted Laida overseeing a woman stepping into a gateway. It was Talem, a genealogy keeper with whom he sometimes played kickball. She turned around, hands clasped together, and waited. Laida smiled warmly and nodded—the most Theran-like form of emotion Ardenis had ever seen on her. It was the warmth behind it that made him think so. Not just a smile because she should, but because she was offering comfort to someone about to experience a new beginning. Or maybe he was seeing things that weren't there.

Just before Talem disappeared to make the journey to Thera, her eyes opened wide, and she gasped. Awareness. Then she was gone.

Ardenis's lips parted.

Laida turned and spotted him. She waved to someone who came and took her place, then walked to meet him at the side of the room.

"Arden! What brings you here?" She absently played with a strand of her golden hair.

He beamed at her nickname for him. "I thought I'd take a break and see how things are going," he said. "The transfer hall is running smoothly today. But I wouldn't expect anything less with you in charge."

Laida gave a soft laugh, and the sound filled him. He'd made her laugh, even if it wasn't a real show of happiness. He frowned and shoved those thoughts deep, deep down. The black gateway loomed on the edge of his vision.

"Yes, things are going well. The line is a little longer than usual, thanks to the update from the council about Prince Isaac's survival. Or should I say thanks to you?" She smiled up at him.

He couldn't help grin back, but didn't answer. He hadn't even bothered to check the bulletins about the prince, though he'd heard the rumor. Laida didn't expect him to corroborate her implied theory that it was his watching which peaked the interest of the people of Acantha. His guilt returned anew; he'd been watching Damian.

"I have a question," Ardenis said.

"What would you like to know?" She scanned the multiple gateways, the line moving as each person left, and nodded to herself.

"Just before Talem left for Thera, she looked surprised about something, pleasantly so." Ardenis shuffled his feet. "Do you know what she experienced?"

Laida looked back at Talem's gateway, then met his eyes. Her beauty struck him still. He'd never noticed before. Her eyes, like all Acanthians, had always been blue, but had they always held such cleverness? Had the way they offset her nose and the curve of her lips been there all along?

"I've been doing this for a long time, Arden. I rarely monitor the actual transfer, because my responsibilities take me elsewhere, but it's my favorite part, you see, and I have a theory." She hesitated, a very un-Laida, un-Acanthian like reaction. "A theory you helped me develop, actually."

"Me?" He raised his eyebrows.

She nodded and took a breath. "I believe, before we go to Thera, we have a moment of clarity."

"Clarity?"

"Yes, that's the best way I know to describe it. A moment where our minds experience Thera before we leave. Everyone reacts differently, but it's as if their eyes are unlocked to something new in the brief moment the gateway is open."

"What does that have to do with me?" He waited with bated breath.

"Well... You've never explained it fully, but sometimes you say you need distance from watching Thera." She bundled her hair and braided it as she spoke. "I've seen some watchers forced to be born because they became too emotionally influenced. I know the watchers are different from the rest of us, though I can't say exactly in what way. More... knowledgeable maybe?" She sighed and tossed her braid behind her. "I'm not explaining this right. What I mean is, there's something in Thera we don't have here. You've seen it, but you don't let it influence you, and the people about to be born see it when they're in the gateway."

He blinked, trying to best decide how to respond. In truth, she'd guessed closer than anyone he'd heard speak of such things before. There was something Thera had that Acantha didn't. Acanthians lived out their time in the premortal world under a kind of emotional veil, with no lies or deceit. But watchers knew. They'd seen the treachery and beauty of mortals for too long not to realize the difference and to know that difference must be there for a good reason.

He controlled his breathing, at a true loss for words. Laida had never been so open before—never voiced this theory. Whether she realized it or not, she knew more than she should. That she'd partly developed her theory because of him meant he wasn't hiding what he knew well enough.

"You don't understand." Laida stated it as a fact, more than as the accusation he felt. "You'd have to see people being born as many times as I have to recognize it, I suppose." She dropped her gaze. "I assumed that as a watcher, you'd understand more than anyone."

They'd entered forbidden territory. He couldn't tell Laida about Thera, or even hint at the emotional veil covering all Acanthians. The veil even he shouldn't know about, except that somehow he did, ever since that fated embrace.

Ardenis ignored her revelation entirely. "Are you attending the dining hall this evening?" He couldn't look at her.

It might have been his imagination, but he thought her shoulders drooped. "Probably. I mean, I don't expect to be here late tonight."

"Good." Ardenis cleared his throat and rubbed the back of his neck. "Well, I'll see you later then."

"Okay. Goodbye, Ardenis." With a smile, Laida turned and walked back to the gateways.

Ardenis sighed and left the transfer hall, nodding to Vinia, who was nose deep in her record book. He ignored the stir he caused among the people waiting in line. Half of them were probably there because of his findings. He hurried away from the impulse to turn around and tell Laida everything.

CHAPTER
FIVE

A rdenis couldn't go back to the tower. Not yet. Now that he'd had some much-needed distance, going back to the young lovers would be foolish. He waited on a bench outside the dining hall as the sun lowered in the sky. The building was long and open, supported by columns and no walls except around the kitchen. People slowly trickled in for dinner.

He wanted to tell Laida the truth, so badly. And that impulse worried him. It had been harder than ever to withhold the information and not tell her he agreed with her theory completely. She'd discovered the truth about their existence—that there was a block, some kind of emotional veil over them that mortals didn't have. The council kept careful watch to make sure Acanthians didn't discover that truth, or worse—become emotionally altered.

Hands in the pockets of his robe, Ardenis squeezed the loose fabric in an anxious grip where no one could see, kneading the material. He had a duty to Acantha, a duty he'd performed without fail or falter for eons. He was Watcher Fater. And he wouldn't allow himself to be emotionally altered.

When he spotted Laida walking down the path, he stood and

entered the dining hall, pretending he hadn't been waiting for her. Inside, rows of long wooden tables with benches filled the room. The smells of baked and roasting meat floated over the din of conversation. Dining workers replenished platters of food.

Ardenis filled his plate with potatoes and pork chops, bypassing Laida's favored fruits and green vegetables, and took his place at their usual table. She didn't look his way as she served herself a vegetable medley then took her seat next to him.

"How was the rest of your day?" she asked, smiling.

"It was fine." Ardenis said, setting down his fork.

He studied her. Unlike him, she didn't seem affected by their earlier conversation. It didn't bother her he chose not to tell her the truth. She ate and chatted with her neighbor while he stared at his plate. Laida was his friend. Even if it didn't bother her, she deserved his loyalty as well as his honesty.

He didn't look up as he whispered, "I believe you."

She dropped her fork and looked up at him. "What?" she said a little too loudly.

He leaned closer, ensuring no one else could hear. "I believe you. I know you've never seen what it's like on Thera, but I wanted to tell you I believe you. What I saw on Talem's face... It's clear a greater emotional awareness awoke for just a second before she left." Ardenis shook his head. Despite his reasoning, he didn't know why he'd confirmed this for her. He shouldn't have.

Laida grinned and picked up her fork. "I knew it. Sometimes I see you with that look. That's what started my theory." She took a bite of carrot.

Ardenis glanced at her sharply.

"Good evening, Ardenis, Laida," their friend Bram said as he sat with Vinia across from them. His kind eyes greeted them above round cheeks.

The three of them, Laida, Vinia, and Bram, were his closest friends. Non-watchers, of course. Much safer company to keep.

"Ready for the match, Ardenis?" Vinia grinned behind her blue eyes and black hair before taking a big bite of her sandwich. "Bram's organized a night match this time."

That's right, there was a kickball match this evening. Kickball was a sport Ardenis had learned from Thera and, with council approval, helped Bram, a recreational coordinator, teach to Acantha. It quickly became a favorite recreational activity, even if they didn't play it like true Therans did.

He finished chewing. "I apologize—"

"He can't make it to the game." Laida finished for him, smiling and tucking her golden hair behind her ears.

He smiled back, eyes lingering on her amused expression.

"Well, you'd probably lose anyway." Vinia grinned again, watching for his reaction.

Ardenis groaned internally, but outwardly gave a rueful chuckle. He glanced around to see if anyone was paying attention to their conversation. He thought he caught Amalia Watcher's eyes, but he blinked and she was looking at her neighbor.

Competitiveness was unusual for Acanthians, especially non-watchers. It was inevitable that he'd pick things up from Thera, things that would affect his mannerisms despite taking the greatest care. Times like these told him he'd passed those things on to his friends. In truth, he enjoyed their rare banter, a diversion from the mundane, but it was best to control the conversation by directing it to neutral grounds when they were in public together.

"I do love a good match," Ardenis said. In reality, he loathed them. The enforcers, particularly Hector, always scrutinized everything, watching for too much emotion, like competitiveness. And without competition, the match was near as dull as watching Damian shuck corn for hours on end. The matches on Thera, though, those he could watch all day.

Ardenis's fork stilled. He'd told them a lie, and not just by omission. Was this the first lie he'd told? Or had there been others?

They'd paused in their eating, waiting for his excuses.

"My instincts tell me this one's important, and I need to work late tonight." Another lie. His instincts were nice and quiet. He just didn't want to go to the kickball match, and it worked because his friends followed their own instincts in their individual callings and were well used to him bowing out of their planned activities.

"I'll be there, but don't count on my help." Bram was a loyal friend, but not much of a sports player.

Vinia's mouth twitched into an understanding smile.

Laida took a napkin to her already clean mouth. "I would be working late tonight, too, but I left Idonea—someone almost as competent as me—in charge of the transfer hall."

Ardenis and Bram exchanged smirks but didn't comment. Maybe one day he'd explain conceitedness to her. Rather than linger, Ardenis scarfed the last of his food and stood at the same time as Laida.

Vinia and Bram bid them goodbye. Full night had fallen, leaving the moon and torchlight to bathe the pleasant evening in pale blues and oranges.

"Headed to the tower then?" Laida asked. Her blue eyes met his, and he forgot how to breathe for a moment. "Arden?"

"Laida." He smiled and looked down the path, hesitating. "Come with me. I want to show you something." Damian would be back on the farm, anyway. No reason to check up on him right now.

Ardenis held his hand out to her, as Damian had to Eva. Heat crept up his neck. She raised her eyebrows, but then smiled and linked her arm through his instead. Handholding wasn't unusual in Acantha, but he'd never held Laida's hand before. He wanted to now, and the thought shook him.

"Okay, Arden, where to?"

He led them down the sidewalk. "I sketched a new picture, and I wanted to show it to you."

Releasing his arm, she clapped her hands. "Oh, I would love that. I love looking at your new work. It's like seeing Thera through your eyes."

Ardenis grinned and rubbed his arm, still warm from where

she'd touched him. It eased the sting of guilt he felt for the rule he was about to break.

When they reached his house, he held the door open for her.

"Wait here, and I'll be right back." He gestured to a wooden chair.

Her mouth quirked up as she sat. "It better not have rain in it."

Ardenis forced away his frown. What could he say? It was true he sketched a lot of rain and weather. But she could never understand why. It represented all the emotions he'd only ever witnessed and never experienced.

Laida knew the facts the council disclosed, and she'd seen his drawings, but she'd never seen war, death, destruction, birth, growth, change, or the joy of a child with his head tipped back to feel a summer rain on his face. For all these reasons and more, the separation between watcher and non-watcher was sometimes hard to bear.

His living area held many of his drawings, though the Thera Museum featured most of his favorites. One charcoal sketch on his wall pictured a quaint cottage on the outskirts of a lush forest, with butterflies gracing a flower garden and thunderclouds in the distance. There was another picture of a woman walking away through the snow. She held a mage staff in one hand, glowing with some unseen conjured spell. An infant strapped to her back peeked out from a cradleboard, locking eyes with the observer.

He darted to his bedroom, grabbing the drawing from under his bed. He had to be sure his friends didn't see them until approved by the council first, of course.

This one was not.

He held it behind him, hesitating, suddenly nervous to show her. Would she like it? Would he be putting her at risk by showing her a drawing the council hadn't approved?

Laida sat up straighter. "Where is it?"

Ardenis cleared his throat. "I sketched it for you. There's a girl on

Thera I see sometimes, and she reminds me of you." This was a bad idea. "Maybe I shouldn't show you."

Ardenis turned back to his room, but Laida stopped him with a hand on his shoulder. The casual touch wasn't anything unusual, but this time his nerve endings tingled pleasantly beneath her fingers. He glanced at her hand, and it drifted back down to her side.

"Please, I want to see it." Her face held no hint of mirth. Of course not.

Ardenis handed her the sketch. It depicted Eva as he'd first seen her. She wore a forest green dress with long sleeves that flared at the cuffs. It hugged her curves and was tied with a gold sash at the waist. Ardenis's favorite feature, by far, was her eyes. The girl in the drawing gazed up with the look of love Eva wore when she looked at Damian. Pure, innocent, trusting love. Ardenis had practiced until he'd captured it perfectly.

He watched Laida. She covered her mouth, and then lightly reached her fingertips to stroke Eva's chocolate hair. It was bound up in a loose bun high on her head, with wisps falling free and blowing as wild as Eva's heart did with Damian.

"Her hair! Is this how they're wearing their hair now?" Laida inhaled sharply. "You don't have to tell me." She closed her eyes. "I mean, never mind." She looked at him and smiled. "This is spectacular work! You hardly ever do them in color."

"The council tends to prefer the drawings without color." He shouldn't have let the conversation continue, let alone considered telling her more about Thera than the council approved. But... he'd already gone this far.

"Yes, this is how a lot of the young women wear their hair now. Some wear it down though." He studied Laida's fine golden hair as it hung loose in waves over her shoulder, crimped from her unbound braid. He just barely fought the urge to tuck it behind her ears.

"This is wonderful. It looks like a great era to be born into."

His breath caught. The thought of her leaving him squeezed his chest, and he didn't know why.

Distance. He needed distance.

"I have to get to the tower now." He put the drawing back under his bed.

She waited at the door. "Thank you for showing me, and for telling me about Thera." She smiled playfully. "I've never known you to break the rules."

"Well, I have a thing for blondes."

Her eyebrows shot to her hairline.

He gasped and clapped his hand over his mouth. What had he just said? He was bringing unapproved Theran dialect into Acantha.

"Please forget I said that." He'd mostly disguised the desperation in his tone. This entire evening was getting out of hand. Now he was telling her to conceal things from the council!

She smiled. "I can't forget, but I won't repeat it."

He flinched, following her out of the house as she walked away. She looked back at him once and smiled.

That smile made it all worth it, to risk getting caught to please her in this way.

When she turned a corner out of sight, he blinked and looked around. What had he just done? The hold on his emotions was slipping away. He needed distance from Eva and Laida, which meant he couldn't go the tower or the kickball match. Sitting at home, fretting over what to omit from his journal wouldn't be much better.

He went to the public baths, his favorite place outside of the watchtower. A light stone building housed the baths, with a high domed glass ceiling that rose above the surrounding houses. The interior featured many areas; warm and cold pools, a massage room, and exercise rooms all boasting tall archways and columns of aquamarine marble.

Inside, he checked his robe and entered the pool room nude. Floor to ceiling windows along the back of the room gave a view of the stars. Lamplight flickered on the surface of the water, reflecting a soothing glow on the walls and the few souls taking advantage of the solitude. He stepped into the warm pool first. The white tiles with blue painted flowers invited him in as much as the soothing water. All was quiet aside from the scattering of hushed conversations and the rippling water as he found a spot along the edge.

Ardenis dipped down into the warmness up to his chin, focusing on relaxing each muscle and trying to keep his mind occupied. He came up and let his arms float and his mind drift. He'd once seen the Fates here—a future war that had already come to pass.

Bare footsteps plodded over tile, disturbing the relative quiet. Amalia Watcher entered the bath and swam over to him.

"Ardenis. Good evening." Her long black hair floated on the surface of the water as she swam. When she stopped and stood, drops drifted off her chin, landing on her bare breasts.

He stood as well, the water level hitting at his stomach. "Good evening, Amalia. Skipping the match?"

"Same as you. We watchers don't have time for sensible things like that. We've seen too much. We've seen the intricacies and emotions of life, and know what real beauty is." She smiled and splashed him. The water ran in rivets down his chest.

It was true. What Bram organized for the people of Acantha was but a shadow of the ardor capable on Thera.

"It's hard to help others understand that," Ardenis agreed. "They wonder why I don't attend the concerts or many of the other activities." It was freeing to speak with someone who understood.

And dangerous.

Amalia picked up her long hair and rung it out. "You mean your friends, Vinia and Bram?"

"And Laida, too." Amalia knew that. Why omit Laida's name?

She dropped her freshly wrung hair back into the water. "Why bother trying to explain? They won't see until their eyes open in Thera. You should spend your time with watchers. At least you'd have more in common with us."

He wanted to cross his arms, a Theran gesture, but resisted. "It helps me distance myself from the emotions of Thera to spend time outside the company of watchers."

Amalia looked him up and down. "That I do understand." She approached, close enough to touch. "I found something interesting today, while you were *distancing* yourself." Her breath drifted against his wet skin.

"And?" He took a casual step back.

She approached him again, glancing around, though there was no one within earshot. "It seems King Zane has fallen ill." She inched so close he swore he felt the touch of her skin. His heart pounded for no reason he could comprehend. "Looks like it will be up to his children to challenge King Tristan's rule."

Ardenis swallowed. "Is that all?" King Zane ruled over Alysies's neighboring kingdom of Daltieri. He'd never had the best health, so it was hardly news he'd fallen ill again.

"Just this. If you change your mind," she whispered into his ear, and her breasts pressed against his arm, "and decide to spend time with your own kind, let me know." She pulled away and smiled.

Ardenis watched her leave, not looking away as she climbed the steps out of the bath, hips swaying. What was happening to him? He knew of lust from watching Thera, but only what he'd read in their books or heard in conversation. It didn't exist in Acantha. His hands trembled beneath the water. Not even the council approved of teachings on the subject. Amalia meant nothing by her actions, surely.

Ardenis raised himself out of the warm bath at the side of the pool, not bothering to use the stairs. He jumped directly into the cold bath, splashing some bathers, and held himself under the water.

"Did you slip?" someone asked as he came up.

Ardenis wiped water out of his eyes. Gunther, a groundskeeper, stood in the bath beside a friend. Their faces adopted smiles.

"Ardenis Watcher Fater, good evening," Gunther said, extending his hand to shake. "Are you well?"

Ardenis's breath caught. Could they tell he was excitable? Gunther pumped his hand in a friendly way, waiting on Ardenis's reply.

"My apologies," Ardenis said. "I didn't see you."

"We will move so you may enjoy this part of the pool." Gunther smiled, and he and his friend waded to the other side.

Ardenis shook his head. Acanthians always asked after each other's well-being, because that's what Therans did. Or at least what the council told them they did. Gunther had meant nothing by it.

Ardenis left after that, concluding that the baths were a bad idea if he was seeking emotional distance. Something was happening to him. These weren't thoughts or feelings he'd had before. He was changing. Part of him didn't want to stop.

CHAPTER
SIX

Ardenis submitted periodic reports to the council, but
nothing he revealed about Eva or Damian had been
deemed important enough to post for the people of Acantha, even though several weeks had passed. Of course, he omitted
most of what happened when he watched the young couple
together, only telling the council that they had a relationship which
frequently forced him to look away.

The council trusted the Fates would reveal the purpose of this
endeavor in time, making no mention of him needing to move on.

One evening, Ardenis sat in the tower, well past his watch, and
found himself alone. The night watchers had not arrived yet. He
moved from his chair to the ledge of the watch window. His hands
gripped the marble as the late-evening sun continued its decent,
plunging the two worlds into darkness. He gazed into the clear pool,
watching Eva and Damian hold hands as they ran through the forest
surrounding Oakrin, Eva's hometown. Another of Damian's cleverly
invented excuses for a trip to market. Evening doves cooed from
branches above and crickets chirped in the tall grass. Somehow, the
two continued to find ways to meet despite their circumstances.

They laughed and looked over their shoulders toward the keep, thick trees with yellow hints of autumn whipping by, their path lit by early moonlight. Eva locked gazes with Damian. She looked so happy. Her eyes gleamed with love.

Even knowing he was fated to be born in the future, the emotional spectrum before him made him long for Thera. He hoped he'd be born into a loving family like Damian's, and grow to fall for someone as deeply as he had. Had Ardenis known the young couple in Acantha before they were born? Had Eva and Damian known each other?

Ardenis touched the image of Eva's face as Damian pulled her in for a kiss. His fingers met cold water, rippling the scene. He let out a sigh. His head snapped up at the rattle of the door, and he stood just as Cammon Watcher entered the room.

"Watching late again, Ardenis?" Cammon carried a lamp and lit the torch next to him, bathing the room in its glow. Several night watchers followed close behind him. He cocked an eyebrow from under his black hair. "What are you doing in the dark?"

"I didn't notice the sun had set. I've been tracking King Zane. I think he is close to making another move against Alysies." King Zane of Daltieri was often plotting against King Tristan, so it was a safe guess, but unease spread from his stomach. Amalia said King Zane had taken ill.

Cammon grunted and glanced at the night watchers trickling in. "When is he not? I thought the same thing. Though those healing mages aren't doing him any good. Let me know when you're ready to submit your findings to the council, and I'll add my notes."

Ardenis nodded. "I will, Cammon. Thank you. I should be ready soon." He glanced out the window at the darkening sky. "Happy watching." He smiled through his guilt and left the tower for the council hall.

He walked the familiar path, hands shaking. He'd lied to Cammon. He hadn't watched King Zane or his wife, Queen Vatrice, in years—was the king sick again? The lie had come so naturally.

He stopped midstride on the path. Music sounded in the distance. He had spent little time with Bram lately and forgot there was a concert tonight. Laida would be there.

Ardenis veered away from the council hall, onward toward the outdoor pavilion. The music grew louder as he neared, and soon the theater came into view. Rows of marble seating surrounded the orchestra in a semicircle. Crowds of blue-robed, black-haired people filled the space, listening intently to the music. Beside the tiered seating sprawled a grassy knoll. Laida's golden hair stuck out in the middle of it like a star in the night sky.

She sat with Vinia and Bram on a blanket spread out in front of the orchestra. Ardenis's steps faltered. He never came to the concerts. What was he even doing here? But he'd come this far, so he kept walking. He stopped when he reached the edge of their blanket. The music swelled in intensity around him.

Vinia was the first to notice him. "Ardenis. I'm surprised to see you here."

Bram smiled.

Laida's face lit up. "Arden! Have a seat."

The way she seemed so excited to see him caused a stir in his belly. He placed a hand against his stomach, unsure what to think. She patted the blanket, and he sat awkwardly next to her, folding his legs crisscross in front of him.

Why, oh why, had he come?

The three of them resumed observing the concert, and Ardenis did the same. He tried to focus on the music. The violinists moved their bows, and the xylophone kept the time, but he couldn't immerse himself in the same tired songs played every few nights from outside the tower. The performance didn't lack in technique, but held no excitement. The music increased in volume, but without passion, nothing like the majesty he'd heard on Thera.

Then he looked at Laida.

She smiled as she watched, and her eyes seemed to glisten. She swayed to the beat of the music, unconsciously. The orchestra rose into a flourish of sound, and Laida opened her mouth and let out a noise that could have been a sob, if crying existed in Acantha. She placed her hand over her heart and closed her eyes as the music swelled out.

This. This was why he had come. Ardenis tore his eyes from her as the crowd burst into applause. He followed a second behind.

"Oh, Arden, you came at the best part. Wasn't that wonderful?" She stared at the orchestra, hand still over her heart.

He watched her. "Yes, it was wonderful."

She looked at him, and he turned away, torn by his mixed emotions of guilt and excitement.

"What made you decide to come?" she asked.

"I've decided I like music." He smiled to make it more convincing.

"Good," Bram said. "I'll be more diligent in reminding you about the next performance."

"Thank you, Bram. I'd appreciate that." He really would.

Days later, Ardenis ate bacon and eggs, leaning over his plate and laughing with Bram at breakfast. The dining hall was full of people and conversation, just as Ardenis liked it. It distracted him from his troubles.

"After the concert the other night," Bram said, "I saw Hector looking around backstage at the pavilion."

"Probably trying to fill his rule-breaking quota." Ardenis chuckled to himself. There was no quota. At least, not that he knew of. He flinched, realizing he'd just used sarcasm, a form of lying.

Bram paused in his eating. "What is that noise?" He glanced around the room.

Ardenis looked up. The usual cacophony of voices had definitely risen in volume. Faces turned toward the entrance, and he followed their gazes, but too many people stood in the way for him to see anything except a brief glimpse of golden hair.

He met Bram's gaze. "Laida," they said in unison, Bram in form of a question, and Ardenis a statement.

Everyone parted as Laida walked through the room toward them. Ardenis's mouth fell open.

Laida had piled her hair up on her head in a loose bun of golden strands. Just like Eva. Just like the picture he showed her. The unapproved picture.

Wisps of her hair tumbled down, framing her oval face and smooth skin. Her eyes gleamed with merriment and a casual innocence.

Around the room, women gaped, then promptly played with their hair, twisting it to mimic Laida's.

This was not good. He squeezed his fork until the handle dug into his palm.

"Good morning, Ardenis. Bram." She smiled and walked past them toward the counter for her porridge and fruit. The crowd tracked her with their eyes, whispering amongst each other.

Bram raised his eyebrow, and Ardenis remembered to close his mouth. He sat back at his plate and ate with reckless abandon, shoveling heaping forkfuls of eggs in at a time.

Laida. He should have known. Of course she'd try something new. Acanthians thrived on new information from Thera, but that information was always pre-approved by the council. With complete innocence, it was only natural she'd act on what she saw. He was immensely glad the enforcers breakfasted earlier in the day. If Hector saw Laida... Ardenis shot out of his seat. He had to warn her.

Laida approached and sat next to him. He glanced down at her hair, then her eyes, and slowly lowered himself back down again.

"What are you doing?" he hissed. If the council found out he'd shown her and they demoted him, he wouldn't be able to observe Eva and Damian any longer.

Bram ate and watched their exchange, but showed no great measure of curiosity or any of the alarm now thrumming through Ardenis's body.

Laida took a dainty bite from her bowl of porridge. "Do you like my hair?" She smiled.

Ardenis grumbled into his plate. "You'll have to take it down before Hector or another enforcer sees it," he said. "They'll never allow it."

"Why not?" She patted her hair.

Just like with technology, fashion trends from Thera required council approval, which didn't always happen. He had to tell her the truth.

Ardenis dropped his voice to a whisper. "The council hasn't approved that drawing. I shouldn't have showed you. I'm sorry." He'd done it to please her, but he'd hurt her far worse than if he'd simply let her curiosity go unsatisfied.

"No?" She tilted her head to him. It was as if he could see her mind working through what he implied and what it would mean if the council found out he'd broken a rule. "It will be okay, Ardenis."

Ardenis looked into her beseeching face and immediately forgot what he planned to say. He rubbed his eyes. "Just be careful."

He stood and dumped his empty plate into the bin, disgusted with himself. "Goodbye, Bram. Laida."

"Don't forget there's a performance tonight," Bram called out from behind a mouthful of bacon.

Ardenis nodded his thanks and headed to the tower. He hadn't considered Laida would mimic Eva. The two worlds were colliding in ways they were never meant to, and he could only blame himself.

CHAPTER

SEVEN

A s time went on, Ardenis watched Damian make the trek to Oakrin, and often Eva would visit her recently favored aunt in the country. Each time, he tried taking his observations elsewhere, but instincts always brought him back. His efforts to remain loyal to the rules of Acantha and not watch romantic love became half-hearted, then ceased altogether. But still he wondered why Damian was important to the happenings of Thera.

When Ardenis arrived at the tower and gazed into the watch window, this time his instincts surprised him and led him straight to Eva. She sat in her room on the top level of Oakrin Keep on a cushioned bench in front of an elaborately carved vanity. Her maid, Mary, finished buttoning a fine cream silk dress with gold embroidery. It flowed over Eva's body down to the fitted sleeves that went all the way to her wrists. As Lord Ferran's only child, she was well provided for. Rich furnishings adorned the room; a huge canopied bed, a plush bear-hide rug, and a desk littered with expensive fineries: perfume bottles, jewelry, and powder boxes.

Eva smiled at her reflection and fidgeted in her seat. Mary, in her plain linen dress and dark brown hair pinned high on her head, grabbed a comb.

"Your father has been very generous with this dress, my lady." Mary grinned making her smile lines crinkle her round cheeks as she worked the comb through Eva's dark hair. "But of course, he had to be! It's not every day you get to have an audience with the king."

Eva caught Mary's eye in the mirror, and they burst into laughter.

"I'm so excited, Mary! I've never been to the castle before." Eva gripped her seat in an effort to sit still, while Mary parted her hair and styled it into elaborate twisting braids.

"Well, you have, but you were probably too young to remember. I can't believe you're already eighteen." Mary sniffled. She'd taken care of Eva since she was just a baby, raising her own children in the process. "Your mother would be so proud."

Eva's smile turned forlorn, and Mary changed the subject. "You're going to have a grand time tonight at your coming out feast." She wound the braids up close to Eva's head, then fitted a golden net dotted with white pearls to hold her hair in place. "Not every young lady gets to have her feast in the splendid capital city of Pavora. You're lucky Lord Ferran is in the king's favor."

Eva nodded, offering a smile.

The time had escaped Ardenis. Eva's eighteenth birthday feast was so near.

Mary put her hands on Eva's shoulders and turned her around. "Now, you mind your manners and be on your best behavior."

Eva pursed her lips and narrowed her eyes, but they lit up with a twinkle of mirth.

Mary laughed. "Forgive me, love, sometimes I forget that just like my own children, you're not a wee one anymore." She sighed. "You'll do fine at the king's dinner."

Eva hugged Mary, then hopped up and stuck her feet into the pointed, matching cream silk shoes laid out for her. She returned to the vanity, opened a drawer, and pulled out Damian's wooden comb with the turquoise stone. She stuck it in her hair, beaming at her reflection.

There was a knock at her door.

"Come in," Mary called.

A servant entered the room and bowed before Eva. "My lady, Lord Ferran requests your presence. The carriage will leave shortly."

"Almost ready." She put lip color and powder on, then left her room and followed the servant and Mary through the dimly lit stone corridor. They made their way down several winding staircases, then through another long corridor lit by sunlight streaming through open windows to the front entrance of the keep.

Two carriages, each with a pair of white horses, waited at the bottom of the stone steps. The attending servants, including Mary, rode in the second larger carriage. In addition, several guards on horseback accompanied the lord and his daughter.

A servant assisted Eva into the first carriage under the watchful eye of her father, Lord Ferran. He wore a black surcoat over his silk tunic, with a longsword sheathed at his side. His brown hair came down to his bearded chin, styled purposefully to curl under—a current trend among wealthy men which Ardenis found strange. His slight frame lent him an aura of innocence, or perhaps weakness. Ardenis reminded himself this was the man who'd tried to assassinate Prince Isaac with the help of Warin.

Eva settled her dress into place on the cushioned bench.

"You look lovely, my dear," Ferran said. "You could pass for a princess."

Eva patted her perfect hair and smiled. "Thank you, Father. I can't wait to see the castle. Will it take long?"

"Not long." He glanced out the window as the carriage pulled away from the keep and traveled under the open portcullis between the towers. "We're off to a late start, but once we leave Oakrin, we'll travel into Pavora woods and stop for a rest. After that it's only another hour."

Eva nodded and pulled a small book out of her pocket. Ardenis was tempted to read it along with her, but she had read it many times, and Ardenis already knew it front to back. It told a story of two young people, forbidden to be together, and overcoming impossible odds in the name of love. He could see the basis of its appeal.

It would take some time to travel through the woods and reach their stopping point. Aside from watching Eva read, there wouldn't be anything to see, so Ardenis checked in on Damian. He was on his family's farm, tilling the ground for autumn planting.

Since all was fine, and he didn't sense an urgency from his instincts to watch anything pressing, Ardenis took a break. He stood and stretched, admiring his fellow watchers; Cadence, Wes, Amalia, and several others. Amalia had kept her distance from him since their conversation in the baths. Or maybe it just seemed that way.

He left the tower in search of Bram and found him near the sports complex. Bram smiled in greeting and spared a moment to play a round of Tafl—a strategic board game Ardenis had picked up from Thera, which had faded from mortal memory—within the large complex building, which Ardenis won. Then they ate lunch with Vinia in the dining hall, something Ardenis didn't normally stop to do. When it was near the time Ardenis estimated Eva would stop for her own lunch, he arrived back to the tower and focused in on Thera.

He nearly toppled his chair at what he saw.

Ardenis beheld pure chaos. They were under attack.

Ferran's guards struggled to fight off a band of brigands armed to the teeth—Warin's men. Ardenis recognized them immediately. Warin was missing, but the rest were there, including Lenard from the tavern, along with a few new faces.

Eva huddled down in her carriage, crying and covering her head, her father beside her. His eyes looked far more calculating than surprised.

Warin's brigands, on foot, engaged Ferran's outnumbered guards on horseback. The clang of swords echoed throughout the woods, scattering birds into the sky. More brigands hauled the servants out of the second carriage. They rifled through trunks, strewing the contents about on the dirt road. The brigands led trembling servants to the side of the trail, forcing their hands in the air with the point of their swords. Mary stood among them, wringing her hands, though not weeping like some of the others. Her horrified glance alternated between her captors and Eva's carriage.

One brigand broke away and stomped to Eva's carriage. His dark eyes shifted around as he latched a greasy hand on the door. Gripping his sword, Lord Ferran stood. He stabbed it through the open window and into the brigand's chest. Eva whimpered beneath the man's screams, but didn't uncover her eyes.

The brigand slumped against the carriage, clutching his chest until he slid to the ground.

Ferran hopped out, shoving the man's body aside, sword at the ready. "Stay put, Eva." He slammed the door and peered at his surroundings.

Lenard and one other stood at attention in front of a covered wagon, as if guarding the contents. Sword up, Ferran strode toward them. With the quick sure movements of an accomplished swordsman, he pointed the tip of the sword at them.

"Flee or perish," Ferran said.

Lenard exchanged glances with his companion, then burst out laughing, no doubt unintimidated by Ferran's fancy clothes and skinny frame. Ferran merely scowled, pressing his blade forward.

Leonard raised his sword. "My Lord?" he asked cautiously, casting another uneasy glance at his oversized partner.

Ferran swung his sword. Both brigands raised their weapons to defend themselves. Metal clanged on metal as they exchanged blows, feinting and parrying. It became clear to Ardenis they were no match for him, even two on one. The brigands' jaws tightened with the increasing effort as they backed to the wagon.

With one hand up behind him, and a wide stance with one foot in front of the other, Ferran thrust like a master. He swept the big brigand's sword to the side and stabbed him precisely through the heart. The man dropped to his knees, dead. Ferran turned his intent gaze on Lenard.

Lenard spat and moved his sword off to the side in surrender.

"Drop it and I won't hurt you," Ferran said, approaching and pointing the blade to his throat.

Lenard dropped his sword. He held his hands in the air as he chuckled with awkward relief.

Ferran's grip tightened on the hilt. In one deft movement, he swept back his sword and sliced. Lenard grabbed at his throat and fell to the ground.

Ferran watched as Lenard choked on his own blood until he lay still, eyes wide even in death. "There now." He wiped his sword in the dirt.

Around the wagon and carriages, the guards killed off rest of the brigands. Ferran ignored his daughter's muffled sobs, and the panicked servants. He sheathed his sword and rushed to the back of the wagon.

Curious what the brigands were guarding, Ardenis moved his gaze inside.

"What in the depths of the Hereafter!" Ardenis shouted at the watch room. He half-left Thera so the worlds blurred together in his vision, allowing him to be in both at once. "Who is watching Prince Isaac?"

His outburst was met with fourteen pairs of wide eyes from the day watchers currently in the tower. Amalia's eyes were the widest, and she shook her head at him. He thrust himself back into Thera, and to Prince Isaac who was tied up in the back of the covered wagon, gagged, and struggling against his bonds.

The brigands had kidnapped the prince, and Ardenis hadn't seen it. His instincts hadn't warned him.

Isaac stopped struggling, eyes narrowed in suspicion when Lord Ferran knelt beside him. Ferran pulled the gag out of his mouth, then cut the rope binding his wrists and ankles.

"You're safe, my prince." Ferran pulled him up and bowed to one knee.

Isaac wiped his mouth and rubbed his sore wrists. He stared at his rescuer. "Lord Ferran, correct?" His voice was hoarse, as if he'd been screaming.

"Yes, My Liege."

"You may rise."

Ferran jumped out of the wagon, then raised a hand to help Isaac down. The prince waved him off, but stumbled slightly when his stiff legs hit the ground. Ardenis couldn't believe the brigands had almost succeeded.

Isaac smoothed his short hair and gave a shaky smile. "I owe you a great deal of gratitude. You've likely saved my life."

Ardenis tilted his head. The brigands just happened to cross paths with Lord Ferran? Of all the ways they could have traveled to escape the palace?

Ferran bowed. "It is my honor, Prince Isaac. Please, you must be distraught over all that's happened this day. Allow me to check on my daughter, and then may we escort you to the castle?"

"Yes. Please." Isaac gestured him on, his overconfidence making up for the fear which showed through in his pale complexion. Though he was tall for his age, and more mature than most, he was still just a boy of twelve.

Ferran took quick steps back to his carriage and poked his head through the open window. Someone had removed the dead brigand's body and most of the blood from the carriage. Eva sat on the bench, rocked back and forth by Mary, who rubbed her back too quickly for comfort. Tears streamed down their faces.

"Eva," Ferran hissed. They both startled and looked up. "Prince Isaac was in the outlaw's wagon. He's safe, but shaken. Make yourself presentable. He rides with us for the castle." And he was gone.

Eva sat up and shot a panicked look at Mary. They both jumped to action. Eva dried her face on a handkerchief while Mary smoothed her hair down with her hands. She fluffed Eva's dress and reapplied lip color and powder.

"What does it matter how I look after what we've been through?" Eva smoothed her hand down her sleeves and rubbed at a tear-stained spot on the silk.

"Of course it matters, dear. And you look as wonderful as circumstances allow," Mary said, patting her hand. She backed her full frame out the carriage door.

"Your Highness," Ardenis heard Mary say from outside the carriage.

Isaac appeared in the doorway, and Eva dropped into a bow—as low as she could, given the confines of the carriage.

He stepped inside. "Please rise."

Eva looked up, and Isaac held out his hand to help her. She took it, smiling shyly as he squeezed and let go. He took the seat across from her, spreading his embroidered cape around himself.

He stared at her.

Eva blushed and bowed her head. She cleared her throat. "Forgive me, I'm still quite shaken up. I've never been through anything like that. Are you well, my prince?"

Isaac looked at his hands clasped in his lap. "I'm not quite sure. I haven't had a chance to contemplate all that's happened." He glanced back up at Eva, and she smiled reassuringly. "I was out hunting—with my guards, of course—and then suddenly I was alone. I heard sounds of a scuffle, and then the outlaws had me surrounded." He took a shaky breath and stared out the window. "I shot one with my bow before they took me. My guard, Peter, he's like a friend... I don't know if he's alive."

Eva's eyes had gone wide, but creased in concern. "How awful." She reached across the short space and patted Isaac's hands like Mary had done to her. "We'll get back to the castle soon. I'm sure Peter is all right."

Isaac smiled, but then Eva seemed to remember who he was. She gave a small squeak and pulled her hand back. "Forgive me, my prince." She bowed her head. "I didn't... I... I'm sorry."

Isaac laughed. "Nonsense. There's no need for apology. It felt nice to be comforted. It's been a trying day." Despite his assurance, Ardenis saw Isaac's hands shaking.

Ferran entered the carriage, bowing. "We're ready to depart, Your Highness." He sat next to Eva across from Isaac.

"Your daughter is very kind, Lord Ferran." He smiled at Eva, and she blushed again.

"Your Highness is generous." Ferran signaled to the driver, and the trek to the castle resumed.

"We need a distraction from our ordeal," Eva announced, leaning forward in feigned delight. "Prince Isaac, what is life like at the castle? I've never been."

Eva's lifetime of social training overtook her distress. A lady of her standing would have been extensively groomed to put the room at ease, even over her own suffering.

Isaac glanced at Ferran. "Castle life is not all that exciting. Mother died last year giving birth to my younger sister, as I'm sure you know, and since then I'm rarely allowed away. Though, I can't blame my father. There have been many attempts on my life." His shoulders drooped.

Ardenis had almost forgotten about that. Isaac's mother had fallen, going into premature labor. The baby did not survive, and it left a strong impression on Isaac.

"My mother left when I was young, too." Eva placed her hand over his, her eyes full of sympathy.

Eva's mother had run away with a timber merchant who she'd known in her hometown before marrying Lord Ferran. He'd sent his guards to retrieve them, and they'd no choice but to flee the kingdom to save their lives. Few knew the true story, though. It was all kept very quiet so as not to disgrace the family.

"Tell me about your life," Isaac said, eyes alight with real interest.

"All right." Eva scooted forward on the bench.

Ardenis watched as a friendship blossomed between Eva and the young prince while they traveled through the woods, swapping stories from their childhoods and eventually laughing together.

Riders had been sent ahead with the news of the safe rescue of Prince Isaac. A whole company of guards thundered up to surround them before they even reached the castle. Lord Ferran ordered his carriage to stop, as if they had a choice. A castle guard dismounted and threw open their door, King Tristan himself at his heels.

"Peter!" Isaac smiled with relief.

Peter nodded, still clad in hunting leathers, his dutiful expression accented by a friendly, relieved glint in his eyes.

It wasn't much of a reunion. King Tristan barged ahead of Peter, filling the door with his large girth. He wore thick, expensive furs despite the early autumn warmth that kept everyone in lighter clothing. Peter bowed to his knee.

"Isaac!" King Tristan yanked his son from the carriage, crushing him in his embrace. "The heir has returned safe and sound." Ardenis knew Tristan's concern was genuine. His capacity for love and compassion started and stopped with his only son.

"I'm fine, Father." Isaac wiggled out of his embrace. "Thanks to Lord Ferran and his daughter, Lady Eva."

Ferran and Eva bowed low from inside the carriage, but did not speak.

"Take the prince back to the castle." Tristan snapped. The castle guard moved to comply.

"If it's all the same to you, Father, I'm enjoying getting to know Lady Eva. She's quite funny. Might I continue my ride with her?"

Tristan examined Eva, then nodded. "Lord Ferran," he said, not taking his eyes of Eva.

"Your Majesty." Ferran bowed once again.

"My son and I will ride with you to the castle."

Ferran and Eva sat back in their seats. Isaac returned to his, but moved over to allow room for the king. Tristan stepped into the carriage with assistance, stooping to clear his heavy golden crown with its shining jewels. His large frame rocked the carriage back and forth. He sat next to his son and ordered the party to continue.

"Your riders informed me you rescued my son from outlaws." Tristan said, addressing Ferran.

"Lord Ferran cut my bindings himself, Father. And Lady Eva, despite being distraught from the experience, found it within her to cheer me up."

Beneath thick eyebrows, Tristan glanced at his son, then to Eva, who blushed and stared at the floor, then back to Ferran.

"It seems the kingdom is indebted to you, Lord Ferran." He played with a gold ring topped with a giant ruby, attempting to twist it though it didn't budge over his thick fingers. "It is fortunate the outlaws chose your path, of all places, for their escape, and that you were on your way to the castle. And I hear you killed every one of them, further helping by ridding me the burden of hanging them." Tristan stared at Ferran. As protocol demanded, Ferran didn't look the king in the eyes. "I will take the remainder of the day to choose your reward."

"I assure you, no reward is needed, Your—"

The king waved his hand. "Nevertheless, a reward you shall have. Lady Eva!" Her gaze snapped to his, then she averted her eyes. King Tristan reached and lifted her hand from her knee. He bent down and kissed it. Eva gave a quick intake of breath. "Thank you for helping my son through his trial. You never know how a man will react when he experiences death for the first time." He turned to the prince.

Isaac smiled at his father and let loose a shaky breath.

Eva's cheeks burned even deeper. "You're welcome, Your Majesty, though Prince Isaac helped me as much as I helped him."

"Your coming out feast is tonight, yes?" he asked. Eva nodded, and Tristan placed her hand back on her knee. He stared out the window for a long while. "Lord Ferran, join me and my advisor in the throne room after you've recovered from your journey. Tonight we'll celebrate your daughter's coming out and the safe return of the prince."

With what seemed like genuine joy, Eva continued to swap pleasantries with Isaac. Only Ardenis noticed her hands curled into tight fists. Like him, her thoughts seemed to be with Damian and what her coming out truly meant—an announcement to the world she was ready to find a *suitable* husband.

CHAPTER

EIGHT

va's party traveled around the outskirts of Pavora, where the
bustle and street traffic thinned compared to the heart of
the city, though the flying royal banners of blue still caused
a ruckus, drawing people like beacons out to see the king. Their party
approached the castle, built at the edge of a vast lake surrounded by
lush forest. Because of the northern lake, aptly named Pavora Lake,
the city had pushed back into the woods south of the castle as the
population grew.

The group passed through two sets of heavily fortified gates set
in stone walls wide enough to house the guards. Eva's eyes lit up at
the sight of the tremendous castle, its stone turrets reaching toward
Acantha. Battlements lined the outer wall all the way around,
patrolled by guards with swords and crossbows. Ardenis considered
it the grandest castle in the region, since the Greygar War turned the
Trula Palace to ruin four centuries ago. Though the palace in
Docimer, the capital of the northeastern kingdom of Kestrea, nearly
matched it in grandeur with its setting in the mountains.

King Tristan exited the carriage first, followed by his son and the rest of the party. Guards lined a path to the entrance. A multitude of castle staff and servants bowed at their arrival.

When they were all safely within the castle, Ardenis ended his watch. He continued to look into watch window, pretending. Preparing his heart and mind. He'd cursed and yelled at his fellow watchers. The sound had shattered the ever-quiet room, bouncing around in a seemingly endless echo. His fingers squeezed around the armrests. Why had no one warned him Isaac had been taken?

He released his grip on the chair and looked up. The same watchers were still in the room. Most were in a watch, but some milled around. When he looked at Amalia, she glanced up, as if she'd been waiting. Why would she have waited for him?

He cleared his throat. "I'm sorry," he said in a loud whisper. Those not in a watch looked at him. "I apologize for disturbing you." He glanced back at Amalia again, but she looked away, as did everyone else in the room. He hoped they'd keep his outburst to themselves, and not see it for what it was—a sign he might be emotionally altered.

It was time to leave—that's what he would have told any watcher in his predicament—but he couldn't. He had to find out what turns this day would take. Why had his instincts led him to Eva and Lord Ferran instead of Damian this time?

He gazed back into the watch window and followed Lord Ferran as he walked down the aisle of the throne room. His steady steps echoed in the vast stone space arched with wood beams and graced by golden candelabras. Few people stood around the room, mostly servants in palace livery at attention beside tables of grapes, cheeses, breads, and rose-colored wine.

Did the aroma of the of the creamy cheeses with their wax coatings smell as pungent as they did in Acantha's dining hall? Ardenis would never know.

Ferran bowed to one knee before King Tristan.

"Rise, Lord Ferran, and sit." Tristan beckoned to him from his oversized lavishly carved throne. Large windows—an overly confident architectural design—lined the back wall, revealing grey clouds moving across the sky.

Ferran rose. His searching eyes looked as Ardenis felt: genuinely in the dark about what to expect from the king. A servant scrambled, carrying over a chair, which he placed behind Ferran on the plush aisle runner.

"Leave us," Tristan said.

Servants filed out of the throne room until only a pair of guards remained at each of the three doors. The king's trusted advisor, Richard, stepped to his side. Ferran didn't spare a glance to Richard's long, neatly cut hair and fine clothes.

Richard ruled over land along the western shore of Alysies, awarded to him by King Tristan when, as an advisor's apprentice, he discovered the former advisor was passing information to spies from the kingdom of Daltieri, their neighbors to the north. Richard, though young for his title, served the king with pride. He stood staring at the back wall, wearing a bored expression, but Ardenis wasn't fooled. He kept his ears open, reporting anything of importance to the king he owed his wealth.

The throne room door shut behind the last servant, the bang echoing in the large space. Ferran licked his lips.

King Tristan smiled. "What an eventful day we've had. The sole heir to the throne was kidnapped by outlaws. Not the first attempt on his life, of course, but definitely the most successful." His words were oddly cheery for such dire news.

Ferran shifted in his seat.

"Did you know, just a few months ago, I captured a man who tried the same thing?" The king chuckled. "I had him tortured for quite some time to discover who hired him." He stared into Ferran's impassive face. Sweat beaded on Ferran's brow and the seconds ticked by in the room. "But he died before learning anything useful. My only son is still in danger." His confident demeanor slipped at the end, voice going rough.

Ferran didn't skip a beat. "I'm sorry to hear that, Your Majesty. I'll do everything in my power to protect him."

Tristan tapped his finger on his armrest. "Yes. Hmm." He sat up straighter and clapped his hands once. "Well," he said in a louder voice. "You're a distant relation of mine, in line for the throne, though way, way down, correct?"

Ferran nodded. "Yes, Your Majesty. Twenty-second if my scribes are correct." He couldn't pretend ignorance in front of the watchful eyes of the king and his all-knowing advisor, even if it implicated him.

"My son seems to have taken a liking to your daughter, and I am in your debt for today's heroics. So..." He snapped his fingers, and Richard, with a barely detectable clench in his jaw, handed over a sheet of parchment. Tristan held it far from his face and squinted as he read. "Against my advisors' wishes, I hereby propose a betrothal between Lady Eva and my son. They will wed when Isaac is of age."

Lord Ferran let out a small gasp. It took a moment, but then his mouth turned up in a grin.

Ardenis blinked, unsure if he'd heard the king correctly. Eva marry Isaac? Eva loved Damian. She couldn't marry the prince.

People married for alliances and advantages all the time, especially in the royal courts. But, the Fates wouldn't keep apart two souls who loved each other the way Eva and Damian did, would they?

Tristan chuckled. "I believe we've caught him by surprise, Richard."

Richard didn't share his king's humor. "Yes, My Liege." He reformed his mask of boredom, covering what Ardenis perceived as anger over King Tristan's decision.

"Well, what say you?" King Tristan bellowed with a sweep of his heavy arm.

Lord Ferran pried his hands off the chair. He got down on one knee and bowed. "Your Majesty honors me by such an offer."

Ardenis narrowed his eyes. This was Ferran's goal all along. He set up a king so his daughter could marry a prince.

"Of course I do." His smiled dropped. "Richard thinks Isaac should marry Princess Caliya of Daltieri, to encourage better relations between King Zane's kingdom and ours." He leaned forward, "King Zane can kiss my arse."

Tristan was being foolish, an unusual move for him. Ferran was a key player in Alysies politics—being aptly situated near Pavora as a go-between the rest of the lords and their territories—but a match with Daltieri was only logical, bettering trade and alliances. Alysies was a strong kingdom, but any princess from the surrounding kingdoms would make more political sense. He acted with his heart, for his beloved son—not his head.

"And what would you ask in return, Your Majesty, to make the contract valid?" Ferran sat back in his chair, rubbing his sweaty hands on his fine linen trousers.

Tristan tugged at the ruby ring on his finger and stared at Ferran. "A simple request. Your fealty and protection for my son and future daughter-in-law, an allocation of your land to be used for farming, and a commitment of your young troops in Oakrin for my army."

Ferran grinned from ear to ear. "You have my word, Your Majesty." He bowed.

"There you go! That's the reaction I was looking for." Tristan slapped his knee. "I'll announce the news at dinner. Keep this to yourself until then." He sat back in his chair and his voice turned dark. "Let us hope Lady Eva continues to make my son happy in the meantime."

Ferran bowed again, and when Tristan waved him away, he left the room with an almost imperceptible skip in his step.

Tristan had ensured Isaac's safety, but Ardenis's thoughts went to Damian. Eva and Damian belonged together. They had true love. Even if this was the way of the world, how could the Fates allow this? Ardenis's heart lurched. How would Eva react when she heard the news?

Ardenis watched, and as requested, Lord Ferran did not mention the betrothal to anyone, not even Eva. After a brief rest, Eva spent her afternoon preparing for her presentation to the king and her coming out feast. The suites they gave Eva and Lord Ferran sat in the west wing of the castle, decorated with painted wood beams and rich carpets. Mary laid out the dresses they'd brought, tsking over the ones ruined by the brigands during the attack. Eva had just settled on a nice emerald green dress when a castle handmaid entered her well-appointed room. She carried a gown and a black velvet box.

"For the kindness bestowed upon the Royal Prince, His Majesty wishes to present you with this gift," the handmaid said, holding the dress aloft. It was a deep blue silk, with a separate petticoat, which would make it impressively large at the bottom and narrow at the waist. The sleeves only came down to mid-forearm, and the neckline hit at the collarbones. It was very modern for the times.

Eva's eyes lit up, and she ran her fingers down the fine material and over the crystals sewn into the bodice. Mary eyed it suspiciously.

"Those are diamonds, my lady," the handmaid said. Eva gasped and withdrew her hand. She glanced back at Mary, whose eyes went wide. The handmaid curtsied. "I will help you dress for dinner."

Eva squealed and grinned. Mary and the new handmaid helped her fit the petticoat and dress over her underclothes. It cinched at the back with a silk ribbon, and the maid pulled it tighter and tighter.

Eva exhaled and grabbed at her middle. "It's too tight!"

"It's the latest fashion, my lady. You'll look lovely once we do your hair."

Eva nodded and sat in the chair the handmaid indicated. The handmaid removed the golden net from her hair, as well as Damian's comb. Eva watched it in the handmaid's hands. Her eyes tracked it faithfully until it was set carelessly on the table amongst the brushes and hairpins.

Eva snatched it up. "Be careful with this. It's very dear to me." She smiled down at it, cradling it in her hands.

"Sorry, my lady." The handmaid unbraided Eva's dark hair, which fell in cascading waves down her back. She then rebraided it, wrapping the braids tight against Eva's skull.

Eva rubbed at her head where her hair pulled at her skin. Mary shot her a sympathetic look.

When her hair was complete, Eva stuck the comb back in it. The handmaid's mouth dropped open, aghast. "I'm sorry, my lady, but the comb must remain in your room with your other things. It would be in poor taste to add your own accessories to the king's gift. Besides, turquoise pales in comparison to diamonds."

Anger flashed in Eva's eyes, but she controlled it. "I'd much prefer to wear it, thank you."

"It would be an insult to the king, my lady." the handmaid replied, eyes going to Mary in search of support.

"Wouldn't want to insult the king, my love," Mary said.

Ardenis frowned. Eva should be allowed to keep the comb—the symbol of Damian's love—if she chose.

Eva let loose a sad sigh of defeat. She reached for the comb and slowly slid it from her hair. "Please take care of this."

Mary wrapped her hand around Eva's and offered a tight-lipped smile of understanding. Did Mary know where the comb came from?

The handmaid lifted the velvet box and opened it, displaying the contents for all to see. Ardenis caught a glimpse of sparkling jewels.

Eva's mouth fell open. "What's this?"

"By King's request. Come, my lady."

She led Eva to a full-length mirror. From the box, the handmaid pulled a tiara glittering with pearls and diamonds and placed it on Eva's head where Damian's comb had been.

"The king is very fond of Prince Isaac. Your father must have made a great impression today." Mary beamed.

Ardenis's frown grew deeper. Unease swirled within. The tiara was as big a statement as any to the king's claim.

Eva stroked her new accessory and glanced in the mirror. The dress accentuated her waistline, and her hairstyle made her look regal. She smiled and twirled, but lacked her previous enthusiasm.

"It's time for the presentation, my lady." The handmaid curtsied again.

Eva followed her out of the room and down several corridors similar to the ones at Oakrin Keep, though longer and filled with servants, scattered tapestries, portraits of past royals, and paintings of Alysian landscapes. The handmaid crossed a threshold flanked by guards where the double doors were wide open. They stopped just inside the throne room.

"Lady Eva Camber of Oakrin," a herald announced, his loud voice resonating within the stone room.

Eva's eyes opened wide as she took in the scene. Torches and candelabras blazed, glinting off suits of armor decorating the room and highlighting the crimson aisle runner leading the way to the king. Several lords and ladies dressed in their finery stood at the back and around the sides, including Lord Ferran. They oohed and aahed at the site of her. Mary beamed as she took her place near the other servants in the back corner of the room.

King Tristan sat in his throne at the end of the long aisle, smiling at her. Ardenis could only assume that the king, who cared more for his son than his kingdom, was doing what he thought best for both. Ardenis's palms went slick at the thought of what was to come.

Eva straightened her shoulders and walked alone to the front. She held her head high and proud, regal in her tiara and sapphire blue dress—Alysian blue, Ardenis realized. It matched the cape the king wore and the Alysian crests hanging on each side of the throne room.

When she reached King Tristan, she bowed to one knee, her dress billowing out around her. After a respectful pause, she looked up, waiting to be released. Tristan smiled and nodded. Eva returned a tenuous smile, then rose and walked back down the aisle, head a little higher.

Courtiers tittered as she passed, some with smiles and some with scorn. They pointed at the tiara gracing her head, voices growing louder until Eva had left the room.

And that was it. Ardenis had seen this tradition many times. Sometimes there was conversation, but King Tristan had never smiled before. The spectators filed out behind her, eager for their meal.

They led Eva into a dining hall where rectangular tables sat end to end in a square around the room. They boasted white linen cloths lined with platters overflowing with food, silver flatware, and goblets of ale and wine. The seats filled with conversing courtiers, wearing dresses and capes as varying in color as their jewels. Many wore shades of blue, the color of the kingdom of Alysies, but Ardenis also spotted deep burgundies, pale greens, and amber yellows representing the various Houses in attendance. They sat eyeing the food or each other, waiting for the king to arrive and take the first bite.

Lord Ferran sat to the right of the king's empty chair, marked by its size and gold-gilded ornamentation. A vacant place for Eva sat next to her father. The chair to the left of the king, reserved for Prince Isaac, was also empty.

Eva took a deep breath, coughing when the dress constricted her lungs. She clasped her hands in front of her and walked slowly to take her place beside her father.

Ferran's eyes flashed to her tiara, and he beamed. "I have happy news, my dear,"

Eva sat, and a servant pushed in her chair. "What news, Father?" Her smile wavered ever so slightly as she smoothed out her dress and her gaze swept the room, taking in the many pairs of eyes on her.

Ferran hesitated and then shook his head. "The king will announce it."

She glanced at him, but he locked his lips together and said nothing.

Ardenis's pulse quickened with fear. How would Eva take such sudden news?

A trumpet sounded from the doorway behind Eva, and she jumped. Everyone quieted.

A servant dressed in rich blue livery entered the room with his chin high and upraised hands clasped before him. "Lords and Ladies, and honored guests of the court, it is my great privilege to present His Royal Majesty, King Tristan Rylandor, and his Royal Highness, Prince Isaac Rylandor of Alysies."

The people stood and bowed as the king and prince entered, making for their chairs. Isaac's light-brown hair was smoothed back beneath a bejeweled crown. He leaned forward, his tunic and vest pressing against the table, and smiled at Eva around their fathers. She looked over and smiled back.

Ardenis rubbed his palms against his legs.

King Tristan wore blue Alysian silk and a fur mantle below his golden crown. He cleared his throat, motioning everyone to quiet, though no one was speaking. "First, I'd like to introduce you all to Lady Eva Camber of Oakrin, as tonight we toast to her coming of age as a lady of the court." He raised his goblet and drank.

Everyone around the room drank as well.

"To Eva!" they said, casting her curious looks and polite smiles. The more influential families took slow sips behind narrowed eyes that stayed focused on her tiara. Such direct attention from the king was unusual, and it seemed many were beginning to suspect.

King Tristan went on. "As some of you know, a band of outlaws kidnapped Prince Isaac today." There were dramatic gasps around the room, though the whole castle would have heard the news. "Lord Ferran defeated those who would seek to harm our kingdom, and tonight we celebrate many things." He raised his goblet, and the courtiers did the same. "To the safe return of the prince, to Lord Ferran's daring rescue, and," Ardenis gripped the ledge of the watch window, "to the agreement I've reached with Lord Ferran." He smiled at Isaac.

Isaac smiled back without a hint of confusion. Ardenis held his breath.

"I'd like to formally announce the betrothal of Prince Isaac of Alysies and Lady Eva of Oakrin." He lifted his goblet.

True gasps of surprise filled the room. Ardenis watched Eva with unwavering attention. She froze. Her goblet, half raised in the air, began shaking in her hands. Oblivious, Ferran grinned triumphantly. Tristan motioned for Eva and Isaac to stand. Isaac stood with a shy smile on his young face, directed toward Eva.

Eva stared straight ahead at nothing. Ferran tugged on her arm, forcing her to stand, wine sloshing out of her goblet.

"Hurrah!" The king drained his goblet down to the last drop.

"Hurrah!" Everyone drank, though some more bitterly than others. Isaac took a swallow from his goblet.

Ferran glared at Eva while she stood motionless, tears forming in her eyes. "Drink, girl, or so help me," he hissed.

She blinked and brought the cup to her mouth. The liquid touched her lips; she swallowed none.

The guests smiled and toasted. Eva and Isaac sat, and the feast and gossip began. Someone filled Eva's plate, but Ardenis doubted she noticed. She stared at it, a forced smile on her face whenever she was addressed. Ardenis watched her dig her nails into the palms of her hands.

He mimicked the action, but felt no release in the lack of pain.

The dinner went on for an agonizing amount of time. Rumors flew among the noble, growing more scandalous, rising in volume and severity in direct correlation to the amount of wine consumed. Blackmail seemed to be the most widely accepted conclusion. Surely, Lord Ferran held something grave over the king's head. Several of the women were in tears, bemoaning the loss of their own daughters' chance to become the future queen.

Ardenis was proud of Eva; she made it through the whole affair without breaking down. Not one tear shed. She pretended to eat while courtiers stared and whispered behind their drinks—some of the bolder ones shouting from their corners. Isaac smiled fondly at her between courses. Her only slip was not staying for the dancing.

Lord Ferran didn't notice as she feigned a headache and followed a servant back to her room, closing the door softly behind her.

And then the thread she'd been hanging onto snapped.

Eva screamed, arms reaching behind her for the satin ribbon, clawing at the dress. Tears poured down her face, staining the blue silk.

Mary startled awake from her chair. "My lady!" She stumbled up and rushed over, grabbing Eva's hands before they could do more damage.

"Get this off of me!" Eva yelled. "I can't breathe."

Mary snatched the ribbon, loosening it from around Eva's torso, then scrambled to lift the dress over her head. With shaking, fumbling hands, Eva stripped off her petticoat. She thrashed against the material, then went for her shoes and stockings. Tears fell in streaks as she grabbed Damian's comb from the table and threw herself onto the plush bed. She ripped the tiara off her head and flung it across the room. Mary's eyes trailed it in horror. It hit the heavy curtain and bounced, clanking to the floor.

Eva sobbed and screamed into the pillow, muffling the noise.

Ardenis was gaping, hands grabbing his knees. An emotion he couldn't identify ripped through him. It bubbled up in his chest, making him want to clutch his hand over his heart. He knew what it was. Anguish. He felt Eva's pain.

Panting, Mary rushed to Eva's side. "My lady, what's the matter?"

"My father made a deal with the king," she said through her tears. "I'm to marry Prince Isaac."

Mary's mouth dropped open. "My girl, this is happy news! You'll be queen." She rubbed Eva's back in a soothing motion.

Eva only sobbed louder.

"It's not fair, Mary," Eva said between sobs. "It's my life."

"It will be okay, dear." Mary's eyes creased with concern. "Isaac seems like a nice prince."

"You don't understand." Eva rolled over to face Mary, make-up running beneath red eyes. "I'm p—"

Ferran burst into the room unannounced, stumbling. His blood-shot eyes drifted across the room, taking in the discarded dress and tiara, then narrowed in fury at Eva on the bed.

Eva looked up, panic filling her face. She flung herself under the covers, drying her nose and cheeks on the pillow.

"Eva," Ferran pointed at her, swaying where he stood. "You will explain your behavior at dinner, or I will have you horse-whipped!"

Ardenis had never seen Ferran raise an unkind hand to his daughter.

Mary's eyes went wide. "My lady isn't feeling well, Lord—"

"That's enough from you!" Spittle flew from his mouth. "Go clean something."

Mary bowed her head and backed into a corner, making herself invisible.

"Father, I'm sorry about dinner." Eva's voice was surprisingly calm. "The news just took me by surprise, and now I am feeling quite ill."

Though telling tears fell from her eyes, her performance impressed Ardenis. The mask of a practiced lady was only slightly askew.

Ferran looked at his outpointed hand, as if surprised to see it still held in front of him. He dropped it. "Don't ruin this chance, Eva. I've worked hard to secure this. The king wishes to wait until Prince Isaac is of age, then you will marry."

"Of age?" Eva sat up, looking hopeful. "Six more years? I'll be twenty-four!"

"Six years for you to truly win the prince's hand and ensure his happiness. You will behave appropriately at future engagements, or you will regret it."

"Yes, Father." She lowered her eyes. A small smile formed on her lips as she rubbed the turquoise stone on the comb still gripped in her hand.

Ferran stared at her for a moment, then pivoted and lost his balance. He steadied himself, hand braced against the wall as he left the room.

Eva fell back against the pillow. Her tears had dried, and hope bloomed in her eyes. Ardenis could almost see her mind churning with implications. Was she thinking of running away? Or that she could use the extra time to convince Isaac not to marry her?

She fell asleep soon after. Mary swept a loving hand over Eva's cheek and then covered her with a thick quilt. She was collecting the tattered dress when Ardenis ended his watch.

Darkness poured through the tower window when his vision fully shifted back to Acantha. The day watchers had left long ago, and the night watch occupied the room. No one paid him any attention, and he took that as a good sign his outburst over Isaac's kidnapping hadn't been gossiped about.

Exhaustion crept over him. His newfound emotion—anguish—weighed him down. He'd seen it before in mortals, how they acted after a shock or disappointment. Their backs hunched, shoulders drooped as if they no longer had the strength to carry their own weight. Sometimes they shook with silent tears, or loud ones, but he'd never understood. Now he did. His insides felt raw, and that rawness filled up the space for breathing, but it was someone else's pain that shuddered out of him with every exhale.

Maybe Eva would find a way to make things all work out. Damian was a part of this, or else Ardenis's instincts wouldn't have led him to the farm.

Ardenis scrubbed at his face. He had to take control of himself before he was caught.

CHAPTER
NINE

Ardenis left the tower and was assaulted by the sound of a wearisome concert already in progress. The noise echoed off the buildings, folding over itself in a mess of racket before fading into the night air. He was late. He attended every concert now that he'd found a good reason for going. Picturing Laida, sitting and enjoying the music, pushed some of Eva's anguish from his mind.

He hurried down the path toward the pavilion. The orchestra neared the middle of their performance, with the rise and fall of the melody, and he hummed along. The council wouldn't allow him to introduce any new songs until the trends dramatically changed on Thera.

Arriving, he didn't see Laida at her usual spot. There was no golden beacon in the sea of black. Bram sat on the second row of marble seats next to Vinia. Ardenis walked in front of the viewers enjoying the show, and squeezed between his friends, forcing a seat. Vinia smiled in greeting. Bram gave him a cursory glance before focusing back on the music.

Ardenis listened to the performance, trying to concentrate on the harmony of the flutists and pianist. It was useless. He leaned over to Vinia. "Have you seen Laida?"

Vinia's kept her eyes on the orchestra, but whispered, "I believe she's with the council."

"The council?" Ardenis said, loudly, just as the music stopped. Several heads turned.

Vinia focused on him. "They wanted to discuss her new hairstyle."

Laida's new hairstyle. She'd worn it up sparingly since he'd warned her to be careful that first time, and no one had stopped her. An enforcer, one who cared, must have finally seen her, or caught on to the gossip.

Hector's grim face flashed in his mind, and Ardenis stood. All eyes nearby went to him, but looked away when they saw who it was. Vinia and Bram raised their eyebrows.

Ardenis ducked his head and hurried off. Laida was in trouble with the council. There was no doubt it involved Hector somehow. Ardenis didn't have a plan, but Laida might need his help. He could only hope she didn't get demoted, or divulge the secret of where she saw the new hairstyle.

Ardenis reached the council hall, where a torch adorned each of the marble columns, blazing with an intensity that matched the council disposition. Firelight washed across the stone sidewalk and into his eyes. He crossed the courtyard, ignoring the urge to read the bulletin of the latest happenings on Thera. Crickets chirped, and the ever-present scent of sweet roses caressed his nose.

Ardenis stomped up the stone stairs and through the wooden double doors. Hector sat behind the tall desk in the foyer, leaning over a record book. He glanced up, but Ardenis ignored him and made straight for the door to the council room.

Hector stood, bumping into the desk and throwing his chair back. "You can't disturb the council. There's a session in progress. As you well know, Ardenis."

Ardenis paused, his hand on the door—not yet ready to let go—

and inclined his head to the enforcer. Was that a note of condescension in Hector's tone? "Forgive me." He pried his hand away and walked to the desk.

What made Hector think Ardenis already knew the council was in session?

Hector picked up his chair and took his seat. He smoothed his black hair back and straightened his robe. "How may I help you, Watcher Fater?"

Ardenis cleared his throat. "I need to report to the council."

Hector glanced at the council doors and narrowed his eyes, a very Theran gesture that told Ardenis to be careful. If there was anywhere he needed to hide what he'd learned about mortal emotions, it was here. Hector made no move to respond, simply watched, as if studying him.

"I didn't know the council was in session. I will return tomorrow." Ardenis's lips thinned. He'd told another lie, this time to an enforcer. It had slipped out without thought.

Hector straightened the book so the lines were perpendicular to the desk. "The council appreciates your dedication, Watcher Fater. You are a loyal citizen of Acantha." His distrusting tone betrayed the niceties.

Ardenis gave a shallow nod. "I'll bid you goodnight then."

He turned and left the room with only one quick look back to the door separating him from Laida. Would they force her to be born for a simple, unapproved hairstyle change? Would she give away his secret?

He went to her house, with only one quick stop along the way. He sat on her sand-colored chair, lamplight glinting over the many flower vases and one of his paintings on the wall. It was of a blue-eyed boy dressed in rags standing on a cobbled street eating a fresh pastry. A heavy snow fell around him. He'd dreamt that one, and Laida claimed it after the council approved it. It was one of his favorites, and a rare color painting.

Eventually, Laida came through the door carrying a bundle of flowers, starting when she saw him. She put her hands on her hips. Her hair was still piled up in the high bun. "What are you doing here?"

His premature feelings of relief confused him. The scent of the fresh flowers she'd picked washed through the room. Roses. She only collected wild roses when particularly stressed—they cheered her up.

Laida turned back to close the door. Ardenis's grip tightened on the flowers he'd picked on the way, then he stuffed them behind a decorative pillow. No one gave flowers to each other in Acantha—it was a courting gesture on Thera—and he wouldn't do so now, even if they made her happy. It had seemed like a good idea, but now that she was here, maybe not. When she found them, most likely she'd be curious, then move on, thinking no more of it.

Ardenis stood and clenched his fists straight at his sides. "What happened, Laida?" he asked through gritted teeth. If the council punished her... An odd sense of anger welled up in him. "Do you like to make me worry like this?"

She looked at him and cocked her head to the side. "Are you in need of distance, Ardenis?" Her tone conveyed genuine worry and curiosity.

No... Yes. Probably. He was angry, damn it all to the Hereafter. He grimaced. Not only had he opened the tight lid he kept on Thera's emotional influence, he'd also begun thinking like them. Ardenis took a deep breath.

"No need to concern yourself." Laida went around the room, replacing flowers in the various multicolored vases. It was adorable the way she always had fresh flowers in her home, something she'd read on a council bulletin and had kept for her own.

He crossed his arms, waiting for her to explain what happened.

She finished her task and faced him. "Hector Enforcer saw me and requested I undo my hair. I didn't see the need." She patted a stray strand in place. "He said I'd have to report to the council, to which I agreed."

Ardenis seethed. She shouldn't contest an enforcer's orders like that.

How much of her innocence had he ruined with his carelessness?

Laida sat in the chair beside him. "I met with the council and told them I came up with this on my own. They took a long time discussing it, but eventually agreed I could keep it." She laughed. He did not. "What's the matter, Arden?"

The problem was, she didn't come up with that hairstyle on her own.

"I shouldn't have showed you that picture," he said. "I didn't think you'd try to copy it. I—"

"I never mentioned you. They don't know it's from Thera." She watched him.

He reeled. Was his presence influencing his friends so heavily? She *lied* to the council! For him. Did she even realize what she'd done, that she'd picked up the nuances of Theran deceit? How did Laida know to keep his indiscretion safe, or that she even needed to?

Ardenis's chest tightened.

He'd told her, that's how. He'd told her the drawing of Eva hadn't been approved, and implied to keep it secret. Now she was caught up in his deception. *He'd* taught her to lie.

"I wasn't worried about myself," he said and looked away. What had he done? Every moment with her only put her in more danger of his stupidity. He couldn't meet her gaze as he hurried for the door. "I'm so sorry, Laida. Goodnight."

Laida didn't call him back as he left for his own house, just a few lanes over. He didn't expect her to.

She was simply doing what she always did—behaving as he was supposed to be; neutral, emotionless. Even so, she'd always pushed the rules just a bit, rather she realized it or not. That's how she'd become transfer leader, finding new and better ways to operate within her calling. He'd always been the opposite, leading by example and following the rules. It was him who'd put her out of order, with mistake after mistake. Bending and breaking rules he never would have even considered before he'd watched Damian and Eva. He had to get back to the right side of the emotional veil, but what if the change couldn't be reversed?

He had to protect Laida from what he'd done to her, keeping her from the enforcer's notice, even if that meant also keeping her from himself.

⊰❖⊱

Needing—though not wanting—distance from Thera, Ardenis met his friends the next morning at the recreation complex. White columns lined the green, grassy space used for all sorts of activities. Today, Bram had organized kickball.

People lined up in pairs all down the field, the sounds of their kicks and low conversation filling the air. They didn't play as Therans did, racing each other to be first to the ball, puffing from exertion. That wasn't allowed. No, they moved at a leisurely pace, lacking any emotion or sign of competitiveness. Instead of scoring points, they simply kicked the ball back and forth to each other. Still, most Acanthians appreciated the recreational time to practice Theran customs.

Ardenis admired the way Laida moved as she kicked the ball to him, her golden hair following her movement. The ball rolled over the short grass and stopped at his feet. Beside him, Vinia kicked the ball to Bram across the field. He missed, and the ball rolled to one of the columns surrounding the field.

"Good kick, Vinia," Ardenis said.

She smiled, then something drew her attention down the field. The claps of sandaled feet hitting balls tapered off.

Hector walked down the sidelines, nearly glaring at the people on the field. He didn't believe kickball was within the realms of the rules—Ardenis's black mark in Hector's book. Hector had once removed someone from the field for kicking too hard. More than one occasion, Hector had brought people before the council for playing aggressively.

Everyone watched Hector's approach. Some even walked off the field.

Ardenis stood quiet, ready for the inevitable.

Laida crossed her arms and traversed the field to Ardenis. "Every time this game is played, he arrives. We're not breaking any rules. The council approved this decades ago."

The remaining players kicked their balls again, some so light as to not even make it to their partners across the field.

"Laida," Hector said when he reached them. "A word."

Laida locked eyes with Ardenis, then followed Hector away to the columns at the edge of the field. Ardenis watched her loose bun bob as she walked. Hector flicked his eyes up, and Ardenis looked away. His heart sped.

"Mind if I join you and Bram?" Ardenis asked Vinia.

"Of course," she said.

Bram recovered the ball and kicked it toward them. Hector stepped closer to Laida. Too close. She didn't flinch, didn't lose her confidence. Ardenis inwardly cheered for her. He couldn't hear what they were saying, but Hector pointed to her hair a few times. Ardenis was supposed to protect Laida from exposing her knowledge, but how could he do that from here?

The ball sped right past Ardenis, rolling toward Laida. He'd missed Bram's pass. She picked it up and headed toward them while Hector stalked away.

Ardenis rubbed his neck. "What did he say to you?"

Laida handed him the ball. "He requested I not try anything else new without first acquiring council approval." She shook her head, smiling. "I saw you miss that pass."

Conversations and play resumed as Hector left the field.

Ardenis breathed a sigh of relief, his worry replaced by irritation with Hector. He was just looking for an excuse to come here and find someone breaking the rules. "I don't think my heart's in kickball today."

Laida shrugged, and Ardenis waved to his friends and walked off the field.

His shoulders hunched in annoyance. The emotions he'd kept in check were getting the better of him. Why had he been so worried?

It was one thing to mimic mortal life, preparing to join the mortal world, but these stronger emotions weren't part of that. As a watcher, he'd always been able to ignore the emotional reactions he'd seen on Thera, because they weren't a part of him. He was outside them, just as every other Acanthian was. Just as he should be.

Now, they came to him instinctively as part of a normal reaction to stimuli. Instead of naturally resisting them, he had to work at subduing them. He wasn't mortal. He wasn't ready to be born. Not with Laida still in Acantha. And his Fating meant he had a long time to wait. Until then, he would have to block his feelings for Laida completely.

CHAPTER
TEN

N o one looked up as Ardenis took a seat at the watch window within the tower. They were all lost in their own observations. The room was nearly full, with all but a few of the twenty seats occupied.

Since he'd begun watching Damian and Eva, his sense of duty and devotion to his calling as a watcher had fallen short of his high standards. He was often late, and he experienced more diverse and complicated emotions by the day. Aside from Eva's betrothal last week, he'd seen nothing of import for months. The only thing he felt sure of was that his instincts wanted him to continue watching the young couple.

He looked at the watcher next to him, Cadence, with her straight, shoulder-length hair. She stared at the water, expressionless eyes unblinking. Sometimes it'd be nice to see what other watchers saw, but only clear water over white marble graced the space in front of her.

He closed his eyes and centered himself, taking deep breaths to calm and clear his mind. His instincts nudged him, drawing him to Thera. When he opened his eyes, an enforcer, Sarafina, stood across the room in the doorway, watching him. She looked around the room at Amalia and the other watchers.

Ardenis ignored her. He wasn't breaking any rules. The watch window glowed in his vision, and he sought Damian. He found him in the small kitchen of his family's humble farmhouse, pacing in front of his parents. He wore a deep scowl.

"I don't care what you say, Pa. I love her." Damian rooted his feet to the floorboards and faced his parents. "I will have her for my wife." His voice rang with determination and finality. This conversation must have been going on for a while. So, Eva's news had reached them.

Ardenis held his breath.

In her linen dress, a scarf covering her pinned-up hair, Damian's mother sat stiff in her chair, eyes on her husband. Her apron, dusted in flour, moved with the rise and fall of her hitched breathing. Damian's father stared at his callused hands, clasped on the worn kitchen table. His shirt and trousers were dirt-covered from the morning chores.

"She's the lord's daughter, Damian," his father said. He looked up to where Damian trembled with rage and crushing grief. "I'm sorry, son, but it's not to be. You have to stop seeing her before you're caught by someone that's not me. You could bring a heap of trouble onto our little farm."

His mother nodded.

Damian's father had caught them? Ardenis had missed seeing that. He'd been too preoccupied with Laida.

Damian resumed his pacing, his stomping shaking the house and the dishes drying next to the sink. He stopped and turned back to them. "I don't care." His father stood. "I'm sorry, Pa, but I don't. She's worth fighting for."

Damian's mother patted his arm. "Your pa has the right of it, Damian." She sighed, and her eyes creased in concern. "I know you love Lady Eva. I've seen it in the whistle in your step, and the way you carry on about, but it's a young love. Even if Lord Ferran were an agreeable man, you must understand Lady Eva could never marry a common farmer."

Damian jerked away from her. "We'll see about that." He grabbed a simple cape off a hook and marched out of the house, slamming the door which rattled the windows.

His mother's wide eyes pleaded with his father. He ran out after his son.

Ardenis tracked Damian to the barn where he bridled their old farm horse. Damian ignored his father as he jogged toward him, grabbing the saddle and hefting it onto the horse.

His father stepped up to him. "I'm begging, son. Don't do anything rash. You've heard the rumors; she's promised to Prince Isaac."

"Prince Isaac is a child!" Damian tightened the girth and mounted.

"They're only six years apart, Damian. Six years won't always be such a big difference." His father spoke calmly and quietly, hands upraised, as if to a cornered animal.

Damian clenched his fists around the reins, glancing toward the road between the trees. The road to Eva.

"I understand, I do," his father said, edging closer. "But... do you think Lord Ferran would allow anything to stand in the way of his daughter becoming the future Queen of Alysies?" He put a hand over Damian's white-knuckled grip. His next words were softer. "You could bring harm to her. Don't you think Lady Eva would be happier in the lifestyle she's always known?"

Ardenis watched as Damian's jaw clenched. He squinted, and tears leaked down his face. Crying didn't exist in Acantha, but Ardenis had seen many tears. Never any quite like these. True love had Damian in its grip and it ruled him completely.

He slumped in the saddle. "Then I'm going to tell her goodbye, Pa. I have to tell her why we can't see each other."

His father hesitated, then nodded, removing his hand. Damian held his father's gaze for a brief moment, then kicked the horse's sides. They sped off, dirt and rocks grinding beneath them.

Ardenis watched Damian's father for quite some time. He stood in place, staring at where he'd last seen his son, not bothering to wipe his tears away.

The love of a parent for a child was a sacred and precious thing.

CHAPTER
ELEVEN

Ardenis wrenched his gaze from the grieving father and followed Damian as he spurred his old horse even faster toward Lord Ferran's keep.

Ardenis's old self would have taken a break for lunch at this point, keeping with Theran customs. After all, it didn't matter who watched, as long as someone did. Just his desire to remain in Thera was enough to indicate he needed distance. Despite it all, he still trusted his instincts. He wouldn't leave. Something important was coming, and it had to be him who watched.

Hours later, Damian arrived at the town of Oakrin. No market or revelers enlivened the dreary street. The packed dirt and hobble homes were made dull by the dark clouds above, promising rain. Damian walked his tired horse slowly down the main road, head down, appearing lost in thought.

He reached a fork in the road. On one side, his secret meeting spot with Eva lay nestled within the woods. On the other, Oakrin Keep towered over the land upon its hill. Damian stopped and stared up. The grey stone walls reached toward the darkening sky. Wind whipped the Ferran banners of red and yellow about in the air. Cawing crows swooped for cover from the coming storm.

Damian pulled his cape tight around him, likely against a chill in the wind. His horse pawed at the ground as he mounted and clicked his tongue, urging them forward at a slow trot. Ardenis had never seen Damian at the keep before, and doubted Damian knew what he was doing.

Please, Damian. Don't do anything rash. It was folly to hope for one outcome or another, but he had to. If only the Fates would listen.

Damian walked his horse up the road and to the keep's entrance. Flanked by two looming towers, the metal portcullis, remained up. Two guards with red plumes spiking from their helms stepped from their posts and approached him, swords clanking at their sides.

One guard walked at rigid attention, the other strutted with a lazy arrogance.

The latter looked Damian and his old horse up and down. "State your business." The arrogant guard placed a hand on the hilt of his sword.

"I've a letter for Lady Eva Rylandor." Damian stared straight ahead, ever the efficient courier. He reached into his saddlebag and indeed pulled out a letter. It was sealed in wax with "Lady Eva" scrawled on the front.

The guard sneered and snapped his fingers. His companion stepped forward to collect the letter. Damian let him snatch it from his outstretched hand, and then the guard walked through the portcullis, out of sight.

Damian nodded at the arrogant guard, who spat in reply, and turned his horse around. He headed back down the hill, and Ardenis watched him loose a long breath.

Ardenis was torn. Find Eva, or follow Damian. He clenched his fists. Damian or Eva. He let his instincts decide, and they pushed him to follow the letter.

The rigid, lanky guard held the letter tight in his grip as he entered a dark foyer lit sparingly by wall sconces. He turned down a narrow hall, stopping at a closed door. The rap of his gauntleted hand echoed off the stone.

"Come in," a gruff voice called out.

Not Eva.

The guard opened the door and a man in rugged leathers, longsword sheathed at his side, sat behind a desk piled with papers. His wavy hair and thick beard didn't hide his scowl.

"A letter for Lady Eva, Captain Intman." The guard handed over the letter, and as soon as the captain grabbed it from his hands, he retreated the room, closing the door behind him.

The man—captain of Lord Ferran's personal guards—grabbed a knife from his desk and carefully sliced through the wax seal.

Ardenis read along with him.

My dearest Eva,
 Meet me in the clearing.

The captain sprung from his chair. "Well, lookit here."

Oh no. Ardenis rubbed a hand over his face. *They know.*

Captain Intman rushed from the room, papers fluttering off the desk. His long strides took to a winding staircase and then a more decorated part of the castle, with rich tapestries and furniture. At a tall door, two guards saluted him as he knocked.

A servant answered the door with an upraised brow.

"Heimer, I need an audience with his Lordship. Now." Captain Intman was near breathless, likely both from his haste and the news he carried.

Ardenis could only watch as the horror unfolded.

Heimer, an elderly servant, opened the door wide. The captain entered to find Lord Ferran seated at a fancy writing desk, a plate of strawberries at his elbow.

"Captain Intman, what is it?" Ferran asked, quill still in hand.

The captain gave a shallow bow and proffered the letter. "A message for Lady Ava, Your Lordship. I came as fast as I could."

Time slowed as Lord Ferran took the letter. His face grew redder the longer he stared at the words. "So, it is as you expected. There is someone else." He looked up. "Heimer, reseal this and deliver it to Lady Eva as requested."

Heimer bowed and accepted the letter. Lord Ferran and the captain waited until he left the room to speak.

Ferran's face contorted with anger. "Take your best men, be discreet. Follow her. Arrest whomever she meets. Protect our future queen at all costs."

Ardenis's heart sped double. *Damian.* This couldn't be happening.

Captain Intman bowed and retreated as quickly as he'd come. Ferran jammed his quill into fresh ink.

Ardenis squeezed his eyes shut. He didn't want to see anymore.

Eva, would she notice the broken seal? He shifted his gaze to her.

She sat alone at the window seat in her room, resting stiffly against emerald and peacock-blue pillows and staring at the wind-rustled woods outside. Lightening flashed, followed by the distant rumble of thunder.

A knock came from the door, making her jump. She straightened her muted lilac dress and swept stray wisps of her brown hair behind her ears.

"Enter," she called out.

The heavy wooden door swung inward, and a servant—Heimer —bearing a silver tray stepped into the room and bowed. "A letter, my lady."

Eva took the letter from the tray and flipped it over in her hand. Her eyes widened. "Thank you, Heimer."

The letter looked crisp, with hardly any signs it'd just been passed from hand to hand, her privacy violated.

Heimer bowed and left, closing the door behind him.

Eva watched the door for a few seconds, and then opened the

letter in a rush, twisting and turning the paper in her haste. She didn't glance at the wax seal that had been broken and remelted into place, but Ardenis did. He read the letter again, even as it shook in her hands.

My dearest Eva,
    Meet me in the clearing.

Eva glanced up and gasped. "Oh, Damian." She smiled down at the letter. Then she cradled her hand over her belly tenderly. "He's come for us."

Ardenis's mouth fell open.

Eva threw the letter into the fireplace where it rapidly burned away. She opened her wardrobe and dug behind poofy dresses before producing a satchel already stuffed with provisions. Opening the door, she paused and glanced back at her room. She blew it a kiss, smiled, then hurried down the hall.

Servants bowed as she wound her way through the keep, but no one tried to stop her. She made it all the way outside and to the stables, where she announced she wanted to go for a ride.

"In this weather, Mistress?" The stablemaster scratched his balding head and looked from her satchel to the dark clouds. The wind whipped loose hay into a flurry. He held up his hand to shield his eyes from the debris. "Begging your pardon, but I wouldn't suggest it."

"Nevertheless, I will go for a ride." Eva stared down the grizzled man until he shook his head and prepared her horse.

She paced while she waited, jumping every time lightening flashed, and readjusting the strap of the satchel on her shoulder. The stablemaster led the black gelding back to where Eva's riding boots had swept trails in the dirt and hay.

"I've thought it over," he said, "and I feel I should warn you—"

Eva grabbed the reins from him. "Thank you for your concern. You've always been kind to me."

Warn her about what? Captain Intman and his men?

She mounted her horse without assistance, her loose skirts allowing her to place a leg on each side of the saddle.

The stablemaster raised his hand and pointed back to the keep. "Wait, Mistress Lady Eva. You don't understand. They—"

"Good day, Alan." Eva raced her horse ahead, not looking back to see Alan waving his arms frantically at her. He covered his mouth and hung his head.

Ardenis couldn't take it anymore. He didn't dare look to see what the stablemaster pointed to. His heart pounded to the point where it'd never slow again. It was too much, too much at stake for the mortals he watched. The mortals he'd come to care about. He needed distance.

He blinked and shook his head. The image disappeared into a pool of water, pristine and motionless. Ardenis ignored his screaming instincts and rubbed his sweaty palms on his robe. Breathing came in shaky intervals.

Amalia caught Ardenis's gaze and smirked. Did she know? Had she seen what he'd seen? He stood and poured himself a glass of lemon water and assembled a plate of food from the buffet table—a Theran practice. He grabbed at random, trying to conceal his shaking hands. He'd missed lunch, so these actions would seem normal. He didn't care. Eva and Damian were in trouble.

Amalia sidled next to him. "Tough day of watching?" She didn't whisper.

He took a drink, relieved his hand didn't tremble.

"You seem tense." She took a grape from his plate and popped it in her mouth. "You just need to distance yourself, Ardenis. You don't want the emotions of Thera to get you."

He glared, and she smiled up at him, batting her eyelashes. "I'm not in need of distance, thank you," he whispered. "Though you'd do well to follow your own advice."

"Your words, not mine." Amalia trailed her finger over his shoulder. He jerked back, sloshing his water. At her knowing smile, he hurried away, back to his seat.

She shouldn't have been able to unnerve him. His instincts—roaring at him to continue his watch—distracted him. They were both in need of distancing, though he'd be damned if he'd admit it.

Just to prove her wrong, he yanked a bite out of a piece of melon, barely chewing before washing it down with water, and then focused back in on the watch window. He hoped Eva was all right.

Ardenis urged his vision as fast as he ever had through the clouds and landscape and straight to the clearing. He found Damian, arms wrapped around Eva in a tight embrace, squeezing the fabric of her dress. They were alone. No guards in sight, just the trees billowing in the wind, and the soggy grass from spitting rain before the downpour.

"Did you tell anyone where you were going?" Damian pulled back and placed his hand against Eva's abdomen. His brows creased with concern.

She covered his hand with hers and smiled up at him. "No one saw me leave. Well, just Alan, our stablemaster, but he won't report me as running away." She patted the bag at her side. "I brought my things and some gold, as you said."

Damian breathed a sigh of relief. "Good. That's good, my darling. It will be rough going at first, but I promise I'll take care of you and our little one. We'll go somewhere King Tristan and his young prince can't find us." Eva placed her head against his chest and sighed into him. He held her close. "It will be okay. I promise."

Ardenis wished he could trust that promise. The Fates were unpredictable.

A strong gust whipped her hair about, and Damian stroked it down the length of her back. The trees protested the wind overhead, and leaves rolled down the path from the road into the clearing.

When Eva pulled back, she looked up at Damian with those eyes again—the eyes which, upon first seeing them, had caught Ardenis's complete attention—wide open and innocent, full of trust and faith in Damian. Eyes of pure love. Ardenis hadn't done them anywhere near justice in his rendering.

Damian stared into her and then leaned down for a deep kiss.

Ardenis's instincts tugged. The guards were coming. He could have pulled his gaze back and watched what was to come for the young couple, but he didn't want to. Seeing would only make it harder. The two lovers would find a way out of trouble, he was sure of it. His stomach churned with dread.

Damian led Eva to her horse on the edge of the clearing. *Too slow. Go faster!* He helped her mount, then beamed up at her, patting her hand. She smiled after him as he walked toward his own old mare on the other side of the clearing.

Lightening flashed with a burst of white light, followed by a clap of rumbling thunder. When it tapered out, the pounding of hooves sounded from up the trail.

"This way! She went this way," a man shouted from the trees.

Eva's smile became a gasp of horror.

Ardenis clenched his robe in his lap. *Run.*

Damian whipped around, wide eyes boring into Eva's.

He gave up on his horse and ran for Eva. Five men on horseback crashed into the clearing. Damian leaped onto the back of Eva's horse.

"Go!" he shouted, pointing to the trailhead.

The riders slowed and spread apart to block the path, hands on the hilts of their sheathed swords. Captain Intman stood ahead of the rest, wary eyes locked on Eva.

Eva met his stare, and decision seemed to snap in place as her gaze went steely. She kicked her horse's sides, plowing straight toward the guards.

Captain Intman cursed. "Move aside! Don't attack Lady Eva!"

At the last second, the guards jerked on their reins, making a sliver of an opening. Eva's horse bounded through them, hooves pounding dirt and rock as it flew up the trail.

"After them!" the captain shouted.

The guards, their horses bearing the weight of only one, raced after them, and the chase was on.

"Stop! Kidnapper, stop!" one of them yelled.

Eva's eyes lost their steel as they broke through the trees onto the road. Her face crumpled as a sob escaped her.

"Keep going, my love." Damian leaned over her. "We can outrun them."

Ardenis hoped with all his being that Damian's words were true. A silent prayer formed on his lips. He'd never prayed for anyone in Thera before—who knew if anyone was listening?—but he did so now.

Dear maker, please watch over and protect the young ones. Let the Fates favor them.

Damian kicked the horse's side with his heels. "Yah!"

The horse put on a burst of speed, its strong legs working furiously against the dirt road. Their pursuers broke through the trees and drove their horses hard, gaining ground with each of Ardenis's rapid heartbeats. Damian tensed as the guards approached. They spread out and surrounded Damian and Eva as they raced onward—two on either side and one behind.

"Give up, boy," the man directly to their left shouted. "Lord Ferran may go easy on his daughter's kidnapper if you stop that horse and surrender. Right now."

"Don't stop, Eva. Never stop." Damian squeezed Eva close. Tears streamed down her face, her eyes wild with fear.

Trees whipped by and lightening flashed in the sky. Eva's horse foamed at the mouth as its powerful legs galloped in vain.

"Ah, this is horseshit," the man on their right shouted. He reached out and grabbed a fistful of the back of Damian's cape and yanked hard.

Everything happened in slow motion, with Ardenis helpless to do anything but watch.

Damian slipped sideways off the saddle. He let go of Eva so as not to drag her down with him. Eva cried out and turned. She dropped the reins and reached for him, but he'd fallen too far. Her weight carried her forward. She lost her balance. They both tumbled off the racing horse. Damian pulled Eva on top of him as they fell. He hit the ground hard, his head bouncing off the road. Eva flew out of his arms. They rolled several feet before stopping.

Ardenis couldn't breathe.

Ferran's men pulled hard on the reins, narrowly avoiding trampling them. The guards skidded their horses to a stop.

"You damn moron!" Captain Intman shouted at the man who'd pulled them down. He dismounted and marched over to the offender, yanking him off his horse.

Ardenis gasped—it was the arrogant guard.

The captain grabbed a fistful of his shirt and shook. "It's your head if Lady Eva is hurt." He shoved him away.

The others dismounted, while the offender looked down the road at Eva's retreating horse, sneering in silence.

Two guards rushed to Eva. She moaned. Blood seeped through her sleeves at the elbows, and her skirts at her knees. A shallow scrape bloomed blood on her forehead. They helped her up. She stood and ripped her arms out of their grip, eyes darting toward Damian.

Two of the men, Captain Intman and another, drew their swords and rushed back to where Damian had landed on the side of the road. He lay sprawled on his back, eyes closed. Ardenis shook uncontrollably, struggling not to cry out in shock.

They studied him, then one kicked at him with a leather-booted foot.

"Dead," the captain said, sheathing his sword.

Ardenis gasped. "No!"

Eva froze.

Lightening crashed in the sky, and the clouds finally opened up. The droplets fell slowly, then in sheets, raining down on the still form of Damian. The water washed blood from a jagged gash in the back of his head.

Eva stood motionless while the rain ran in rivulets down her face, soaking her hair and dress. With wide eyes, and body trembling, her mouth contorted into despair.

The dam broke. "Damian!" She ran, slipping in the mud. She flung herself on top of him, grabbing his face and shaking him. "Damian, answer me!" She threw her head to the sky and screamed, "I forbid it! No! No, no, no."

Eva looked toward Acantha, blaming the Fates for this outcome. Her eyes seemed to lock with Ardenis's, accusing him, forsaking him. He shuddered from the horror and fear that stretched over him, suffocating. Her screams pierced him straight through. The Fates were to blame. Even his prayer had done no good. Bitter anger coated his shock and fear.

Eva vomited. The men grabbed her arms and hauled her backward.

"No, no, no, no." She shook her head and screamed, wrenching away and back to Damian once again.

Ardenis extended his shaking hand, trying to reach through their distance and comfort her. *This happened for a reason, Eva. It will all be clear in the end, surely.*

She cradled Damian's face, weeping over him. "This can't be. It can't be real."

A jagged pain ripped at Ardenis's middle, as if he was breaking inside. It was his soul, his emotions, turning ragged and reforming to normalcy, then jumbling again. He couldn't breathe for not knowing how to contain these new feelings.

Captain Intman shook his head, a flicker of sorrow on his bearded face. "Get her back to the keep," he said above the pounding rain. "We'll clean up this mess."

A burley man reached for her, and she grabbed onto Damian's hand. The man lifted her away. She screamed as Damian's fingertips slipped from her grasp.

Eva's grief turned feral. "Don't you touch me!" She kicked and punched and scratched as the man threw her over his shoulder. He took countless elbows to the face as he walked back to the horses, trying not to injure her.

"Damian! Help me!"

A tearless sob escaped Ardenis's mouth.

The arrogant guard sat astride his horse, and someone handed her up to him. A blank mask had replaced his sneer. He held her tight to his chest as she thrashed.

"Let me go!"

They rode off toward the keep, followed by two more of the men. Two remained behind. They loomed over Damian's body as the rain washed mud and blood in streams down the road. The captain grabbed Damian's foot and dragged his lifeless form toward the horses.

The rain poured down, and the world continued on, unaffected by the horrors.

CHAPTER
TWELVE

Ardenis couldn't watch anymore.

He tore his gaze from the marble pool, squeezing his eyes shut tight. His breathing came too fast and his heart raced. A pain he'd never experienced before ripped through him. He rocked his body back and forth. When he opened his eyes, his arm was outstretched over the marble, trying to comfort Eva through the vast expanse separating their worlds. He slowly pulled it back and looked around. The tower was still full. No one looked at the watch window.

All eyes were on him.

Their expressions betrayed a vast array of emotion. Most of them, like Cadence, wore relaxed expressions, heads cocked to the side. They must not have crossed the line and become too involved in Thera. Those with more emotional awareness viewed him with raised eyebrows or gaping mouths, a couple with narrowed eyes.

Amalia looked at him with understanding.

Ardenis cleared his throat. The echo reverberated in the profound silence. "I must report to the council." He stood. All eyes tracked his movement. He'd forgotten to whisper.

He turned away from their prying stares and calmly walked out of the room. When he left the tower, he ran. He didn't know where he was going; he just ran.

He ignored every curious look until he arrived at his house. He burst through the door, slamming it closed behind him. Rushing through his living area, he hurtled through the bedroom, past sketches of his favorite sites on Thera. He flew through the door to his private terrace and jumped into his bathing pool, fully clothed. He sank until the water covered his head and he touched the bottom. Bubbles rose around him, swirling his blue robe.

In the depths of the water, Ardenis screamed. He screamed and tore at his hair and kicked off his robe until he was out of air and was forced to reemerge for breath. He dragged himself over the side of the pool and lay nude on the tile, panting. Evening sun shone through the trees above his stone privacy wall. The irritating brightness contrasted with the dark of the clouds he'd left behind in Thera.

Ardenis had always wished for rain in Acantha. He doubted he'd ever see rain the same way again.

He lay there until his breathing calmed and his heart resumed its normal pace.

Damian was dead. He was meant to die. It was his fate. His journey began in Acantha, where he chose to be born on Thera, and then he died like he was supposed to. Ardenis couldn't shake the emotions he'd witnessed, the emotions he'd been a part of that had absorbed into him so fully. Would he ever see the light of love in Eva's eyes again? He could only picture her despair, the way she looked with her tear-streaked face and dress ruined by rain. Her eyes held only agony and anguish of the purest kind. She'd clutched herself like she feared she would break apart.

Ardenis pulled himself up and methodically dressed in a dry robe. He squared his shoulders and left home, heading straight for the council hall. An image of the black transfer gateway flashed in his mind. He couldn't be caught. The damage done must be repaired.

When he entered, he approached the desk where Hector sat

speaking with Cadence. Their conversation stopped. Hector straightened his quill. Cadence stared at the floor.

"I wish to report to the council," Ardenis said. His voice sounded hollow.

"Very good, Watcher Fater." Hector's voice sounded off too, like hung with a note of caution. What had Cadence told him? "It's been some time since your last useful report."

Ardenis said nothing, too numb to offer excuses.

Hector frowned. "Cadence Watcher will wait. Ardenis Watcher Fater may enter the council chambers."

Ardenis didn't give them the courtesy of a nod. He pushed the doors open and entered the familiar entry hall. A few steps brought him into the council chambers where the dark wood paneling matched his mood. Taking his place behind the podium, he faced the council members as they filed into the room. He knew what to say, the only thing that might excuse his behavior.

Ardenis bowed to them as they were seated at the tiered benches. He recognized, but didn't know, any of them, a product of the men and women of the council maintaining a separate existence from the rest of Acantha. Gharum Head Councilman entered last. The insignia of the northeastern hemisphere with a gavel stitched into his blue robe caught Ardenis's eye.

Gharum was the judge, and Ardenis the criminal.

"Ardenis Watcher Fater. What news do you bring from Thera?" Gharum leaned forward in his thick wooden chair, which sat just ahead of the rest of the council.

Ardenis took a deep breath. "I bring word of happenings in the Kingdom of Alysies." He forced his voice to remain calm and emotionless, burying his pain deep, deep down. "And also... I've seen the Fates."

Eyes snapped to him and heads swiveled. It was the most reaction he could expect of the council members.

Gharum smiled. "That is promising, indeed. Please, continue."

"My report concerns Lady Eva. Her father, Lord Ferran, rescued

Prince Isaac of Alysies from a band of brigands who used to be led by Warin before his death. Lord Ferran is the one who hired Warin to do the assassination, and possibly master-minded the kidnapping of the prince. As a reward, King Tristan arranged for Lady Eva to be betrothed to the young prince." Ardenis's fists tightened. Emotions threatened to bubble up to his impassive face. *Damian's dead.*

Gharum's nod accompanied the scratch of a quill as Ardenis's words were recorded.

"With the announcement of the betrothal, Prince Isaac now has the assured protection from Lord Ferran against future threats to the crown. When Prince Isaac is of age, he and Eva will be wed. A mere six years."

His next words came quieter, which was just as well. It helped to disguise the tremor in his voice. "Damian died today." He paused and swallowed a lump in his throat.

Gharum tilted his head, studying him.

"He and Eva tried to run away, but Lord Ferran's men stopped them. Damian died in the attempt."

"Who was Damian again? The simple farm boy?" Gharum asked.

Ardenis nodded, not trusting himself to speak. Damian died. Damian was dead. "Eva is carrying his child."

"That's almost unworthy of council notice." Gharum shook his head. "But what of the Fating?"

Unworthy? The word slammed into him. Nothing could be further from the truth. Damian's love had meant something, to more than just Eva. It had opened Ardenis's eyes to a world of beauty and torment he was only beginning to understand.

The room watched Ardenis expectantly. Did they see the turmoil within? "I was deep in a watch today when I had a vision." Another lie, and straight to a council in session. "I've fated myself. In the future."

Gharum's eyes opened wide. "Yourself, you say?" Murmured conversations broke out around him.

"Yes. I didn't appear as I do now, but I know it was me just the same. It is an innumerable number of centuries from now. So, clearly, I won't be born soon."

"Can you describe your Fating?"

Ardenis told them of his vision, omitting only one thing. For reasons he couldn't explain, he felt the need to keep his future wife a secret.

The council, especially Gharum, listened with rapt attention as Ardenis described the future city and himself. Someone brought paper and drawing pencils, and the council had him sketch the details of the surrounding buildings and unusual snow. His abnormally bright blue eyes. When finished, they carried the drawing through the door only council members could enter. His eyes trailed the drawing until the door closed behind it.

Ardenis voiced one last detail, one more thing that might save him from exile. "My Fating caught me off guard, and I was a little out of sorts when I came out of my watch. It was jarring to see myself in the future."

Gharum raised an eyebrow. "Jarring?"

Ardenis inwardly cursed himself. He'd used a Theran expression. He didn't correct his mistake, not wanting to call more attention to it. Instead, he nodded. "That is all I have to report."

Gharum paused, staring through Ardenis. "We thank you, Watcher Fater. The council will deliberate and release the pertinent information to Acantha."

Ardenis bowed and left the room. When he entered the foyer, Cadence still remained at Hector's desk. Once again, she didn't meet his gaze. Hector stared at him with open curiosity gleaming in his eyes.

Ardenis left the council hall without a word. He'd secured his position. Despite what damage his actions had done, lying about the timing of his Fating had presented a plausible explanation for his behavior in the tower. If the council released his report—and they likely would—his reputation would remain protected. It helped that

121

it was forbidden to discuss the happenings in the tower among non-watchers.

He stepped out into the clear night. The warm air surrounded him, but offered no comfort. He let his head hang as he walked down the stone pathway, leaving the council courtyard and heading straight home. Light flickered over manicured lawns and flower bushes of the residential section.

A few houses vanished beside him, turning into an empty field, but he ignored it. Just another sign of more souls leaving Acantha, with none to replace them. Their homes no longer needed. He'd never wondered before what happened when there was no one left. The end of the human race? Another Acantha somewhere to take their place? So many unanswered questions now that his mind had been set free.

He prayed the council wouldn't find him emotionally influenced and force him to be born. Maybe they would simply demote him to be a gardener, or the torch lighter. It was no less than he deserved after he'd let himself get wrapped up in the emotions of Thera.

Not even the oldest souls in Acantha knew the consequences of Theran emotions permeating their world. It had never come to that. Watchers turned themselves in when they knew it'd gone too far.

Ardenis had seen wars, and death, and destruction. He'd seen birth and new growth, and the changing of countless seasons. He'd watched it all from a healthy emotional distance, as he should have.

But not Damian and Eva. Their moment in time had changed him irrevocably. He was awash in emotional turmoil. No matter how many calming breaths he took, or how many times he scrubbed his face, he couldn't slough off the weight of Damian's love or his death. He'd been blessedly, and rightfully, blind before. There was no way to unsee what he'd seen, to put the veil back where it belonged.

He'd tried, oh how he'd tried, to move forward as if he hadn't been affected, but when he opened his ears to the night, and the swell of the music from the orchestra hit him, he didn't want to go home. There was only one place he wanted to be—only one person who could break through the pain of Damian's death.

"Laida," he breathed, and just her name lifted his spirits.

Ardenis followed the music all the way to the pavilion. He spotted her with her golden hair immediately. She had it piled up on her head in a bun, as did most of the women in the audience. Even some of the men had their long black hair up. Laida sat on her blanket alone this time, smiling and swaying to the music, away from the others who'd chosen to lounge in the grass instead of sit on the benches.

Ardenis took a deep breath and marched straight toward her, but slowed on the outskirts of the crowd. He shouldn't be here, shouldn't want to be with Laida or to long for her to look at him as Eva had looked at Damian, but, damn him, he did.

He weaved through the onlookers and sat on the blanket next to her without waiting for an invitation. She waved with a casual flutter of her arm and a warm smile. He paused, waiting, but she didn't turn from the orchestra. Ardenis let his shoulders slump. He stared at the blades of grass waving gently in the night breeze.

Was he fated to spend the next few centuries longing for someone who didn't know how to long for him back?

His heart ached as his thoughts turned to Damian and Eva. They loved each other, fiercely. Despite the consequences, they weren't afraid to follow their hearts and act on their love. Should he follow their example and put aside everything about his world he knew to be true? But look how it turned out for Damian. He'd died and left Eva behind with her heartbreak.

Ardenis couldn't do that to Laida. Watching Eva would only lead him to more turmoil, more exposure. And that would only lead to more trouble for Laida. More than anything, he wanted to check on Eva, to see her grief without her love. But he couldn't. He'd have to observe someone else, even if his instincts demanded otherwise. For himself, and what it might do to his last thread of emotional distance. Who would he become if he continued down this path?

Already he was unlike any other Acanthian. An outsider. A rule breaker, when duty to his calling had once been the most important thing.

Most of all, he had to stop watching Eva for Laida, for what he might do if nothing bound him, if he was free to follow his heart and act on his love.

His love.

Is that what this was? Had he learned to love Laida?

He brushed the beginning of a smile off his face. This couldn't be love. Could it? Love, romantic love, didn't exist here.

And look what the Fates had done to Damian for his love.

Laida clapped, and Ardenis blinked. The music had ended. She turned to him, smiling.

"Wasn't that spectacular?" she asked. "You ought to get here on time if you want to see the whole performance." She shoved his shoulder playfully.

Her touch washed over him, lifting his dark mood from the deepest recesses of his melancholy heart. The green of the grass and white of the stars brightened along with all the other colors around them. The blue of her eyes. The red of her lips.

He returned her smile. Yes, he'd live in loveless agony for the chance to see her happy.

CHAPTER
THIRTEEN

Though instincts warred against him, heartache had won out, and Ardenis had stopped himself from watching Eva. He couldn't bear it. Five years passed while he maintained his distance from her and let the other watchers take over. He'd even reduced his time spent writing in his journal—unusual for an Acanthian—unable to bear combing through his own thoughts. Even the council bulletins about her life were too much.

He didn't regret his decision. The pain and agony Eva had endured in the aftermath of Damian's death would only have exacerbated his. And, as he'd done before, he would have turned to Laida. His only bright spot.

No. She wouldn't be called to unnecessary council sessions, or be subjected to his emotional awareness more than he could help. Not even Vinia or Bram could cheer him, though they provided the excuse to hide his emotions. With them, he could pretend Damian's death never happened, and forget what had followed.

The day after Damian died, Ardenis had left the rain behind to view the bleak sunshine in northern Thera. He'd been just coming out of a watch when he'd received another shock. The watchers had been gossiping in whispers, when one of them stated casually that Eva had lost the unborn child. Damian's child.

One of the watchers, Amalia, whispered loudly, "Only Mary knows, and she's taking care of Eva. She'll be okay." She glanced over at him.

Ardenis had barely escaped the tower before crumpling in anguish. He never found out if it was the fall from her horse, or her grief that had caused the miscarriage. The council didn't bother posting about it. It had been the Fates' design for that soul to bypass Thera and go straight to the Hereafter, but where once that might have comforted him, now it did nothing.

The shock of Eva's news only strengthened his resolve to watch another kingdom entirely—Daltieri, Alysies's northern neighbor.

But even in Daltieri, he couldn't escape the whole of Thera revolving around Eva in some way. The more he'd watched, the more their paths seemed increasingly intertwined.

King Zane of Daltieri, who was known to be a sickly king, never discovered it was his wife, Queen Vatrice, who was responsible for his illness. Poison. He lay on his sickbed while she, round with child, ruled in his stead, concocting new ways to expand their kingdom.

Ardenis now focused into Thera and found the queen pacing the throne room—a smaller and less lavish version of King Tristan's. Dark stone outlined the room, absorbing what little light the sparse torches emitted.

Queen Vatrice held her thin arms clasped behind her back. Her stern eyes narrowed beneath groomed eyebrows, red lips set in a pinched line of deep concentration. A cape of fine black cloth billowed behind her as she reached the end of the room, turned, and continuing pacing. The flowing deep green dress accentuated her stomach.

"Your Majesty," her husband's advisor, Timothy, said, "It is customary to send a gift to commemorate the engagement, now that they've entered the celebration period."

The year leading up to the wedding of Eva and Isaac had arrived.

Until now, Ardenis had avoided any information about the elaborate festivities. He couldn't bear to see Eva forced to spend time with someone other than her love.

"Obviously, you blasted fool." Vatrice stopped mid-pace and shot an annoyed look at Timothy.

He flinched and glanced at the armed guards flanking the exit. "Forgive me, my queen."

She followed Timothy's gaze and gave a satisfied smirk.

Ardenis frowned, sighing. Vatrice only kept Timothy around because she could cow the young man with the flick of a look. All it took was a vicious threat to Timothy's wife and child, and she'd enslaved him ever since.

Queen Vatrice's monarchy made Ardenis miss Eva and Damian, and even Prince Isaac, with each passing day. Their love and innocence, when not marred by agonizing memories, contrasted with the foulness he'd witnessed over the past five years. Vatrice's behavior would never have bothered him before Eva. But even watching the corruption of Daltieri wasn't as hard to bear as watching Eva live her life without Damian.

Loveless, just like him.

Vatrice continued pacing. "Summon General Maken. And Allister."

Timothy bowed, hands shaking, and rushed out of the room. Vatrice touched her stomach and crossed the dim space to the dais. She walked up the single step, bypassed her own throne, and eased herself down onto her husband's. The worn wooden chair had been in use for decades, though all the gold and jewels were long gone, sold or stored away for safekeeping in their recent hard times.

A smaller kingdom than Alysies, Daltieri's northern mountains made it impossible for goods to reach them by sea. They relied heavily on trade with the surrounding kingdoms, especially Alysies, with its rich forests and sea access. Daltieri produced mostly coal and were known for a special cheese made from goat's milk. The circumstances produced hardy, but poor people, and even more hardened leaders, as was the case for as long as Ardenis had watched them settle these lands.

Until recently.

King Zane's predecessors had nearly ruined the kingdom in a fruitless quest for expansion—a problem Queen Vatrice had solved just within the past few months. They had discovered gold in the North Mountain, and the queen was hiding it, making big plans for their newfound wealth. She wanted sea access badly.

Queen Vatrice tapped her jeweled fingers on the chair's arm with increasing impatience, until Timothy reentered, followed by General Maken, who bowed on one knee before his queen. Allister entered silently behind them, with only a nod of his head. His black mage robe hung to the floor, and he carried a wooden staff topped with a mage crystal. No glow emanated from it, indicating Allister wasn't using magic at the moment. The Daltieri monarchy always had a mage in their courts—even more in their army—unlike King Tristan of Alysies who unwisely didn't trust them.

Ardenis still believed Thera was overdue for an explosion of magic in the population. So few had been born with the gift lately, like the Fates were holding it back for something incredible.

Vatrice smiled, the kind that chilled the soul on the receiving end. "General Maken. As my advisor has pointed out, we must send a gift to honor the engagement of the young prince of Alysies." Timothy shrunk under her attention. "He has provided a few options."

She pointed to a table on the edge of the room Ardenis hadn't noticed. It contained three items: a place setting of blue glass rimmed in gold, a golden statue of a tree with intricate golden leaves fluttering in the drafty room, and a small chest opened to reveal dozens of little diamonds and a smattering of rubies and emeralds.

General Maken rose from his bow, face expressionless. He wore leather armor with tassels indicating his rank as general. His entire being radiated confidence, from his large frame to his wide stance. He didn't speak, for his queen had not asked him a direct question.

They had trained him well at Monhaber, a renowned military school in Daltieri, which produced some of the best swordmasters.

"Leave us," Vatrice said, staring straight ahead.

Timothy retreated from the room, practically running. The bang of the heavy door echoed in the stone hall. Allister stood by the wall, silent and motionless. His intense eyes looked as if he concentrated on something far away. Maken remained standing at attention.

Vatrice hoisted herself up and resumed pacing. "King Tristan is vulnerable. He has but one son, and we have an open invitation to deliver a gift to the happy couple, whom my sources say are not equally happy with the arrangement." She stopped and faced Maken. "Where does our army stand? Could we defend ourselves if an attempt on the prince's life went foul?"

Maken stared ahead at the empty throne, arms rigid at his sides. "With the recent influx of gold from the mountains, the army is steadily growing, but we aren't ready for a direct attack." His facial muscles rippled where his jaw clenched. "Your rule could be placed in jeopardy as well—"

"Because I don't have any sons?" Vatrice's sharp voice cut through Maken's baritone as she grabbed her stomach. She pointed an accusatory finger at Allister. "You best hope this one's a boy. My husband is not long for this world."

Ardenis had heard this before. The queen blamed Allister for her lack of sons; she had five daughters already. Though no amount of magic could force Fates' hand, Allister had studied at the best school of magic in all of Thera—Thomats, in Alysies.

Neither Maken nor Allister reacted to the outburst, not even to blink.

Vatrice smiled. "Send the chest then. A simple gift for a simple boy, one whom I'll delight in defeating when the time is right. No need to divulge our recent discovery of gold."

Maken bowed. "Yes, Your Majesty."

Vatrice waved him away, and he left the room.

She eased back down on her husband's throne and beckoned

Allister forward, eyes raking him up and down. "Have you found a way to see into their castle?"

"It's too far, my queen. Even augmenting my power with another mage crystal hasn't helped. Perhaps closer, no more than an hour's ride away, I might see something."

Ardenis expected an outburst, but Vatrice nodded. "I don't want you that close until the time is right. We'll find another way in." She stood and crossed over to him, then grabbed him by his robe and pulled him into a rough kiss.

Allister kissed back willingly, winding fingers through her hair. This was not the first time Ardenis had seen this behavior, and even then, he hadn't bothered to distance himself as he would have before Damian and Eva.

Queen Vatrice sat back with a triumphant smile on her lips. She rubbed the goosebumps on her arms. "Start a fire before you go."

Allister bowed without speaking. The mage crystal encased at the top of his staff lit up, casting bright light through the dim room. Ardenis watched the large hearth to the side of the room, already stacked with fresh kindling. A moment later, fire erupted, adding an orange glow to the crystal's light. A simple spell, but Ardenis hadn't realized Allister could control the element of fire. His specialty was gateways—opening magical windows to spy on others. A dual ability was uncommon.

"Thank you, Allister." Vatrice retreated to her throne. "Prepare something new, in case my husband decides to recover."

Allister nodded and left out the throne room doors.

Ardenis left Gadren, Daltieri's capital, to report to the council. It was draining to watch so much depravity all the time. Their corruption clung to him like a viscous poison trying to worm its way into his mind.

As he walked down the stone path, the warm light of midday soaked into his blue robe. Over the past five years, he'd pretended to be content in his role, as he once had been. When performing his watcher duties, or spending time with Laida and his friends, he feigned emotional neutrality. To all outside appearances, he was his old self again. Inside, he was in constant turmoil.

Each night as he fell asleep, he let his final image of Eva burn in his eyes—the way she looked being hauled away after the brutal death of her true love. Damian had been meant for her. Ardenis could not stand to think of how Damian's poor mother and father would have reacted to the news of their son's death.

He shook off the dark thoughts and entered the council hall. Fortunately, someone besides Hector sat behind the desk. He gave his report to the council and then went to the dining hall for lunch. Laida was not there, so he ate alone, sipping his beef soup.

Midway through his bowl, a murmur circulated around the room. The volume of conversation reached him through his melancholy. From the sound of it, the council had posted a new bulletin—a significant one. He dumped his half-eaten food and followed the stream of people to the council courtyard.

As with all council information, they nailed the news to a bulletin board in the center of the courtyard. Ardenis remembered a time when it was carved in stone because paper hadn't been invented in Thera yet.

Several people stood around the bulletin. Ardenis waited patiently for his turn to read the council's censored news. As he drew closer, he spotted Vinia up ahead, reading the document. She turned and smiled when she saw him.

"I'm going to be born!" she said, easing through the crowd to meet him. "I feel it. It's my time."

Ardenis's eyes widened, and then he grinned and clapped her on the shoulder. "I'm happy for you, Vinia. This is a good time to be on Thera. Let me know when, and I'll be there at your sendoff."

"Tell Bram he'll have to find a good kickball replacement." She smiled and walked off.

An ache formed in Ardenis's chest, but he rubbed it away. He was glad for his friend. He'd have been born long ago if it was the Fates' design, and if Laida wasn't in Acantha.

When his turn came to view the bulletin, Ardenis stepped up to it. The Watchers' Edict loomed in his vision. He used to read them every day as a reminder. *Do not observe mortal love.* He'd broken nearly every rule since laying eyes on Damian. Now, he ignored the edict and read the new post.

His mouth gaped open.

King Tristan of Alysies had fallen ill and died. Isaac was to be crowned king.

He was meant to watch it, but he had not. His instincts had raged, as they always did, but he'd ignored them.

A second bulletin announced there would be an event each month in Alysies leading up to the wedding to celebrate the union between Lady Eva and King Isaac. The wedding was a mere year away. An aching coldness chased away the afternoon's warmth. Ardenis vowed not to watch the wedding ceremony. He would not. Eva was meant for Damian. He couldn't trust himself not to arouse suspicion again with his emotional reaction.

He pivoted and headed toward the tower. A bit of corruption ought to clear his heartache away.

"Ardenis!"

That singular voice rooted him to the spot and lifted his spirits. He peered through the dispersing crowd, easily spotting her. Her golden hair hung down today, flowing behind her as she jogged toward him. His personal sunshine, breaking up the monotony of their uniform, unchanging world.

He broke into a grin. Laida caught up to him and tugged the edge of his robe.

"Your hair is longer. Are you going to wear it up like the others?" she asked.

His grin grew bigger at her attention. He always wore his hair jaw-length, but had let it grow longer since Damian died. He felt better that way, like his secrets would be guarded behind his hair somehow. The length reminded him not to let his newfound emotions get the better of him.

"I like it this way, though I don't think I'll wear it up." *Like Eva.* That style seemed more a woman's style on Thera anyway, not that the people of Acantha made that distinction.

"It certainly helps you stand out." She smoothed down her blue robe.

That's when Ardenis noticed the gold sash. She'd tied it tight around her waist, shaping her robe into a dress. He froze. It was so similar to a dress Eva had frequently worn. All he could do was stare.

"What do you think?" Laida gave a curtsey.

He cleared his throat. "I like it. It suits you. Though I don't recommend spending time in front of the council hall if you don't want to get caught." He glanced around them. Others were already pointing at her makeshift dress and whispering amongst each other.

Laida laughed. "The council won't mind. Mortals wear it this way, after all. It was your drawing of Eva that inspired me, you know."

Changing her hairstyle was one thing—they had *some* choices over how they wore their hair—but altering her dress was completely different. The council would never allow it. Appearances didn't matter in Acantha like they did on Thera, but there were too many emotional decisions involved in dressing differently from one another, which is why they all wore matching robes.

"What drawing is she referring to, Watcher Fater?" Hector asked from behind them. Ardenis flinched.

Laida faced Hector with flawless self-assurance. "Have you not seen Ardenis's collection at the museum, Hector? You really should visit. It's a wealth of Theran information." Laida fluffed her robe-turned-dress. The Thera Museum did feature portraits of women wearing dresses, but still, Laida had never tried to mimic them before.

Hector noticed it then and he jumped back, aghast.

Ardenis watched him carefully.

"Laida!" Hector said. "I cannot allow this blatant rule violation.

To the council hall, at once!" He pointed, arm outstretched toward the building behind them, the other hand clenched to his side.

Laida smiled, unperturbed. "Goodbye, Arden. Perhaps I'll see you at dinner." She walked past Hector toward the wooden doors with the council engraving.

Hector flicked his gaze Ardenis, who responded with a slight incline of his head. When Hector turned to follow Laida, Ardenis's eyes turned to daggers he bore into the back of his skull. Laida disappeared into the building.

There was such anger, such hate, emanating from Hector. Where had it come from?

Ardenis discarded his plans to return to watching and took a seat on a nearby stone bench surrounded by rosebushes. He'd be damned if he could focus at the tower now. He waited for a long time, staring at the council doors, idly picking roses and shredding them. People came and went, and not only watchers. Several areas reported to the council, but none as important to the people as a watcher.

When at last Laida emerged, night had fallen without him noticing. The pile of shredded petals had grown in size, enough to cover his sandaled feet. He stood and kicked at it, scattering them as Laida walked toward him. Her robe was no longer shaped into a dress. The sash was gone.

He picked a fresh pink rose and handed it to her when she stopped in front of him. Her lips formed a smile, and she brought the flower to her nose, inhaling the fragrant scent.

"Do you recall how you sometimes mention the need to 'distance' yourself?" she asked, tucking the rose behind her ear. They had no thorns in Acantha.

Ardenis nodded.

"I believe Hector needs some distance. I almost had the council convinced that wearing the sash in such a matter was acceptable, when he came into the room. He entered so fast the door banged against the wall. I feel he'd been listening at the door. The council allowed him to speak as if he was a member, instead of an enforcer."

"What did he say?"

She walked toward the dining hall, and he stepped quickly beside her.

"He presented arguments about how it was a rule violation and how it would start the people of Acantha on a path of dress altering. All very good points, but the way he said it felt off. Something in his tone of voice caught my attention. It sounded how you've described mortals being harsh and mean." She glanced up at him. "The feeling it gave me reminded me of the way I perceive you sometimes."

"Me?" Ardenis held his breath. Laida was too perceptive.

"You've never used that tone of voice before, but I've become adept at predicting when you're going to say you need some distance." She smiled. The pink of the rose and the flames of the night torches mixed with the blue of her eyes, turning them the color of a lavender sunset.

Ardenis kept his hands loose at his sides, though he yearned to reach for her. "Hector's not a watcher, though. Thera can't influence him the way it can a watcher."

"Oh, I know. It's just the way I perceived his actions."

"So you can't wear the sash anymore?" No surprise there.

"No, and the council demoted me."

Ardenis gasped, and Laida raised an eyebrow at him. He turned his attention forward.

"There. Right there." She placed her hand on his arm, stopping him in the middle of the stone path. He glanced from side to side, but no one else was around. "So these things I witness you do sometimes... That's Thera's influence. How much has Thera affected you?"

Ardenis gritted his teeth. He shouldn't discuss this with a non-watcher.

She stepped closer. The edge of her robe brushed against his, taunting him. "I won't tell anyone," she whispered. "I didn't tell anyone about your drawing."

She shouldn't want to know more than she was allowed. She shouldn't know to keep secrets. He'd done this to her.

"Secrets are lies, Laida. If you were wise, you'd report me and yourself to the council." He watched her, waiting for her to agree, but her lips curled up into a small, innocent smile.

"It's not a secret that Thera can affect watchers. That's why most choose not to become one, assuming they can't resist. I want to know how much you've resisted."

Ardenis sighed, half relief and half weariness, and shook his head. "You ask too much."

She stepped back. "I'm sorry, Arden, if I've overstepped my bounds."

Laida turned and walked away. Before she could get too far, Ardenis caught her fingers.

She stared down at their joined hands.

Ardenis let go. "Yes, it's from Thera, these things I do sometimes." He sighed. "I spend most of my time watching their world, and it's hard not to be influenced by it. I've been a watcher the longest out of all the watchers. There's a reason so many of us are forced to be born."

"How much has Thera influenced you?" she asked.

He rubbed his fingertips together in the lingering bliss of Laida's touch. "A bit. But it's not my time to be born. I will endure what I must to follow the Fates' design."

She nodded, and they continued walking.

"Laida, what are you waiting for? Why haven't you been born yet?" He didn't meet her eyes, afraid of the answer. The thought of her being born and leaving him forever tore at him.

She smiled and stared off at the star-filled sky. "My instincts tell me there's something special ahead for me. It just hasn't come yet." She paused. "I have a secret too, you know." She glanced up at him.

This was the most open he'd ever seen her before. "You don't have to tell me."

"It's only fair." She frowned. "I fear being born into an ordinary life, or being born without magic."

"Magic is rare on Thera. More so than it used to be. Few are born with it."

"I remember the reports from the council when magic was everywhere. I've thought about it more and more, lately." She pulled him into a stop. "I want to be the girl in the drawing you made for me—Eva, the future queen of Alysies. Not the women I see in the museum who lead unimportant existences."

"I've often thought of that very thing." Ardenis smiled and reached his hand toward her. He tilted her chin up. "The Fates don't know who they're trifling with if there's anything in your future that's less than extraordinary."

Laida pulled away, but laughed. She linked arms with him, and they walked to the dining hall together. His heart danced the entire way.

CHAPTER
FOURTEEN

Ardenis tracked the progress of Eva's engagement, but only through council bulletins and discussions overheard from fellow watchers. He doubted Thera had ever seen celebrations equal to the elaborate parties he heard described. There were many feasts, and parades, and extravagant gifts of gold, furniture, and rare spices from neighboring kingdoms. For the grand finale before the wedding ceremony, newly crowned King Isaac sent bread to all the major towns in the kingdom, feeding the hungry in the name of Lady Eva.

In the midst of all the revelry on Thera, Ardenis met his friends outside the transfer hall for Vinia's farewell. Amongst the columned portico, sun shining in at just the right angle, Bram, Laida, and a few others who had arrived to wish her well, lined up to take their turns. One by one, they spoke words of 'good journey,' or 'travel well.'

When it was his turn, Ardenis shuffled forward to say goodbye. He meant to clasp Vinia's hand, but he caught them both by surprise and embraced her in a hug. She opened her eyes wide, and he laughed, chasing away some of the ache that'd been building in his chest all morning.

"I've no doubt you'll be a great kickball player in your life on Thera," he said.

Vinia grinned. "I want to be a mother. Maybe I'll teach my children to play."

Ardenis nodded. A mother was a noble calling. He hoped her wish came true. "Farewell, my friend, and may we see each other again in the Hereafter." Vinia had been his friend for a long, long time.

The ache in his chest renewed. He would miss her. He'd never thought that of anyone he'd seen born before. His new emotions made that possible. But as much as it hurt, it was a gift, allowing him to see just what he was losing, and to appreciate a friendship he wouldn't have known to appreciate before.

Everyone waved goodbye as Vinia took her place in line. He stood beside Laida, feeling equally guilty and thankful beyond measure it was Vinia leaving and not her. They stayed until she entered the transfer hall, out of sight.

Laida turned to him. "Well, as I am trying to earn my rightful place as leader again, I better get back to work."

"Are you still organizing transfer records?" Bram asked.

"Yes. I'm also responsible for the numbers and making sure we don't exceed our daily quota of borns. Almost what Vinia did before. It shouldn't take long to move back up." Laida pushed her blonde hair over her shoulder and walked toward the transfer hall.

She stepped quickly, likely feeling the pull of her instincts to her calling. Slender hands graced her sides, swinging with her pace and the movement of her hips.

Bram cleared his throat. "Back to the tower, then? I'm off to finalize the plans for the chess competition I'm coordinating."

Ardenis reluctantly focused on Bram. "That sounds fun." Though he'd never label it a 'competition.' "Goodbye, Bram."

"Goodbye." Bram smiled and headed toward the recreation center.

Sighing, Ardenis made his way to the tower. He wished for rain in

Acantha, the first time he had in a long time. It would be appropriate. He'd been dreading this day for years, and losing Vinia wasn't the worst part.

Today was the day Eva married King Isaac and became queen.

All the day watchers would be on hand to witness the momentous occasion. And Ardenis wouldn't even have the refuge of watching Queen Vatrice and staying well away. She would be in attendance while her ailing husband, King Zane remained home with their children. Only a few months ago, Vatrice had given birth to the son she'd always wanted; Samuel, now heir to the throne of Daltieri. Her son and daughters remained at home, and Ardenis had tracked her slow journey to Alysies, each passing mile like a stone dropped into his gut.

Ardenis walked with slow steps, further delaying the inevitable. Too soon, he entered the tower and the white domed room. They filled every chair except his. The room was silent, as all gazed deeply into the clear pool in the center.

Hector stood at the side of the room, observing everyone. Of course they'd have an enforcer present today.

Ardenis took a shaky breath and hid his trembling hands in the folds of his robe. Sitting, he focused on the watch window. Too soon, it glowed in his eyes, and his vision zoomed through the Theran landscape. Bypassing Oakrin and Lord Ferran's keep, full of so many dark memories, he ignored Queen Vatrice of Daltieri walking with her entourage from the west wing to the castle chapel, and finally let his instincts take over after six years of holding them back.

Tension released from his shoulders and breathing became easier. His instincts took him straight to Eva. No other watcher knew her like he did. He'd avoided her for far too long.

Six years had passed, but Eva looked much the same, aside from a hollowness and a shadow that seemed forever draped over her skin. She sat in front of an armoire while servants put finishing touches on her makeup. She wore a flowing ivory gown of delicate lace, and they'd twisted her curly brown hair into an intricate updo, topped with a veil of sheer fabric that flowed down her back. Her cheeks had lost all the roundness of youth, almost hollow now, and she'd filled out in places that marked her as a mature woman.

It was her eyes that had changed the most. There was no love or life in those eyes. Ardenis would have wept for her if he could. Eva gazed at her reflection with empty despair. Handmaidens hastily dabbed makeup to cover the dark circles, but they seemed a permanent part of her. The pain threatened to overtake Ardenis anew.

"You look beautiful, my lady," a portly servant remarked. Ardenis recognized Mary, Eva's maid from Oakrin, though she wore more silver in her dark hair. Mary sprayed Eva with perfume from a clear crystal bottle.

Eva smiled, but it didn't reach her eyes. "Thank you, Mary." Her voice was soft and weak, defeated.

A servant knocked and entered the room. "It's time," he said.

The handmaidens squealed and raced around the room, grabbing flowers and last-minute necessities. The elaborate buildup to the big day had everyone excited, everyone except Eva. Ardenis watched as she opened the drawer in front of her and pulled out a comb. It was brown, intricately carved, with a turquoise stone adorning it. She squeezed it in her fist.

"Perfect, my lady!" a maid exclaimed, snatching the comb out of her hands. Eva reached for it, but the servant slipped the comb in Eva's hair underneath her veil. "Something blue." The maid smiled.

Eva breathed a sigh, muscles relaxing. She rose, holding her dress up with both hands so as not to trip, and followed the servants through the winding maze of Isaac's elaborate castle. Lilac and freesia tied with white gossamer ribbons decorated the glowing wall sconces in each hall. Ardenis imagined their lovely, happy scent, contrasting with Eva's mood.

She licked her lips and pulled at the high collar of her dress. Perspiration beaded on her forehead, and her tight gown rose and fell in succession with her rapid breathing. The servants tittered around her, unaware of the state of their charge.

They went like this all the way to the castle chapel. A choir, accompanied by a string orchestra, sung a most extraordinary musical masterpiece. The voices rang clear and full of depth, harmonizing with the melodic symphony of the violins and cellos. The Acanthian performances he'd endured to be close to Laida would never achieve such beauty.

The doors opened at the back of the chapel, revealing Eva to Isaac and the beaming spectators. Her veil hid her silent tears. Her father, Lord Ferran, came to her side dressed in the finest fabrics; tight black trousers beneath a loose, blue and silver top cinched with a belt at the waist. His black shoes were extra pointy. He gripped Eva's arm as they began their slow march, his fingers digging into her silk glove, ensuring she'd make it to the end of the aisle.

The chapel was several stories tall, buttressed in wood beams. Stained glass windows let in plenty of colorful light. Men and women of noble birth wore their fine clothes, elbow to elbow in the pews. Their enraptured gazes alternated between Eva and Isaac. Queen Vatrice sat near the front, her guards disguised as nobleman. She'd left her baby behind in Daltieri. With a sneer beneath her painted face, the queen watched Isaac—her son's future rival—as he waited at the front of the chapel.

Isaac had grown into a man in the years since Ardenis had last watched him. His light-brown hair was long and swept back into a low tail. He stood tall, a broad chest puffed up beneath his navy tunic and cream cape. A ceremonial sword hung at his side. His eager eyes tracked Eva down the aisle. Ardenis appreciated the irony as the man who'd tried, on several occasions, to endanger Isaac, now walked his bride toward him.

Isaac had always been a good prince. Even from a young boy, he'd shown promise. Through the council bulletins, Ardenis knew Isaac had continued to make good decisions as king over the past year. Poverty was on the decline, and trade with neighboring territories steadily increased. He'd continued his studies and proved quite intelligent, in addition to his renowned skills with a blade. It was a good match. But Eva had already found and lost her true love.

Ardenis grabbed at his chest and held his breath.

When they reached the front of the chapel, Ferran released Eva, bowed, and retreated. Isaac stepped off the dais and smiled. Eva didn't meet his eyes when she took his proffered hand, but Isaac continued to gaze warmly at her.

The priest spoke his piece, the same words heard a thousand times, and Ardenis watched Eva. She stared straight ahead, somewhere on Isaac's chest, her face dead to the world, though her tears had stopped. When Isaac squeezed her hand, some color returned to her cheeks.

A young page produced two coordinating diamond and sapphire rings—Alysian colors. Isaac slid Eva's carefully over her finger, caressing her hand before letting go. Eva put Isaac's thicker band on with brisk efficiency, though she met his eyes and blushed.

"By the power vested in me by His Majesty's holy church, I now pronounce you man and wife." The priest clasped his hands. "You may kiss."

King Isaac pinched the edge of Eva's veil and lifted it over her face. She stared at his chest again, unable or unwilling to look at him. When he smiled and tilted her chin up, she met his eyes. The emptiness was a fierce contrast to the warmth when she'd gazed upon Damian.

She didn't flinch when he skimmed her cheek with his fingertips. And when he cupped her face in one hand and leaned down to her, he paused just before their lips met. An invitation? Eva gave in to him. She shut her eyes and then closed the minute distance between them.

They kissed sweetly, husband and wife.

Ardenis's vision snapped. White light flashed before his eyes.

He no longer viewed the scene at the royal chapel. Faster than ever before, his vision shifted into a new scene. A Fating of the future. Ardenis gasped, struggling to calm himself.

A pregnant mother. Her face was a blur. She cried out in pain, so much pain. People gathered around her, mopping sweat off her forehead as she screamed. She lay in a bed, in labor, in a sweat-soaked nightgown of fine cloth. She pushed and yelled. More people ran around what appeared to be a large bedroom, but with the furniture cleared away. The edges were dark, as if his vision wanted him to focus only on the mother. The room was chaos, and inside him, his instincts screamed.

"That's it, push! He's almost here," a familiar female voice said.

With a scream of effort, the mother pushed with all her might. Her voice quivered as her baby was born. Ardenis held his breath as the newborn's first cry filled the room. The mother sagged back against the bed, exhausted.

Someone cut the umbilical cord and wrapped the newborn in a blanket, hiding all its features, save one. The ears.

The infant had elongated, pointed ears.

What was he seeing? Certainly no ordinary baby. Was it a birth defect?

A word sprang to his mind, a foreign word he'd never heard before.

"Elf," he said out loud.

His instincts caressed him, showing him this was true. A new word to define something unique to their worlds.

He trembled, trying to understand what this meant, what his vision was showing him. This baby was unlike any in existence.

He'd fated the birth of a baby, and not just any baby, the first elf.

All that magic absent from the world... was this what it was saving up for?

His vision started slipping. The mother sagged against her pillow, reaching for her baby, but the scene went blurry. With an audible grunt of effort, Ardenis focused hard on the mother's face. She came into focus just before the vision fell away completely.

Eva.

CHAPTER

FIFTEEN

Ardenis blinked, and his vision shifted. He once again viewed the chapel, where King Isaac and Queen Eva walk down the aisle, arm in arm. Eva wore the hint of a smile, though just a hint. Her eyes still held sadness, but also a touch of guilt. The rest of her looked the same as the Eva from his Fating of the firstborn elf. Soon, then.

He ended his watch and abruptly stood. All faces turned toward him, staring with variations of unguarded curiosity.

"You've seen the Fates, haven't you, Watcher Fater?" Cadence asked with wide eyes.

He thought back. Had he reacted emotionally? Cried out again, or shown signs of distress? By their expectant faces, it was likely. They attributed his last outburst to a Fating, even if that was a lie he'd given the council to explain his behavior.

Choosing not to deny it, Ardenis nodded.

"Well done, Ardenis," Cammon said. "Well done, indeed."

It was a curious reaction, but one he was used to. Fatings bolstered watchers' esteem even higher in the eyes of the rest of Acantha. It meant more information available to them. Amalia, her long black hair

147

hanging loose over her shoulders, nodded at him, but there was something more than respect in her eyes. Suspicion? He quickly looked away.

The others inclined their heads in a sign of respect. No one did him the discourtesy of asking what he saw. He wasn't allowed to share his Fatings with anyone but the council.

"I must report this." Ardenis avoided their eyes, then turned and left the tower.

He did not go to the council hall. He forced himself into even, calm steps, concentrating on the placement of each foot so as not to alert anyone to his emotional state. They couldn't see his racing heart and the doubt that sprung to his mind. Arriving home, he shut the door tight and sank into a chair. His head hung in his hands.

The Fates had given a name to the race of the pointed-ear infant. Was it truly the beginning of a new race? The magnitude of this admission had far-reaching consequences. Only one concerned him now.

Laida.

When the council released his Fating, she would be first in line to be born as the elf. He knew it without a doubt. This was the opportunity she'd been waiting for—the chance to be more than ordinary, even if there was no guarantee it would be her. The probability was small. Acantha had never seen an event as big as this one would be—the potential to start an entirely new race in Thera. If the council approved sharing this information with the people—and they would—many would be unable to resist. Especially Laida.

She'd be born. No matter if she became the elf, or a mage, or a thieving street urchin, Laida would be gone from Acantha and out of his existence. She'd be long dead before his fated born time came.

He slammed his hands onto the armrests. That couldn't happen. He'd lie. He'd make up a story to tell the council. He pressed his palms into his eyes. It would be the biggest lie he'd told, affecting everyone. How could he even think such a thing? Duty came before *everything*. He had to share his Fating. He *had* to.

He groaned in frustration, something he'd never done before. The emotions whirling inside felt so foreign, yet so familiar as they mirrored every Theran sentiment he'd witnessed for most of his existence.

Eva had lost Damian. He wouldn't lose Laida. He straightened his robe and smoothed his black hair where he'd pulled at it.

The best choice that would cause the least damage was to say nothing to the council and say nothing to the watchers. Let them think he'd passed on the information and the council chose not to share it. The elf would still be born, and Laida would remain in Acantha. A tinge of happiness colored his heart, but guilt trapped it before it had a chance to bloom.

He'd made up his mind, so why did he feel worse than before? His steps were heavy as he headed back to the tower, trying to pretend all was well. He entered the rose garden, tower door in sight. Beside the door, Amalia leaned casually against the stacked stone with her arms crossed. When she saw him, she pushed off the wall and intercepted him on the stone path.

"Amalia, how may I help you?" Ardenis stopped before colliding with her, then backed to a polite distance. He met her eyes with neutral indifference, though his heart thumped wildly. She'd always differed from the other watchers—knowing, or at least suspecting, more than she should about him.

"Did the council enjoy your Fating, Ardenis?" Amalia smiled up at him. Her eyes and voice held a hint of warning.

"I'm sure, but I'm not at liberty to discuss my Fating or the council's reaction." His even tone and unremarkable statement sounded normal, unemotional. His heart steadied just a bit.

"Oh yes, as I well know." She picked at her nails. "I also know you didn't go to the council." His head snapped up. Amalia raised an eyebrow. "I propose we meet somewhere more private at a later time. Your home after dinner?"

Ardenis was sure she heard his uneven breaths. He'd lied, in a world where people didn't lie, and Amalia knew it. "Why are you doing this?" His words tumbled out. "Why can't you leave me be?"

Amalia glanced around, then stepped closer. "Since you asked so nicely, I'll tell you this evening." She smiled and walked down the path, away from the building.

He wasn't about to follow her, so he entered the tower, willing his steps to slow. He felt like fleeing. Maybe he wouldn't go home—simply watch all night. Why should he trust Amalia? He didn't need her, or the friendship of any watcher. He only needed for things to go back to the way they were before he'd witnessed mortal love.

Ardenis sat in his chair. No one looked up at him now, though a few shuffled around the room. The wedding celebrations must have ended. The wedding. Normal, everyday things. Safe things. Eva had seemed almost happy by the end of the ceremony. Isaac had been kind and patient, traits he'd exhibited since his childhood. Perhaps there was hope of love for Eva yet.

Ardenis looked at the watch window, and that's when it dawned on him. His instincts hadn't led him to Damian, all those years ago. They had led him to Eva. She was the start of the important moment in history his instincts wanted him to watch. The birth of the elf would be the most profound thing to ever occur in Thera. Perhaps it was Eva's goodness and capacity to love that would grant her such an extraordinary gift. And maybe some of Isaac's magical heritage as well.

Or, maybe... he was led to both Damian and Eva, to learn of love. Had the Fates meant for him to break the rules and fall for Laida? So far, it'd only led to torment and agony, more lies upon lies.

He stared at the smooth water within the marble pool and prayed Amalia wouldn't turn him over to the council. She must be emotionally influenced herself to recognize his lie. And the way she'd looked at him, so knowing and full of emotion. Just like a Theran. His hands trembled. Evening would come quickly, and he hoped to puzzle out Amalia and what she knew.

CHAPTER
SIXTEEN

Ardenis ate roast chicken and vegetables with Laida and Bram in the dining hall that evening. Vinia's absence was keenly felt, but only by him, it seemed. They didn't talk about her, didn't comment on how much they missed her. He almost mentioned it several times, but Laida and Bram didn't seem to feel the same sense of loss. Is that how he'd reacted when his friends had been born before?

They sat across from him, and he snuck glances at Laida. If he reported his Fating, their time together would be reduced from centuries to mere months.

The fork shook in his hand. It could be as little as days if Eva were to get pregnant right away.

Amalia dropped her plate next to him, causing him to jump. Laida and Bram smiled in greeting as Amalia sat. She didn't utter a word.

"I found a slight flaw in the transfer records," Laida said. She stared straight into Ardenis's eyes, as if he were the only one in the room. He reminded himself to breathe, ignoring their interruption and his trembling fork.

"Really?" he asked, recovering.

Bram scribbled on a sheet of paper. Amalia ate her food and acted invisible. Ardenis was well aware of her and her knowing gaze, studying him.

"Yes," Laida said. "I believe we'll be able to let more borns go each day than previously. It seems we hadn't calculated for the recent increase in population. I'm hoping this discovery will earn my position back."

Bram looked up from his writing. "Good work, Laida," he said, beating Ardenis to it.

Ardenis felt a surge of irrational jealousy.

"Thank you, Bram. I got the idea when an enforcer brought the third forced born this week. It made me think, with more souls on Thera recently, there would be room for more to be born—more mortal women to bear children."

The third this week? Ardenis peeked to gauge Amalia's reaction. She stared at Laida, speared carrot stopped midway to her mouth.

Laida spoke over his thoughts. "What are you working on, Bram?"

"My journal. I had an idea to hold a Tafl tournament. What do you think?"

Laida clapped her hands, smiling. "Oooh."

"That sounds great, Bram." Ardenis smiled as well, focusing his emotions. He enjoyed Tafl.

They chatted until dinner ended, Ardenis forcing polite conversation to distract him from what was to come. Amalia remained silent, not even pretending to care. The others didn't seem to notice. When she stood to leave, Ardenis followed her away from the table.

"You're not coming to the concert, Arden?" Laida asked.

Ardenis glanced at Amalia, who smiled and winked at him. "Not tonight, Laida." He clenched his jaw. It was the first time Laida seemed to care if he went to the concert, and he hated to disappoint her, even if that disappointment was all in his head. Amalia was making him waste precious time without her.

"Okay, goodnight then." Laida turned and walked toward the pavilion with Bram, taking his arm.

Or maybe she didn't care at all. He seethed.

Ardenis watched her go until Amalia cleared her throat.

"You're in more trouble than I thought, *Arden*," she said.

His cheeks burned.

Amalia's eyes widened. "Come." She grabbed his arm and paced toward his house, not bothering to disguise her eagerness.

Without stopping to wait for him, she opened his door and went inside. When he caught up, she stood in the middle of his living area, hands on her hips.

"You've let Thera influence you, my friend. Your emotions are replicating theirs."

Ardenis opened his mouth to deny it, but couldn't. He sighed, hanging his head. He thought he'd done well enough disguising it these past years. But they couldn't force him to be born yet; it wasn't his fated time.

"It's your Theran reactions that give you away," she said. "Like what you're doing now."

He glanced up at her sharply. She stared at him hard, shifting her weight from foot to foot. The seconds ticked by, and Ardenis bore her gaze with silence. Dread pooled in his stomach. Amalia was on the edge of some great precipice.

She blinked and looked away. "Look, Ardenis. I'm sure you already suspect, which is why, after all this time, I'm willing to share what I know with you. I've kept my secret well these last 150 years." She hesitated. "I recognized the signs in you, because, I'm emotionally altered as well." She finally looked up, jutting out her hip and sweeping her black hair around to the front of her shoulder. Theran gestures.

"150 years?" He sat in his wooden chair, resting his forearms on his knees. He'd been sure she was about to turn him over to the council. "I had no idea. Until recently—"

"I know. It takes being emotionally influenced yourself to recognize the signs in others. I have to commend you. You've done well hiding it. You've passed all my tests, but it's becoming apparent."

Tests? Amalia had accused him of needing distance, sidling up next to him in the baths, unnerving him. The feelings she'd invoked had alarmed him; his emotional awareness was so new then. He hadn't known how to handle those sensations. And of course, the threat of being caught was as real then as now.

Ardenis considered Amalia's admission and the truth in her words. He found himself angry. "Why were you testing me? And why are you telling me this now?"

She stepped closer. "We are the same, and I want to help you. I'm trusting you with my secret because I feel it's not your time. You need help if you're going to last without being discovered."

He wanted to be angry at her actions, her attempts to tempt him into revealing his darkest secret. But, here she was, telling the truth and trying to help him. He needed someone on his side so badly. Someone who understood what kind of prison he had locked himself into. A prison of the mind and of the heart.

"It's so hard, Amalia. My eyes are wide open," he swept his hands in the air, "and I want more than anything to close them, except..."

"Except for Laida." She stared at him. Ardenis dropped his arms and looked away. "I know, Ardenis. Truly, I do."

Amalia walked straight to a drawing on his wall. It was of a herd of wild horses, trying, but failing to outrun a summer storm. She lightly caressed the sheets of rain falling from the sky. She must love the rain as much as he did, one more thing just beyond his reach if he followed his instincts and stayed in Acantha.

Amalia moved over to a more recent drawing of a two-hundred-year-old tree. A small farmhouse sat in the background, barely visible through the rain. The great-great-great grandmother of the woman that lived there had planted the tree for her husband and son, lost to the Creaban War. She didn't know, but the army was a mere two days' march from reaching her house when they signed the treaty ending the war. It still stood, just south of the Alysian border.

Alysies, Eva and Isaac's kingdom.

"I loved someone, too." Her voice rang with a grief unknown to Acantha.

Ardenis's mouth gaped, but he said nothing. Her pain tore at his own.

"I was more foolish than you," she said. "I tried to get him to love me back. Of course, he didn't understand. Couldn't. He wasn't a watcher. When he chose to be born, my world ended. I tried to watch for him, to see who he was on Thera, but it proved impossible." She faced him. Her eyes held a sadness Ardenis had only recently begun to understand. "He's long dead and in the Hereafter now."

Ardenis swallowed. "Why didn't you follow him?" It was the first thought that came to his mind because he'd thought it many times. He'd follow Laida if he could.

She remained quiet for a long while before answering. "I know you lean heavily on your instincts, Ardenis. All watchers do. I suppose all Acanthians do, following the call to leave Acantha for the great unknown." She sighed. "I wanted to follow him. I did follow him. I stood in line next to him for the transfer, but something told me it wasn't time yet. My instincts. It was almost like pain to remain in line and go against them. At the last moment, I stepped away, and he waved goodbye to me with a smile on his face. Two friends parting ways until the next engagement." She pulled a chair up to him and sat.

He swallowed. "How could you stand it? Laida, she doesn't see me the way I see her."

Amalia patted his knee. "Don't take it personally. Laida lights up your life, and she doesn't notice whether you come or go. Remember, it's the way things are supposed to be here. We're the exceptions. The emotionally altered."

Something cautioned him not to press her for more. It was the way she wouldn't meet his eyes, and the way her words sounded so rehearsed, like a mantra she'd been repeating to herself for over a century. It was clear she still keenly felt her pain under the bravado.

"What do I do?" Ardenis held his breath, praying she had all the answers—that she could make it all go away.

"You learn to control your new awareness as best you can, and you continue to do your calling according to the Fates' design." Amalia shook herself and put her hands on his shoulders, turning him until he stared straight at her. "That means no hiding things you've fated from the council."

Ardenis looked away, ashamed. Amalia snapped her fingers in his face, and he glanced back at her with wide eyes.

"I'm serious, Ardenis. The Fates gave you a gift. Why you and no one else, I'll never know, but they gave it to you. When you see what they want you to, it's not so you can keep it to yourself. No matter what it is, no matter how much it may hurt you in the end," she took a deep breath, "you must share it."

Ardenis stared at the floor for a long minute. "I know. You're right. It feels wrong to keep it inside." He tugged at his sleeves. "It's big though. It could change a lot of things on Ther—"

"Ah!" Amalia hit his shoulder. "Don't say another word. Remember, do your job. Obey the rules. Don't give the enforcers a reason to become suspicious." She stood and smoothed her blue robe. "Now, I suspect you have somewhere you need to go."

Ardenis stood. "Thank you, Amalia. Truly. I would have done something terrible by keeping this to myself, if not for you."

She straightened, and a smile of contentment reached her eyes. "Thank you as well, Ardenis. I feel lighter than I have in decades. I've fulfilled part of my purpose for staying in Acantha, I believe. My sacrifice is being justified."

Ardenis inclined his head toward her and strode out of his house. Though it pained him, he walked purposefully toward the council chambers. It was time to divulge of the fated born.

CHAPTER
SEVENTEEN

Hector sat behind the desk in the council foyer, immediately darkening Ardenis's mood. Many watchers stood around the room, still waiting to report on what they had witnessed of the wedding ceremony. Hector looked up, setting his quill down perfectly parallel to his paper.

Ardenis had the irrational urge to snap it in two. "I need to report to the council." His voice rang authoritatively in the otherwise quiet room.

"Ardenis Watcher Fater." Hector inclined his head. "Word reached me you'd be here. You've had a Fating, I suspect?"

Ardenis blinked. How had he heard about that? The only ones who knew were his fellow watchers, and it was not their place to divulge the information.

He gave no reply, except to maintain a steady gaze on Hector.

Hector scowled. "As you can see, there is a long line of watchers waiting to report after the events of the day. You're one of the last of the day watch to arrive. I'll add your name to the list, and you'll be summoned when it is your turn." He scribbled something in his book.

Ardenis nearly bristled. They always moved him to the front because of his gift. Perhaps Hector was trying to force him to admit he'd had a Fating. What Ardenis had seen was timely and couldn't delay.

"Have the rules changed, Enforcer? It is my understanding the Watcher Fater takes priority with the council." Ardenis kept his posture relaxed, neutral. Indifferent.

Hector clenched the quill, feather quivering. "You haven't fated anything of use in years, Ardenis. What makes you so special?"

Ardenis watched him, giving nothing away. Laida was right. He wasn't the only one being affected emotionally. Hector had learned anger—perhaps envy. But not from Thera.

"I also witnessed you speaking to Amalia earlier at dinner." Hector sniffed and scribbled something else. "Are you two friendly now?"

Ardenis raised his eyebrow. Had Hector overheard something he shouldn't? "What business is it of yours whom I befriend?"

Hector slammed the record book closed. It jarred the oil lamp, causing firelight to flicker in the dim room. Heads swiveled his way.

Ardenis didn't know what to think. How had the council not noticed Hector's behavior? The doors opened, and Cadence walked out of the council room.

"The council will see you now, Watcher Fater," Hector said as if nothing unusual had occurred, though he didn't look up.

Ardenis sneered and entered the room without a word.

The council members sat on their benches, Gharum in front, but as Ardenis took his place behind the podium, more filed in. What started out as ten, soon became twenty. Then thirty. It seemed every councilor who ruled over this part of Acantha had joined his session.

Word had traveled fast where it should not have. Ardenis clenched his sweaty fists behind the podium. He prayed he was wrong about Laida, that she'd choose to stay. He forced his face into the impassivity of a guiltless watcher.

Ardenis lost count, and soon it was standing room only in front of him.

Gharum Head Councilman nodded to him. "Watcher Fater, we are pleased to gather to hear your report."

Ardenis nodded in return and cleared his throat. "I will begin by giving my account of the wedding ceremony."

"There's no need of that, Ardenis," Gharum said. "We've already heard from your fellow watchers and will continue to do so well into the night."

Ardenis couldn't help gaping. So, they weren't going to deny they knew why he was here. He waited for Gharum to explain himself, but no explanation was forthcoming.

"I've seen the Fates." His announcement was met with stoic faces, though some council members in the back whispered among themselves. "As I watched King Isaac and Queen Eva wed, the Fating came to me. It was of Queen Eva. She will bear a child and give birth."

"A cause for celebration. Heirs to the royal line." Gharum smiled. "How far in the future is your Fating, Watcher Fater?"

"Not far, though I cannot say exactly. Eva hadn't changed much. No more than a year or two."

"Any details you'd like to add?"

Ardenis hesitated for only a second, thoughts of Laida clouding his mind. This was the hard part. Every admission had been easy up to now. "Yes. The baby... I couldn't see very well, but one feature stood out as clear as I see you all before me. The child had elongated ears."

Gharum glanced up. "The child was deformed?"

"This was no deformity." Ardenis resisted fidgeting in place. "I struggled to understand what I saw, and a word came to me. I know it was of the Fates' design." He breathed slow, shaking breaths.

Gharum frowned. "What word, Ardenis?"

Everyone in the room leaned forward.

"Elf."

Several brows creased in confusion. They glanced at each other.

"Elf?" Gharum looked to the side, and Ardenis followed his gaze to the hall that led out of the council room. "What is that?"

"I believe it is a new race of human. The Fates have destined Queen Eva will bear the first of its kind in Thera. The first elf."

Gharum's mouth gaped open. "This is unprecedented." He looked around the room as if it held the answers. He silenced the rise in volume of conversations with an upraised hand. "Why, I wonder. Why now?"

"I do not interpret the Fates, simply report them." Ardenis didn't know the answer to his question. Perhaps only time would tell.

"Yet you interpreted that the elf would be the start of a new race." Gharum narrowed his eyes.

Sweat beaded Ardenis's upper lip. "It was part of my Fating. I was given the word and meant to know that it wasn't a word to describe a deformity, but a new race."

Gharum nodded. "We, of course, trust your Fatings. Thank you for your report, Watcher Fater."

Ardenis gave a shallow bow and left the room. Shouts rang out behind him before the door cut off the noise. The intensity of Hector's gaze trailed him the length of the foyer. Something in Gharum's words echoed strangely with him. He said they trusted his Fatings, which almost seemed like confirmation they had reason to doubt them. The whole thing was disconcerting.

Night had fallen by the time Ardenis stepped outside, and the gentle breeze chilled his clammy skin. He breathed a sigh of relief. He'd done it. Though there'd only be anguish in his future, he'd made the right decision. It was in the council's hands now.

From the courtyard, the familiar racket of the concert was absent. He let his feet carry him home, while trying to decide how best to prepare for the coming pain.

CHAPTER
EIGHTEEN

Ardenis passed the council courtyard on his way to the dining hall for breakfast. A large crowd had gathered around the bulletin board. He didn't get near the front before the rumors circulated. It wasn't his Fating everyone talked about. This bulletin took him by complete surprise.

King Zane was dead. He'd died overnight in his castle in Daltieri, which meant one of the night watchers must have seen it happen. They reported his death was surprisingly devoid of outside influence and simply a matter of natural causes. Ardenis suspected Queen Vatrice had finally succeeded. Now she'd rule with absolution.

Ardenis spotted Laida's golden hair in the crowd, bouncing its way toward him. His heart leaped for no obvious reason.

"Arden!" she called. "That's big news about the king, but the wedding happened without incident, so it will be a busy few days at the transfers."

Ardenis smiled. He loved seeing the things that excited her. This influx at the transfers was nothing compared to what would happen if the council released his Fating.

Laida left for the transfer hall, and after breakfast—which he didn't touch—Ardenis went to the tower. He felt Amalia's gaze on him, but wouldn't meet her eyes. Having her know the truth about him meant it was real, and he could no longer deny he'd been emotionally altered. The guilt and shame still throbbed like a mortal wound.

He paid little attention to watching Queen Vatrice's happiness over her husband's death, or her quick departure to return to her kingdom. That afternoon, as he ended his watch, he could almost hear the hammering of the nail into the bulletin board from his chair. That was impossible, of course, but he knew nonetheless. This was what he'd feared. Ardenis knew this bulletin intimately.

He stood, his chair scraping back loudly against the floor. Not caring if anyone reacted, even Amalia, he retreated to his house. There he sat and waited, head in hands, for the inevitable.

He first heard it in the sound of multiple footsteps on the stone pathway, and the voices that carried tones of curiosity leading to the council courtyard. The rumor of a second announcement must have spread. Any Fating was always big news. This was the biggest of all. He could imagine the reactions as people realized they were reading a Fating. They'd be happy, perhaps questioning. They'd share the news of the Fating, but nothing more. They weren't capable of reacting in a more profound way.

The sound he expected, but dreaded, took shape in the form of a knock at his door. Laida entered just as he stood.

"I'm going to be born!" She grinned and threw her arms open wide. So full of emotion, or the appearance of it, anyway.

He sat back down heavily, staring at the floor. There was a squeezing in his chest—a physical and mental ache he didn't think existed anywhere else in Acantha.

"Arden, did you hear me?" She shuffled forward.

"Yes," he said hoarsely. He cleared his throat and forced himself to look up at her.

She'd dropped her arms and looked at him with polite concern.

"You know the odds, Laida," he said. "The likelihood of it being you is small."

Her smile turned into a frown. "You've given Acantha a great opportunity, Arden. I've always known your gift was special. Don't discredit your ability."

"Don't you want to wait for something more guaranteed?" he pleaded, knowing nothing was ever guaranteed. But what else could he say?

He held his hands, palm up, before him—a Theran gesture. He had to convince her to stay with him, but he had nothing to offer she wanted. If not for Amalia's words, reminding him Laida wasn't to be blamed, he might have been angry. Instead, he felt incredibly empty.

She looked at his hands. "I've been waiting for the right time to be born, Ardenis." Her tone remained polite indifference. "It might be a small chance, but it's a chance I'm willing to take. To be born at such a momentous time in history, even if I'm not the elf, would be tremendous."

"They said it was a boy." Ardenis grasped at clouds. He stared at the floor again.

"What?"

"The elven child. In my vision, they called it a boy." He stood and grasped her shoulders. "So, you see, it can't be you."

At the beginning of humankind, when Acantha was crowded with souls awaiting their time to be born, the genealogy keepers noticed a keen correlation between gender associations for those who transferred. Whichever they identified with in Acantha, they became in Thera. That was the theory, at least.

Laida shook him off and backed up. "Why did you tell me that? It's forbidden for you to share your Fatings with anyone but the council."

Ardenis straightened and stepped away, putting more distance between them. He was losing it. "I'm sorry, Laida. You're right."

Her eyebrows wrinkled in thought, then relaxed. "I understand, Ardenis. Perhaps you haven't read the bulletin and didn't realize that wasn't included." She put her hand on the doorknob, preparing to leave.

More than anything, Ardenis wanted to pull her into his arms and sigh her name into her hair.

"Thank you for your concern, but I've made my choice," she said. "My instincts tell me it's time. Since you didn't say you saw the gender for yourself, you can't be certain the Therans were correct. We don't know if there will be other elves. I still choose to be born." She opened the door and smiled. "Good day."

He couldn't think of a counterargument before she closed the door. He grabbed his robe, pulling it so tight he thought the fabric might rip. He wanted to chase after her, yell for her to open her eyes and see what he could. How many more months, or weeks, or days until she was born and gone from his existence?

Ardenis paced his living space, trying in vain to control his breathing. What was happening to him? He couldn't calm down. The squeezing in his chest threatened to choke him.

He ran to the terrace, stripped off his robe, and jumped into his bathing pool, sinking to the bottom. The water muffled his screams and acted as the tears he didn't know how to shed.

<hr />

Ardenis emerged from his bathing pool and swam to the side. When he looked up, Hector stood above him. His eyes were narrowed, feet apart, and arms crossed. He had let himself in unannounced.

How much had he seen?

Ardenis wiped all signs of surprise off his face. Placing his hands on the side of the pool, he vaulted out. Dripping wet and naked, he straightened and met Hector's unwavering gaze. "Enforcer, I didn't expect to see you. In my house." He reached for a towel from the table behind Hector, and Hector flinched.

"I don't normally meddle in the affairs of the watchers, as you know," Hector said, stepping away.

Anger and annoyance overrode Ardenis's sense of dread. He scrubbed his face with the towel to avoid rolling his eyes.

"I read the bulletin regarding your Fating." Hector paused. "I'm intrigued."

Ardenis turned his back on Hector and entered his bedroom. He grabbed a dry robe from the wardrobe, hiding his trembling hands. After putting it on, he wiped water from his damp hair and turned to Hector in the doorway.

"Intrigued, Enforcer?"

"Yes." Hector paced forward, so close he had to tilt his head to look up into Ardenis's face. "I was wondering. Why would a Watcher Fater lie about the Fates?"

Ardenis took a half-step back. Hector smirked.

"I didn't lie," he spat, no longer masking his anger. "And besides, Enforcer, that would be for the council to decide, and not for you to pass judgment." Ardenis couldn't help the venom in his voice. Who was Hector to accuse him of lying, when he'd sacrificed so much to tell the truth?

"You're lying right now." Hector raised his voice. "I can see it in your defensive emotional reaction."

Ardenis leaned over Hector. "And what would you know of such things, Enforcer?"

"There is no way," Hector said through clenched teeth, "it's in the Fates' design for an elf to be born on Thera." He took a deep breath and straightened his already perfect robe. He backed up a step. "Therefore, the obvious conclusion is you must be lying."

Ardenis shook with fury. "You disrespect me greatly with your blasphemy. I am Acanthian. I do not lie, as well you know." Ardenis looked away, clenching his fists to control his anger. Then his head snapped up. "What do you know of lying, Hector? You're not a watcher."

Hector smiled. "I'm an enforcer of the council. There is much that we know."

"Does the idea of an elf being born disturb you?" Ardenis asked sarcastically. "Perhaps you should concern yourself less with what watchers see, and more with your own calling."

"Two humans producing someone of a different race? It's not possible." Hector narrowed his eyes. "And you will not tell an enforcer how to conduct enforcer business, Ardenis."

"And you will not accuse a Fater, the only Fater, of lying." Ardenis crossed his arms and raised himself to his full height, towering above Hector. "It is not up to you to question the Fates' design."

Hector balked, then glared. "You'll slip up. Then your Fating will lose all credibility, and the people who are hailing you a hero of the ages, and declaring this an unprecedented time—the people who are throwing themselves at the transfers in a race to be born the elf— they'll see your Fating for what it really is. A farce." His voice was laced with heat. He practically spit the last word.

Ardenis's nostrils flared, and he took an unintentional step toward Hector, who wisely backed to the front door.

Ardenis clenched his fists. "Get out of my house." He wanted to hit him. He wanted to hit him hard.

Hector made it to the door, then backtracked and ripped Ardenis's drawing of a Theran child off the wall. "The council did not approve this for viewing. I'm taking it." He rolled it up, creasing it in his haste.

Ardenis strode forward, breathing heavily with eyes wide. Hector took one look and rushed out the door. Ardenis slammed it.

"So this is anger," he breathed, clenching his fingers into a fist and examining it. "I kind of like it." He smiled. He punched the door —feeling only the pressure of his knuckles impacting the wood, no pain—and paced the room, his heart still racing, and his muscles tight. It felt good to release his rage.

A short while later he sat in his chair, cursing himself for his stupidity. He shouldn't have lost control. Hector had gotten to him.

Maybe that was his purpose in coming—to see how emotionally influenced Ardenis had become. Maybe it was a test.

Hector couldn't turn him in to the council without risking getting himself in trouble. He'd been influenced as well. But Hector could certainly find fault in Ardenis's actions in other ways. Why did Hector assume he'd lied to the council? Ardenis rubbed his temples. If he could experience pain, he'd surely have a headache.

CHAPTER

NINETEEN

Ardenis shirked his watcher duty for the rest of the afternoon. Except for one quick errand, he waited at home until dinner, when he thought the excitement would have died down. Leaving his house, he shut the door and turned.

He'd been wrong thinking the excitement had passed. Very wrong.

A crowd of Acanthians milled around in front of his house. They chatted among themselves, or sat in circles playing cards. Their mass extended at least five houses down both directions. When they saw him, all conversations ceased, and every face turned toward him. They smiled.

Ardenis gazed at the people, not knowing how to react. Acanthians didn't do this. His Fating was unprecedented, yes, but it was a gift from the Fates, not from him. He considered saying something, but didn't know what, and it would be out of character for his pre-Theran influenced self. So, he took a deep breath and stepped forward down the path. As he did, the people parted and inclined their heads.

He reached the end of the walkway and turned toward the dining hall. The people there made way for him, too. No one said a thing. It seemed a silent show of gratitude for his service. The only sounds were soft whispers and the rustle of sandaled feet. A warm and peaceful feeling enveloped him, and he smiled, grateful for his ability to see the Fates and for what it provided the people of Acantha.

The last person moved aside revealing Hector on the path, blocking the way. His eyes betrayed his fury, and his lips parted into a snarl, revealing his teeth. As Ardenis walked steadily forward, it became clear Hector had no intention of moving.

Ardenis locked his gaze on Hector, and though he probably shouldn't have, he smiled and waved to everyone. Hector clenched his fists. Ardenis strode forward confidently. He would barrel Hector over if he had to. He came closer, bracing himself for impact. At the last moment, Hector stepped off the path, glaring. The nearby Acanthians exchanged glances.

Ardenis grinned in triumph.

"I'll just be doing a routine inspection while you're out, Ardenis," Hector said.

Ardenis lost his grin, but didn't turn around to give Hector the satisfaction of a response. He had several unauthorized drawings he did not want the council to see.

Fortunately, he'd expected this of Hector.

Halfway toward the dining hall, he spotted Laida from a distance. She looked to be in a hurry.

"Laida!" She glanced over to him, and he jogged to catch up. "I put some drawings under your bed today, but don't look at them. They haven't been approved yet." He grinned. Something had told him Hector would try something like this eventually, so he'd hidden them earlier.

"I'm sorry, Ardenis. I don't have time to talk right now. I'm in a hurry." She focused on the path before her.

He walked quickly to keep pace, furrowing his brows with concern. He almost reached for her hand. "What's wrong, Laida?"

They arrived at the dining hall, and Laida entered ahead of him without replying.

Ardenis's mouth dropped open as Laida climbed on top of the nearest table. Diners paused in their eating and conversations ceased. Laida straightened and looked around the room, then cupped her hands around her mouth. "I apologize everyone, but I need to make an announcement." Her voice carried through the room as everyone watched her. "I need all transfer workers to report to the hall immediately, and please bring those you know whom aren't here." She inclined her head. "Thank you."

Ardenis held out his hand to help her, but she jumped down and walked out the building. He stuffed his hand in his pocket, following her.

"What is going on?" he asked gruffly.

She glanced over her shoulder at him, but didn't smile as he was accustomed to. This was the most stressed he'd ever seen her.

Laida kept up her fast pace. "We've had an exceptional amount of people sign up to be born. There are more than the transfers can handle. We need order while we come up with a solution."

More than the transfers could handle? That had never happened in all his long years.

"We have at least a few months before Queen Eva conceives, if we're correct about your Fating, but no one seems to care," Laida said. "They all want to be a part of this time in history, and I'm not the only one who wants a chance to be the elf." She stopped and turned to him, placing her hand on his arm. He trembled under her touch. "This many people cannot be born at once. Thera can't sustain the numbers."

Ardenis had no response, other than to gape at her helplessly. "What happens if more people are born than there are mothers to bear them?"

Laida blinked. "They would miss their chance to go to Thera. They'd go straight to the Hereafter instead." She turned and marched toward the transfer hall.

Straight to the Hereafter? Still better than the Dark Unknown, the one thing he feared above all else.

Taking long strides, he caught up to her, though he didn't know what he planned to do. More than anything, he wanted to ease some of her burden and smooth the worry from her brow.

When they arrived, chaos was exactly the word he'd use to describe the scene before him. Acanthians were everywhere, and though their reactions were a muted version of what he'd seen in Thera, Ardenis could feel the tension in the air. Where there was typically an orderly line or a smattering of fond farewells, now there were clumps of people that became thicker and thicker as they moved closer to the building. Transfer workers issued commands, trying to corral people into order, but there were so many. It seemed impossible to know where to begin.

Though no longer in charge because of her demotion, several workers and would-be borns called out to Laida, looking for leadership and guidance. She brushed past everyone with brisk efficiency, and Ardenis followed. She didn't tell him to do otherwise.

They entered the building, and inside, the transfers were already full. Every gateway had someone in it with long lines behind. The black gateway was the only one unused. Ardenis shivered and looked away. The transfers were indeed running at capacity. Laida stepped into a back room ahead of him, and he registered several sighs of relief.

Ardenis stopped, unsure if allowed to continue. Shrugging, he followed. He caused all this anyway. Maybe that gave him the right to be here.

The room was large, almost as large as the watch room, but sky-blue instead of white. Skylights let in streams of sunshine from the two-story tall ceiling. White-painted floral woodwork decorated the light blue walls. They'd arranged the white tables similar to a Theran classroom. All chairs were occupied, and the transfer workers trailed Laida with their eyes as she walked to the front of the room. Most smiled at him as he awkwardly stood at the back. Several people offered him their chair, but he politely declined.

Laida stood before them, looking each in the eye. Several more people filed into the room.

"Idonea Transfer Leader is overseeing the transfers in progress, and so I will preside over this meeting. You know why you are here, and why we've spared so many when we have such a pressing matter outside." Laida glanced up at him. "Ardenis has fated an unbelievable occurrence to take place on Thera." She smiled. "It is understandable why we've seen such an increase. I include my own born in that number."

She stood calm with her arms relaxed at her sides, and no hint of tension in her face. She didn't even pace, displaying the fine qualities of every great leader he'd seen on Thera.

"Normally, if we exceed quota, it's only by a few, and we simply turn the last ones away until the following day. That will not work this time. There are too many here, and too many more to come." Her smiling eyes scanned the room. "I open the floor to solutions we may present to the council."

"Does the council have any suggestions?" someone asked.

Laida's smile faltered. "Hector Enforcer has approached the transfers as council representative under Gharum Head Councilman's authority." Her eyes met Ardenis's. "He says it is up to us to find a solution."

Ardenis didn't like that Hector was involved. It didn't seem consistent that the council would send an enforcer as a representative and not allow a transfer worker the job. But nothing like this had ever happened.

Everyone whispered amongst themselves. Ardenis had nothing to offer, and selfishly didn't try to help. If the transfers remained backed up, there was a good chance Laida wouldn't choose to be born. She'd stay to see the problem resolved.

Hopefully.

The thought sent his cheeks burning with shame. Laida wanted this. How could he not support her in something her instincts clearly required her to pursue? He should have left the meeting. It wasn't even his area of expertise. But it may well have been his last moments with her. He studied her, and she stared off in the distance, tapping her finger against her lips. Her soft, perfect lips.

She dropped her hand. "That's it..."

Conversations ceased, and they all watched from their chairs.

"I believe I may have a solution," Laida said, eyes lighting up. "We can have a drawing. Those who want to be born can write their names, and we can draw until our quota is filled for the day."

"A lottery," Ardenis said, smiling with pride. Laida was a genius.

Several people turned to him.

Laida grinned. "Yes, a lottery. Like they've done in Thera to determine their leaders. That's the only way it's fair and everyone gets the chance they seek."

"Where will they put their names?" a woman asked.

"We can put a large box outside the transfer hall. We'll fit it with a small hole, only big enough for a strip of paper, then draw names that morning for the day."

Ardenis admired her more with each word she spoke. He'd never had the privilege of seeing her lead the transfers. She possessed such admirable traits: her confidence and ability to take charge, her selflessness by including the transfer workers in a solution to the problem, her level head and unique ideas. He understood, more than ever, how she'd become the leader of the transfers.

Everyone smiled and thanked Laida for her idea.

"If there are no objections, I will present this to the council. In the meantime, let's organize everyone as best we can," she said.

Laida nodded to Ardenis and left the room. He pushed off the wall and followed her, leaving behind the sounds of chairs scraping against the wood floor as people left their seats. With the meeting adjourned, Ardenis and Laida went straight to the council hall.

"Do you want me to join you inside, Laida?" he asked.

She tore her eyes from the council hall and turned to him.

"Thank you for your assistance today, Arden. I can handle the council just fine." She pulled the door open and entered the building. Ardenis glimpsed Hector behind his desk, smirking, before the door closed.

Ardenis ignored him. He had no say in the council's decision. They would not turn down such a wonderful plan.

He wanted to do something nice for Laida, so he retrieved a storage box with a hinged lid from his house—dumping out some spare drawing supplies—just suited to her needs, and had a craft-worker cut a hole into it.

When Laida came out of the council hall, he sat waiting, the box beside him on the bench. Her smile became a grin.

"Did you bring this for the lottery? How did you know what the council would say?" She ran her hand over the box and opened and closed the lid.

"I knew the council would agree with your idea. It's a brilliant plan," he said.

Laida reached her arms around him and gave him a hug. Warmth flooded him, and Ardenis stopped breathing. It was a brief, friendly hug, but it meant everything to him.

He carried the large box back to the transfers for her, and she chatted the entire way about her plans.

"They gave me my position back." She beamed. "My idea earned me my place, even though I told the council I'd only be leader for a little while."

Ardenis swallowed hard. "That's great, Lade." He forced a smile.

"I like that," she said.

"What?"

"You called me Lade, kind of like I call you Arden sometimes." She grinned. "I like it."

His heart soared. He'd cheered her up and connected with her, even if it was on a superficial level. His lips curved into a smile, and he brushed aside the thought he may be influencing her emotions with his own. She would have reacted that way to the nickname before. A sense of pride filled him to have made her smile.

They delivered the box to the transfers, and by nightfall the council had nailed a new notice to the bulletin outlining the details of the lottery. The transfer workers put the box in place, and people were already putting their names in.

Laida did not enter her name that day. She said it wasn't time yet, and Ardenis could breathe again for a little longer. He fell asleep without the need to scream his frustration and pain beneath his bathing pool.

❖

Ardenis headed to the dining hall for breakfast, but stopped when he reached the council courtyard. An enormous crowd clamored around the bulletin board. Laida stood in the center, and the wooden lottery box sat on a small table next to her.

It was time for the first drawing. A transfer worker with medium-length, straight hair, Idonea, pulled out a name and handed it to Laida.

"Trinia," Laida said, her voice loud and clear, carrying over the crowd amassed for the drawing. She passed the paper along to the transfer worker seated next to her, who marked the name in the record book.

She accepted the next paper. "Runald."

And the next. "Aniva."

Those nearby smiled and shook hands with the people whose names were drawn as they left for the transfer hall. Ardenis watched as Laida shined in the spotlight of everyone's rapt attention, a silly smile on his face.

Laida accepted the next strip of paper from Idonea and gaped at it. "Ardenis."

Ardenis's mouth dropped. He hadn't entered the drawing.

Someone must have put his name inside. Someone had been dishonest.

Laida's eyes found him in the crowd, and she smiled, then continued reading the names passed to her. Bram walked over and patted him on the back.

"Ardenis, I did not know you planned on being born. I thought you'd seen your fate in the future." Bram smiled. "I wish you well, my friend."

Ardenis couldn't speak, even to respond. This kind of under-handed treachery did not exist in Acantha. Someone wanted him gone. He thought he knew who.

"There's been a mistake, Bram. I didn't put my name in the lottery." His voice sounded detached while his raging emotions tried to keep up with the implications of this new development.

What was happening to Acantha?

Bram raised his eyebrows. "Mistake? You don't want to be born?"

Ardenis took a deep breath. "No, not yet." He pushed his fists into his pockets.

"So you changed your mind. You better go talk to the record keeper."

Ardenis didn't argue with Bram. There was no point. He moved through the crowd toward the front where the record keeper was still busy writing the names as Laida called them.

"I didn't put my name in the drawing," Ardenis whispered.

The record keeper finished writing as he spoke. "Of course you did. It's right here." He pulled Ardenis's name out of the pile. Ardenis took the strip of paper from him and pocketed it.

"Please remove my name from today's list of borns and advise Laida to draw another." He strode away from the courtyard without making sure the keeper complied. He needed to find Amalia. Of everyone in Acantha, she was the only one who might believe him.

He went straight to where he thought she'd be and found her in the tower. She sat gazing in the watch window, and he approached her.

"Amalia," Ardenis whispered. She was deep in the middle of a watch, and she jumped at his words. She shook her head, and her faraway gaze slowly focused on his face.

"Ardenis. Can I help you?"

"Can we speak outside, please?" He recognized the urgency in his own voice. None of the other day watchers looked his way, thank the Fates. His request hinted at secrets.

She stood and smoothed her long black hair. Ardenis left the room, peering back to see that she followed. When they reached the garden outside the tower, Ardenis pulled her down next to him on a bench.

"What is going on, Ardenis?" she asked, her voice harsh and impatient outside the quiet of the tower.

"Someone tampered with the lottery."

Amalia studied him with pursed lips. "That's a heavy accusation."

"I know. It implies a lot, but it's true. My name was in the box, but I did not enter the drawing." He brought the strip of paper out of his pocket.

Amalia looked at it with wide eyes, then at him. He nodded.

"It's not my handwriting. They picked me to be born today. And I suspect Hector is behind it."

She let out a long breath. "You better mind yourself, Ardenis. Hector is not one to trifle with. I wouldn't be surprised if your assumption is correct."

"Why isn't he to be trifled with?" He cocked his head.

She gave him a tight smile. "That's a story for another time."

He nodded, though he wanted to press for more.

"Look, he can't force you to be born unless you make a mistake and the council authorizes it. Just mind yourself and don't give him a reason to single you out. He'll move on in a few decades or find someone new to pick on. Oh, and be selective about what you write in your journal each night, if you haven't already."

Ardenis groaned and let his head fall into his hands.

Amalia tugged his arms from beneath him. "Hey! You must resist that kind of reaction."

"I'm sorry... I mean, I apologize. You're right." He placed his hands on his knees to keep them from forming fists.

"Keep your head low. Do your duty. You'll be all right. Also..." She hesitated. "You've been missing meals and other recreational activities. You can't drop the pretense of mimicking mortal life or the enforcers will notice."

"What's the point of mimicking them if we're all just going to forget everything anyway?" He'd never cared to question it before, but everything was different now, and the worry and anger of the lottery had him wound up.

"How else would we know enough about Thera to choose when to be born? Knowing their ways isn't the same as living them, even without emotional awareness."

He nodded. She'd had more time to ponder these things.

She squeezed his shoulder. "And I like to think we keep some of ourselves when we go there, so it matters in that way too."

Ardenis sighed and stood. "Thank you, Amalia."

She smiled and went back into the tower, leaving him alone with his thoughts. He'd have to be more mindful of his actions, but what could he do about Hector that wouldn't put himself in danger of being born? What did Amalia know that she was keeping from him? Too many questions swarmed through him, when only one really mattered to him.

How could he convince Laida to remain in Acantha?

CHAPTER
TWENTY

W eeks went by without another incident. Laida's lottery system worked splendidly, and she had yet to enter herself. Ardenis attended every drawing, usually with Bram. He was there mostly to ensure Laida hadn't entered her name, but also to ensure his name wasn't drawn again. He'd reported the incident to the council, after enduring Hector's seething glare, but Gharum assured him he must have forgotten he'd put his own name in. It was impossible that an Acanthian would tamper with the lottery.

"There are no lies or dishonesty in Acantha."

Ardenis stopped watching Queen Vatrice, instead watching Eva daily, hoping for a Fating to help him narrow down the timeframe, but there was none.

Eva adjusted quickly to her new life. She spent most of her time being pushed and pulled between the ladies of the court. Everyone wanted her ear to promote their own conquests and agendas, but she handled it with finesse. Whenever a party monopolized her time, she politely excused herself and moved on to a different activity. She had advisors, but didn't seem to need them often. She took to queen-hood well.

Eva's nights were spent with King Isaac, who was loyal and loving to her. Ardenis saw her slowly soften toward him, going from separate rooms, to opposite ends of the bed, to much more. Her smiles grew more genuine in Isaac's never-failing patience. Her eyes still didn't hold the love she'd once had for Damian, but it was close. Ardenis wondered if in time she'd grow to love Isaac as she had Damian.

Every time they kissed, it pained Ardenis that she would betray Damian in such a way. He'd learned so much from them—to feel, to love, and what it meant to fully embrace the emotional capabilities of his soul. Their love had changed him forever, and in his mind he would always see them as one; Eva and Damian.

Then one day, Eva told Isaac she loved him. Isaac had never looked happier. Ardenis had struggled to breathe.

When Ardenis found Bram at the council courtyard the next morning for the lottery, he knew his shoulders slumped and feet dragged, but he didn't have the heart to care. If Bram noticed, he didn't comment. The usual crowd waited to see if their name would be drawn, but his thoughts were consumed by Eva's words. He reminded himself Damian was gone. Though it seemed a short time to him, six years was a long time for Eva.

Ardenis peered through the crowd to the front where he knew Laida would be. When he saw her, her eyes were wide and darting about. His melancholy instantly forgotten, he straightened up, alert. Laida chewed on her lower lip and wrung her hands, which trembled ever so slightly.

Ardenis clenched his fists. He'd destroy whoever had made her feel this way. He strode forward through the crowd, bumping people out of his path. He made it halfway to her before she cleared her throat.

"I regret to inform everyone the lottery box is missing." Laida met his eyes, and he stopped midstride.

The crowd muttered amongst themselves.

"Was it misplaced?" Bram, who had followed, asked.

"We're not sure," Laida said. "It was there last night, but when we went to collect it this morning, it was gone." The muttering grew in volume. "I apologize, but it's likely someone mistook it as their own property. If anyone sees it, please return it as soon as possible." Laida stopped wringing her hands. "In the meantime, we are placing a new box outside the transfer hall, and I would invite those of you who wish, to re-enter your names for today's drawing."

Laida turned and led the way back to the transfer hall, and the large crowd followed. Her golden hair flowed against a sea of black. Ardenis walked next to Bram, muscles tense. The box wasn't missing. Someone had stolen it.

"Things must be busy at the watchtower lately." Bram cut into Ardenis's dark thoughts.

He tore his gaze from Laida. "What do you mean?" Did he suspect something?

"I haven't seen you at any of the recreational activities lately, besides the concerts." Bram smiled.

His tension released in a whoosh. "I apologize, Bram. I've been very busy watching Thera." Not entirely a lie, but not the truth either. Pretending to be the same person as before was proving increasingly difficult. It took more energy and focus to make sure he didn't say the wrong thing or act the wrong way. It was best to stay away when he could.

"I understand, Ardenis. You have a very important calling."

Ardenis offered his friend a warm smile of appreciation. Bram had always been kind and generous. He'd make a fine soul for Thera one day.

An acrid smell stopped him short. He raised his nose to the air.

Smoke rose in front of the transfer hall. Ardenis left Bram behind, rushing to reach Laida at the front of the group. She froze, holding a hand over her mouth. The new lottery box was burning. Fire snaked along its wooden post. As Ardenis reached her, the burning box gave way and crashed to the ground, sending embers and ash flying.

Everyone was stunned into silence. Ardenis put his arm around Laida, and she didn't deny him. She grasped his hand where it rested on her shoulder.

"Arden," she whispered. "Why are these things happening? Are the Fates unhappy with the lottery?"

He squeezed her fingers in tandem with the squeeze in his heart. "No, Lade. I think... I think someone is tampering with the lottery."

She glanced up at him. "Tampering?" Her gaze drifted toward the smoldering remains. An enforcer Ardenis didn't know stepped out of the crowd to inspect the scene. "What does that mean?"

He swallowed. "It means interfering. Wrong-doing."

"That's not possible."

"It does seem impossible." He looked around to make sure no one listened. "I know this is going to be hard to hear, but listen. Hector does not want an elf born on Thera. He told me so himself when he came into my house uninvited."

Laida gaped.

"There's something wrong with him—a hatred I don't understand." He leaned closer, relishing the warmth of her nearness. "I believe Hector is sabotaging the lottery."

"What is sabotaging?"

Ardenis gritted his teeth. He'd used another Theran word not approved by the council. "It's like tampering. It means he's purposely trying to ruin it. By entering my name, stealing the box, and even burning this one."

Laida shook her head. "Those are things not of Acantha. The council would never allow them to continue."

"And there is where the true question lies." He spoke his thoughts aloud. "Why is the council allowing these things to continue? They must know of the goings on, yet they do nothing."

Laida pulled away. Her glare—something he'd never seen her do —penetrated straight through him. "Ardenis, I realize you are wise beyond me in the ways of rule breaking on Thera." The subtle heat in her tone was unmistakable, nearly enough to pass as Theran. "And while I may have believed you and your suspicions of Hector, I won't sit by and listen to you blindly accuse the council of wrong-doing."

Too far. He'd tested Laida's limits and had chosen the wrong words to do it. He should have told her he loved her.

The thought hit him in the gut. He really did love her, like Eva loved Damian.

She stared at him, waiting for him to respond.

"I'm sorry. You're right." He sighed and looked at the ground. "I'm going to report this to the council." He didn't look at her as he left.

"Ardenis," Laida called out to him. He turned back around. "I will sort out this lottery problem. And I thought you should know. I've decided when I will enter my name. Two weeks hence." She turned and walked away, past the burned-out box and into the transfer hall.

Ardenis stared after her. His jaw clenched and unclenched. His eyes burned. He couldn't see straight, couldn't think straight. Two weeks? Two weeks to convince her to stay, to tell her he loved her? Two weeks for the Fates to intervene and keep her in his life? Two weeks until he never saw her again.

Bram touched him on the shoulder, and he jumped.

"What is wrong, Ardenis?" Bram looked at him with concern.

Ardenis blinked. The crowd that followed Laida to the transfer hall milled about, surveying the burning box. They didn't look uneasy, despite the implications of what they'd just seen. Some even smiled, probably assuming it was another random accident. A couple of watchers caught his eye, but he ignored them.

He took an uneasy breath. "Laida announced she is entering the drawing in two weeks." His voice sounded pained.

Bram smiled. "She told us at the Tafl tournament last week. We're very happy for her."

Last week? She'd known for an entire week and hadn't told him?

"Excuse me, Bram. I need to report this incident to the council."

"Very good. Will you be at the concert this evening?"

"I'll do my best." Ardenis forced a smile and walked away. It took all his concentration not to run, screaming.

Hector was slowing down the lottery—maybe even stopping it—which, Ardenis supposed, he should be thankful for. It could delay Laida's born, but it was wrong. It violated the rules of Acantha. And it hurt Laida. She was committed to this task. Ardenis doubted she would allow Hector to stand in her way now that she knew about the opposition.

When Ardenis entered the council hall, he didn't bother to hide his disdain, glaring and nearly groaning out loud. Hector. It was always Hector. Why couldn't it ever be a different enforcer? His millennia of relaxed composure was slipping, and he didn't care.

"I need to speak to the council," he said, heat in his voice.

Hector didn't look at him, but scratched notes into a book with his quill. Ardenis remained still, waiting for Hector to speak.

Hector stopped writing. He didn't glance up, but said, "For what reason do you need to see the council, Watcher?"

Ardenis tensed at the misuse of his proper title. "That is between me and the council, *Enforcer*." With low, clipped syllables, he threw Hector's title at him like an insult.

Hector glanced up. His expression was neutral, but Ardenis could see the hate in his eyes. "Very well. The council will see you now."

Ardenis entered the room, throwing the doors open too forcefully, and took his place behind the podium while the council filed in to back of the room. When all were seated, he noticed only ten were present instead of the usual for him—double or more.

Gharum Head Councilman stood, fluffing his robe behind him. "Ardenis Watcher Fater. What do you have to report?"

Ardenis inclined his head. "I come to you, not on watcher business, but as a witness to today's events." He looked around the room. All eyes were on him with expressions of polite interest.

Gharum steepled his fingers. "And what do you have to report?"

"Someone has taken the lottery box from the transfer hall. Laida

Transfer Leader put a new box in its place. When we arrived, the replacement box had been lit on fire. It was destroyed."

"Anything else?" Gharum asked. There was no surprise, no whispers amongst the council. It was not the reaction he expected.

Next was the difficult part. Ardenis placed his hands on the podium, gripping it to steal himself. "It is my belief these acts were the result of wrong-doing in Acantha."

The council members' eyes went wide, and they all looked to Gharum.

Gharum smiled, which seemed innocent enough, but there was something off in his expression. "Thank you for your witness, Ardenis. We'll look into the matter. It most likely was a simple accident."

Ardenis gritted his teeth. He couldn't argue. An unaware Acanthian wouldn't know to. He was supposed to accept the councilman's word and move on.

"Ardenis, before you leave, I'd like to ask you a few questions."

"Of course, Gharum Head Councilman." His voice sounded calm, but his heart raced.

"Hector Enforcer brought the council a drawing he confiscated from your house. It was of a young child in Thera. Do you know that of which I speak?" Gharum glanced up at him casually.

"I do." Ardenis's palms turned slick.

"The council did not approve that drawing. We expected you to plead your case for it, but you haven't been here to claim it. Why not?"

"I've been busy." He'd forgotten about the drawing, lost in the distraction of Laida. "My instincts have kept me in the watchtower."

Gharum paced the room. "You are a good contributing citizen of Acantha, Ardenis. Your gift of Fating has been invaluable. It's not like you to break the rules." He stopped and faced him.

Ardenis didn't know what to say, or how much Hector had told them. He kept his face relaxed, but his knuckles turned white against the podium still locked in his grip.

A smile played on Gharum's face. For a moment, it appeared almost calculating. "Is Thera's influence proving to be too much?"

Ardenis's heart rose to his throat. He'd never been asked that before. They suspected him. If the answer was yes, they could force him to be born. If they knew the truth, they'd send him through the black gateway into the Dark Unknown. He'd only broken one rule they knew about, and somehow Gharum had concluded Thera was influencing him.

"No." He took a deep breath. "I know this for certain, because it is not my time to be born. As you know, I have fated myself in the distant future. If I was on the verge of becoming susceptible to Thera's influence, then my fate would be different."

Gharum frowned, but the other council members nodded their heads. Ardenis didn't celebrate just yet.

"There is no shame in admitting you need a break, Ardenis."

Ardenis didn't speak. What did the council know of shame?

Gharum nodded. "Considering your contributions, and because subsequent inspections yielded no results, the council forgives your indiscretion." He turned his back on him. "You may go."

Ardenis bowed to the rest of the council, and left. Blessedly, Hector was absent from the desk.

He walked with deep breaths back toward the tower, ignoring the beautiful sunshine and ignorantly happy Acanthians he met on the path. The council didn't believe him, and now suspected him of being emotionally influenced. Perhaps it was time to go beyond them and straight to the High Council. He'd need evidence to take his accusations there, though.

Or maybe Thera had made him paranoid. Maybe this was the way Gharum had always acted and Ardenis just never noticed it before becoming emotionally altered. Was he seeing things that weren't really there?

Amalia said to keep his head down. Do his duty. He was a watcher, so he'd watch.

CHAPTER
TWENTY-ONE

That evening Ardenis waited outside the council hall, watching for Hector to leave. He sat on a stone bench on the other side of a rosebush, just out of sight from the council doors. If he caught Hector breaking the rules, acting irrationally or setting more fires, he'd have something to take to the High Council. He pretended to collect roses, but stared through the bushes as the sun set to night.

Finally, Hector emerged from the building. He looked left and right, then headed in the opposite direction of his house. Ardenis stood, scattering rose blooms. He followed at a discreet pace, but Hector never looked back. After a while, Ardenis noticed they were walking toward the transfer hall. When he arrived, the line outside the hall was steady, as transfers happened at all hours of the day, but it was quiet in the courtyard. The burned-out remains of the lottery box had been cleared away, with a new one in its place. Curiously, no one waited to enter their name.

Ardenis watched Hector skirt around the line, then enter the building from a side door Ardenis hadn't known existed. When anyone, including enforcers, needed to visit the transfer hall, they used the front entrance.

Ardenis jogged to catch up. He reached the door and paused, listening for Hector on the other side. He didn't hear anything. He grabbed the handle and turned. The room was a dark, but Ardenis's eyes were already adjusted to the night. Hector was not here. Ardenis could make out shelves full of record books. Light peeked out from under a door, and he crept forward and opened it. The busy, open room of the transfer hall had him blinking with the contrasting light. Wooden beams divided people into long lines, and every gateway was full and manned by a transfer worker.

His palms sweat. His instincts flared, like a punch to his gut. Something was wrong. He scanned the room of faces, some more recognizable than others, but didn't see any sign of Hector.

"Ardenis!"

He jumped and swiveled to face Laida.

She smiled. "What brings you here?"

He shook his head to clear it. "Have you seen Hector?"

Laida raised an eyebrow. "No, but he could be here somewhere. He's been here off and on since the lottery began. Trying to find something to infract us for, no doubt."

Her sweet, innocent sarcasm blanketed him. His instincts calmed to a dull buzz in the back of his mind. Luckily, and predictably, she seemed to have put aside their previous disagreement.

Ardenis put on a smile. Maybe there was nothing to fear. It was Hector's duty to check on these types of things, after all.

"Should I say you're looking for him if I see him?"

"No, that's okay," he said quickly. "Goodnight, Laida."

"Goodnight, Arden." She turned and walked away, so he did too.

He went out the main exit, keeping an eye out for Hector, but he'd disappeared. He thought about going to Hector's house, but he needed distance. He nearly went to Amalia's instead. She'd know what to do. But, he couldn't. She'd only help by giving his newfound emotions a place in this world, normalizing them when they shouldn't even exist, when they were best kept secret.

His steps quickened toward home, and he wiped at his face.

Laida was right. Who was he to doubt the council? One lone enforcer, maybe, but the council trusted Hector. Shouldn't he? Learning of love and emotions had pushed him closer to the wrong side of the emotional veil more than he'd ever seen another watcher.

His Theran emotions escaped his grip more every day, swarmed and plagued him, cropping up when he least expected or desired. Haunting him. He couldn't ruin the last of his time with Laida. He had to do better. He'd make it right again.

⁘

When he awoke, Ardenis went to the council courtyard for the morning name drawing, but the courtyard was nearly empty. No one had arrived for the drawing. Dread filled him, and he glanced back and forth in panic. Was Laida okay? Something was wrong, and Hector was behind it.

Ignoring the stares of people on their way to their daily callings, Ardenis jogged, then ran, then sprinted all the way to the transfer hall.

He arrived breathless. Everything seemed... normal. The lottery box sat in place, the lines stood full, but the people wore calm, smiling faces. He slowed his pace to a walk. Then he hunted for Laida. He breathed a sigh of relief when he found her a short while later, addressing another worker. He stopped a polite distance away.

"I know, Idonea," Laida said. "It will put more pressure on the lottery system than we've seen thus far, but it will work out." Idonea was Laida's second in command now that Vinia had been born and Laida had secured her old position as leader. Idonea wore her black hair in a bun, though she didn't execute it quite as well as Laida.

Idonea nodded, then glanced up at Ardenis. Laida followed her gaze and smiled.

"I'll announce the meeting time later. You may go," Laida said.

Idonea gave a quick bob of her head and hurried away.

"Is this going to become routine, Arden?" She walked forward and grinned up at him.

He studied her face, but didn't see any stress in her eyes. "I went to the courtyard this morning, for the lottery, but no one was there."

"Did you read the bulletin?"

No. He hadn't been able to think through the panic that had blinded him when he thought something might have been wrong with her.

She didn't wait for him to respond. "Only a small amount of people entered the lottery, so there was no need for one. Everyone wanting to be born today got a slot, assuming we don't have any extra later."

Ardenis stared at her. Why the sudden lack of interest?

"I know that look, Arden. You're trying to puzzle this out." She smiled again.

He was giving a look? "Okay, yes. Why the sudden disinterest? The elf hasn't been born yet." That he knew for certain. All the watchers were on the lookout for Queen Eva. She hadn't even shown signs of being pregnant yet.

"Well..." Laida looked around, and her cheeks turned red. She was embarrassed. He'd never seen that in her before—or any Acanthian—even when she got in trouble for her new hairstyle. The subtle blush deepened the blue of her eyes in an endearing way. Would it feel warm if he caressed her cheek?

"Laida?"

She lifted her face to him, and her eyes sparked with something he swore was real for just a second—some moment of passion, of fire. Then she blinked.

"It seems word has got around I've picked my date for the next new moon. So everyone is waiting until then to put their name in as well." She tossed her unbound golden hair behind her shoulder. She seemed irritated by the thought, though it was muted irritation.

He smiled, amused. "What makes everyone so sure you're correct?"

She threw up her hands. "I have no idea, Arden. I'm just as mystified as you." She sighed and looked toward the active transfer gateways. "We should be able to continue the same lottery routine, even with this new development, but we're having a planning meeting this afternoon, just in case." She looked at him. "With the numbers we anticipate entering that day, and since I won't be helping, because I'm entering myself, it is likely to be a little chaotic."

Ardenis nodded. "That it will be." He chose his next words carefully and took a deep breath. "Laida?"

"Mm-hmm?"

"I'm going to miss you when you're gone." The words poured out as the thought of losing her hit anew. But he couldn't leave it at that, not without tempering it with something more customary to cover his indiscretion. Acanthians didn't miss each other. "I know I'll tell you again, but journey well, my friend."

Laida stepped to his side and linked her arm with his. He could have sworn she closed the distance between them just a bit more than usual. He forgot how to breathe.

"Miss me, Arden?" she teased, laughing. "You don't need to miss me. We're here to do our duty until our time comes to be born in Thera. We live our lives there to the fullest, making mistakes and learning to rise above them. Then we die, and who knows what will happen, but I believe we'll all be together again in the Hereafter. So don't miss me." She leaned her head against his shoulder. "It's only for a short while, after all."

She squeezed his arm, and his heart lurched. Then she let go. He went back to feeling like half a person without her touch.

"I better get back to work," she said. "Will I see you at the concert tonight?"

He stared into her eyes. "I wouldn't miss it."

She smiled and walked away, and even that sight filled him with joy. She turned a corner out of view. His shoulders slumped, and he sighed. The days of seeing her come and go were numbered.

CHAPTER

TWENTY-TWO

In the morning, Ardenis went to the tower to spend the day looking in on Eva, but he frequently had to move his gaze elsewhere. She and Isaac were indeed trying to produce an heir. Aggressively trying. As much as his instincts had pressed him to witness love, lovemaking was a different story. His cheeks burned, and he looked away each time. Many times.

Ardenis suspected Laida's prediction for when the baby would be conceived might be too late.

He watched Eva again later that afternoon. She slept naked in Isaac's arms while he smiled down at her with eyes full of love. True love. He stroked brown curls off her face.

"Eva, my queen, my wife." He kissed her neck behind her ear.

"Mmmm," she mumbled, with closed eyes and a smile on her lips.

He kissed along her bare shoulder and moved up against her.

"Not again, my love," Eva said, without opening her eyes. "I'm so very tired."

He chuckled and rose out of bed. "Later, then." He donned a red velvet robe. "Rest, my queen. Our son is depending on you." He shut the door quietly behind him.

Eva's eyes popped open, and she sat up. She scooted over to the edge of the bed, and placed her hands on her abdomen, smiling down at herself. Then her smile turned forlorn. A long sigh escaped her. She donned a matching red velvet robe and sat at the vanity. After a long look back at the door, she opened a drawer and pulled out a brown comb with a turquoise stone.

Damian's comb. Ardenis's heart lurched.

Eva held it in her hands, almost as tenderly as she'd held her stomach. She kissed the stone, her lips lightly brushing against it.

"I have to believe you'd want me to be happy, Damian." Her voice held sadness, and a pleading edge that begged forgiveness. "You can rest well knowing I am. Not a day goes by I don't think of you, though I remember the details of your face less and less each day."

Eva wiped a tear off her cheek. "I have to let you go now. My kingdom needs me. My future son needs me." She dropped a hand to her belly, a wavering smile forming on her lips. "Take care of our baby."

She hunched forward and covered her mouth against a sob, then whispered, "You would have been a great father. We'll be together again in the Hereafter."

She wrapped the comb in a soft cloth embroidered on the corner with pink flowers and placed it in a silver box. "Sleep well, my love." She kissed the box, then pushed it deep into a drawer of the desk.

Despite the pain it clearly caused her, Eva was moving on with her life. Ardenis envied her strength.

She stared at her reflection for several minutes. Taking a deep breath, she dabbed at her eyes with a handkerchief, put on fresh powder, and rung the bell for a servant. With an obvious force of will, she sat up taller and lifted her chin.

A servant entered the room and bowed deeply. "How may I be of assistance, my queen?"

"Tell the king I am prepared to see him at his leisure."

"As you wish." The servant bowed again and left the room.

Ardenis leaned back in his chair. Yes, they may well reach their goal before Laida's prediction.

He ceased his watch. Eva had learned to move on from the loss of Damian. Would he be able to find it within himself to do the same when Laida was born?

Never.

Immortality meant he had a long time to grieve for the loss of the only soul he'd ever love. Laida would be on Thera, falling in love with someone else, and he'd be left behind, forgotten and alone, with nothing to do but wait for his time to come. The mere thought of the precipice between them was crippling. He understood now the human desire to forget. Though even as sweet as leaving the pain behind would be when his time came, he hoped to take a piece of Laida with him. He would rather remember.

⟡

The days passed, and soon the gossip concerning the burning lottery box died out. Ardenis watched Eva, but saw no signs of her expecting, despite their continued efforts. He spent every evening with Laida, who had more free time now that the transfers had temporarily died down. There were no more mysterious incidents, and Ardenis put aside his efforts to gain evidence in order to spend his last few days with his friend.

They went to concerts, played kickball with Bram, or simply spent time together at Ardenis's house. He sketched her a drawing of the three of them—they wouldn't understand it if he had included Vinia, though it felt wrong not to—and he talked of inviting Amalia into their close-knit group to make them four again, pretending for a time that Laida wasn't leaving.

When the day before the new moon arrived, Ardenis could hardly breathe. The sun rose in the sky outside his window, and his heart sank with each new ray that touched upon his room. He wanted to shut his eyes and pretend a new dawn wasn't occurring, but it was. So, he forced himself to dress, hands shaking.

His efforts to remain positive and emotionally distant had failed. Utterly. There was no denying that now. Finally ready for the day, he didn't go to the tower. Instead, his feet carried him to the transfer hall, the foreboding sun at his back. The early morning passed while he paced, eyeing the horde of people standing in an endless line, all waiting their turn to enter the drawing.

Laida had not arrived. He picked a bouquet of roses to give to her, then thought better of it and hid them behind the water fountain in front of the transfer hall. Then he changed his mind and picked some more. When she finally strode into the transfer courtyard, he stood in the nearby garden, gathering his third bouquet. He looked down at the large yellow blooms in his hand, then tossed them over his shoulder and walked to her.

"Arden!" She smiled. "What brings you here? Decided to defy the Fates and enter your name?"

He forced a grin and stood next to her at the back of the long line. "Even I know better than to defy the Fates. I was walking past and wanted to say hello." The lies came easily now.

"It's been nice seeing you so much. Usually you are busy watching."

"Not much going on lately." At least not that he knew about. A world war could have broken out on Thera and he wouldn't have noticed; he was too wrapped up in tomorrow's event. "Do you still feel good about your chances?"

Several people turned to look at her as she responded. "Yes, but I'll tell you what feels odd, is standing out here in line instead of in there working." She sighed. "I don't know what to do with myself for the rest of the day."

Ardenis peered ahead of them. "You may very well be in line the rest of the day."

She laughed, toying with the piece of paper in her hand, the strip with her name on it for the lottery. "It's not moving that slow."

And indeed, it was not. Ardenis's gut filled with dread as they stepped closer and closer to the horrible box. "I'm not needed in the tower today. Maybe we can spend the afternoon together after this."

Laida smiled. "That sounds nice."

One of the moments he'd feared since he fated the first elf's birth had finally arrived. Laida stepped up to the box, strip of paper held aloft.

She smiled and stuck out her hand, so confident and sure. Just before she put the paper in the slot, she paused and glanced up at him. He caught a flicker of fire in her eyes—a passion he thought he'd never see—then it was gone, and she dropped her name in the box.

"What should we do now?" she asked.

"Umm." He stood there for a second, mystified, contemplating ways to get her name back. She pulled him out of the way of the next person in line.

Ardenis didn't want to waste a second of his precious time with Laida. He forced a grin. "How about we visit the museum?"

"The museum? But I've seen all the drawings there."

"But you've never seen them with me as your personal guide." He watched her, waiting for her to give in. "I'll tell you all the things you've ever wanted to know about Thera."

Laida gasped. He'd never allowed himself to break the rules before like this. It was forbidden, but what did he have left to lose? It was his final gift to her—his acceptance of her choice. He was going to let her go.

He held his hand out. "Maybe you'll learn something you can use on Thera in your new life as an elf."

Laida looked at his hand, smiling. Then she took it and laughed, swinging their arms back and forth. Her smile reached all the way to her eyes. The wispy bun on her head bobbed with her laughter.

She took his breath away. The feel of her hand radiated up his arm, directly into his heart. He didn't think he could be any happier than at that moment. He locked this image and the feel of her touch away in his mind. It would help him through the dark times ahead.

"Okay, Arden. The museum it is." She laughed again, and they walked side by side.

She didn't let go of his hand. Nothing could destroy his contentment. Not even Hector eyeing them as they passed the council courtyard.

The museum was not close. At halfway between their region and the next, more people could enjoy the benefits of it. They left behind houses and community buildings, walking along the stone path flanked only by trees and grass. They passed few people. The smile never left his face.

The museum was the most modern building in Acantha. He'd seen the structure in a Fating he'd had of the future. It postdated current architecture in Thera, but the High Council had approved it. They built it with poured concrete with support columns spaced further apart than the current style. It featured floor to ceiling glass windows, letting in an immense amount of light, which didn't destroy the art like it would on Thera. He wasn't the only watcher who donated to the museum, but he'd contributed a good amount. He liked to visit to see the parts of the world he wasn't privy to watch.

Ardenis and Laida ascended the concrete stairs and entered the museum through the wood and glass doors. Inside, partitions divided rooms displaying the various paintings, drawings, and sculptures of Theran culture. Quiet conversations drifted from a few other visitors, but they'd be easy to avoid.

"Where would you like to start?" he asked. The museum was separated by region and date, from when humans first appeared on Thera until the present. Soon, there would be a new chapter —elves.

"Let's start with yours." Laida smiled and clapped her hands.

He grinned in return, leading the way. He'd only taken an interest in drawing his Theran watchings a few centuries ago, so that's where they began. These consisted mostly of landscapes and rain. He'd loved the rain, once.

"This," he said, pointing to a bird's-eye view of Thera, "is a map of our region in Thera." Laida leaned closer to the map, studying it. "Not much has changed in the last few hundred years, at least not to the landscape. There are new cities and roads, and some cities were lost to war, but the mountains are still there, and the rivers mostly still flow the same courses."

He smiled and pointed to a plot of land in the center of the northern continent. "If your prediction proves correct, this is where you'll be born, nine months from now." She smiled and her eyes twinkled. "This is the Kingdom of Alysies. The land extends all the way to the coast here." He traced his finger to the west coast. "Its southern border ends here." He indicated the thick forest dividing Alysies from its neighbor to the south, Creadel. "Your father will be King Isaac, a fair and just, but newly appointed king. And your mother will be Queen Eva." He looked away. "She has an immense passion and love for life. She loves your father dearly."

Laida sighed with delight. "Tell me more."

"You'll be the firstborn, which means, in this day and age, if you don't have any brothers born after you, you'll be heir to the throne, which will make you queen someday."

"Why wouldn't I be the heir just for being the firstborn?" she asked, raising her voice.

Ardenis glanced around and stepped closer to her. "Sadly, it doesn't work that way right now. Men view women the weaker sex and they rule over them."

Laida scoffed. "Well, that will be the first thing to change once I'm queen."

Ardenis bit back a smile. "If anyone could establish gender equality, it would be you." He glanced back at the map. "I must warn you, if you somehow take any of this with you, to watch out for Queen Vatrice's heir, Prince Samuel. He'll only be a year older than you, but the kingdom of Daltieri has been trying to find a way to take over

Alysies for decades." He tapped his finger on the map, where Daltieri sat above Alysies to the north. "Vatrice employs a mage, Allister, and he is very powerful."

"I don't recall Isaac employing a mage."

Ardenis nodded. "Right. Isaac's ancestors once had magic in their blood, enough they didn't need a mage to perform their spells and such. It eventually bred out of them, but the lack of a mage became tradition. Stubborn pride—and former King Tristan's hatred—kept them from acquiring one. I expect Isaac to follow the same pattern."

She nodded. "I'll remember that."

"I hope so, Laida." They both knew she'd take nothing with her into her new life on Thera.

She smiled and walked on, so he followed. She passed one he had drawn of Thomats, the most popular school for magery on the continent, with its white marble columns and people milling in their black mage robes. She passed by one of his favorites—the beautiful town of Docimer at the base of a mighty mountain in the kingdom of Kestrea. Then she eyed one drawn of students learning swordcraft from a master swordsman in southern Daltieri.

Finally, she stopped in front of one of his particular favorites. It was a drawing of a man trying to save the last of his crops from a rising flood. He'd gathered an armful of the precious food and seeds. Face to the sky, he held his corn and potatoes. Rain battered him, but his expression seemed to say, "Do what you must. I will rise above." He looked just as Ardenis remembered him.

"Life is hard in Thera," she said, staring at the drawing.

"Yes, it is, in more ways than we can understand. There are floods and drought, wars and hunger, but there are the emotional difficulties as well." He gazed at the drawing, deep in thought. He'd only begun to understand just how difficult that part of being mortal could be.

"Surely the emotional part can't be that bad." She linked her arm through his and squeezed.

Warmth flooded him. "No. It's not all bad."

"Then tell me what is good. Give me something to look forward to."

He held his breath and looked into her eyes. "There's love."

"We have love here."

"We have love that we emulate from what we know of Thera, but it's different from real love, the love between friends who miss each other when they're gone. Or even greater, the love of a parent for a child, or the romantic love between two people. Unshakable and pure." She furrowed her brows, so he went on. "Do you remember the drawing I gave you of Eva?"

She nodded.

"Her hair enraptured you, but it was her eyes that drew you in. Those are the eyes of love. There is no denying it when you see that look in someone's eyes."

She stared at the floor, finger to her chin for a long while. "I've seen that look in your eyes before."

His lips parted. "You have?"

"Does that mean you love someone?"

His cheeks burned. "Must be a coincidence." He cleared his throat and left for the next room. Laida followed.

For over three hours, Ardenis told her everything he knew about Theran life. It was the most fun he'd ever had. He'd never felt so free, finally sharing all his secrets with his best friend. As they traveled from room to room, he noticed the drawings changing slowly over the years, from landscape, to human towns, to people displaying emotion. Maybe Thera had influenced him sooner than he thought. He also noticed, elatedly, that Laida never showed interest in drawings by other watchers, only his.

As the sun set over Acantha, the light changed angles through the windows. Soon, it gave way to the shadows of night, and it was time to go home.

He held the door open for her, and Laida smiled up at him as they descended the steps. To his utter shock, she reached for his hand and held it. He didn't dare breathe for fear of scaring her away, but she didn't let go the entire walk back to her house. Indescribable flutters of happiness ran through his body the whole way. He knew he'd never forget it.

When they reached her house, he walked her up to the door.

"Laida, what do you know about the Hereafter?"

She blinked, tilting her head. "I know we all go there after we live our lives on Thera."

"Do you think we'll all be together there? Bram, Vinia... me and you, afterwards?"

She smiled. "I do." The conviction in her voice eased a tightness within his chest. But, she went on. "It's our duty to be born and supply the souls to Thera. How can there not be something as glorious as the Hereafter waiting for us on the other side of that journey?"

He stood there, contemplating her words. Yes, it was an Acanthian's duty to be born, with an emotional veil and unique instincts to propel them to make that leap. But, she'd looked beyond those simple reasons and came to a conclusion he'd never considered. Maybe the Hereafter was their reward after it was all over.

But what kind of reward could there be for someone who broke the rules? And if they caught him, he'd never reach that glorious Hereafter. Or Laida.

She squeezed his hand and released. "Goodnight, Arden. Thank you for keeping me company all afternoon. It's hard not being in the transfers when so much is going on, but you made it better. I think I enjoyed our visit even more than being at the transfer hall. You're a great friend."

Despite that damned word which haunted his every action, he wanted to hug her. He wanted to hug her badly, but he didn't—or else he'd never let go. He'd promised to say goodbye, and he would keep that promise, for himself and for her.

"Goodnight, Lade." He smiled. "You know, you're the only one who calls me Arden."

"Well, it suits you."

"I'll see you at the drawing in the morning," he said.

"All right, see you then." She turned and entered the house, shutting the door.

A lamp lit up inside, and her shadow moved within the front room. He sighed and walked way.

He went to the public baths, but the long dip in the warm pool did nothing to help him relax. His face refused to form a smile for the people who stopped to bid him good evening.

He left and went to the one person who could understand.

Ardenis knocked on Amalia's door. She opened it, concern already deep in her eyes.

"Ardenis, I was hoping to see you. Come in." She held the door open, and he stumbled inside, collapsing on a chair.

He hunched over his knees, head in hands. Amalia's comforting arm wound around his shoulders. Words stuck in his throat, but it didn't matter.

"I understand, Ardenis. I know your pain. I've been exactly where you are. You are going to be okay."

He could only nod, grateful she didn't poke or pry like she normally did. His pain was her pain. It reflected in her deep frown and compassionate blue eyes as she watched him.

They sat in silence together until he knew he must go. Amalia gave him a hug and a wavering smile, and he left.

Once home, Ardenis tried to sleep but couldn't. He drew several renderings of Laida, but it didn't clear his head. The sun was long gone, making it hard to breathe again. Only now, it accompanied an ache in his chest. He'd been a fool for lamenting the rising sun. This was worse, much worse. His mind couldn't find a way to protect itself from the coming pain. He lay in his bed staring out the window, praying for endless night.

TWENTY-THREE

Ardenis awoke before the sun. He threw off his covers and shoved his arms into the first robe he touched. Rules be damned, he was going to give Laida roses. He set out into the blue predawn light, picking the loveliest blooms he could find. Acantha was just waking up when he knocked on Laida's door.

He held the bunch up high in front of him so it would be the first thing she saw, and so he wouldn't lose his nerve. Pink roses filled the bouquet, as well as pale pink peonies and sprigs of lavender, and he'd even tied it off with a length of twine—in a bow, no less.

He knocked again and inhaled the sweet scent of the flowers. Laida would love them.

There was no answer.

Ardenis opened the door and entered. "Laida?"

He moved into the front room. It was empty. All the things that made this her home—her flowers, and the drawings he'd given her, her personal touches—had been cleared away. It could have been someone else's house.

The pain struck right into his heart. The flowers slipped from his grip and hit the ground, bursting from their binding. Not yet. He wasn't ready for this goodbye. He grabbed at his middle and slumped back against the door.

Laida was so sure her name would be called this morning, sure enough to pack up her house. He stood and took a deep breath. He was wasting time. There were only mere hours left to be with her. The door opened and hit him in the back of the head.

"Hello?" Laida said.

Ardenis jumped out of the way. "Laida! I was looking for you."

She opened the door, smiling. Air rushed freely into his lungs. He could breathe again. "I was looking for you, too. I put your drawings back under your bed."

"Oh, um, thank you." He shifted to stand in front of the flowers on the ground. "I see you're ready to go." His voice nearly cracked on the last word.

"Yes. You know, just in case I'm right." She grinned. "I came back to make sure I got it all. I don't want to leave more work than necessary for the shifters."

The shifters—Acanthians called to remove a person's belongings, shifting them out of the home so it would be empty when Acantha replaced the empty house for a garden or a new building. There were no new souls to take the places of the ones who left, after all.

Laida stepped past him into the front room. He followed her gaze as it dropped to the floor. She pointed at the flowers. "Did you pick those?"

His cheeks burned, and he reached down to scoop up the colorful blooms. Resting them on his knee, he retied the twine. This bumbling farewell was not what he'd had in mind.

He stood and held them out, only slightly smushed, forcing his doubts aside. "I couldn't let you leave without giving you flowers, just once." He looked at her, holding her gaze.

She smiled, and Ardenis saw something new in her eyes, a tenderness that had never been there before.

She'd given him certain looks or gestures before that spoke of emotions beyond Acantha. He'd easily dismissed them as a trick of the mind—his hope that they were true. This tenderness, however, was soft, and sweet, and unmistakable. Ardenis forgot how to breathe—didn't want to if it meant this moment might pass.

Laida took the flowers from his hand, and her fingers brushed against his, sending sparks up his arm. Bringing the roses to her nose, she inhaled deeply.

"They're beautiful, Arden. I wish I could take them with me." She rubbed her cheek against the soft petals, then looked into his eyes. "Here." She went to her bedroom and returned with the flowers in a glass vase. "Your house could use a little color." She smiled and held out the bouquet. It was a precious gift, but he didn't want to waste time on them now.

He set them down on the table next to the door, not taking his eyes off her for a second. No longer able to help it, he pulled her in for a hug. Her body fit snug against his. Safety, and a feeling of home he'd never fathomed, warmed him to his core. He squeezed his eyes shut. She hugged him back for a quick moment, then drew away. It took everything in him not to pull her back.

"Let's get to the courtyard. I want to hear them draw my name." She smiled and left her house without looking back.

He followed, shoulders slumped. They walked side-by-side to that blasted courtyard with that blasted lottery. His peace and comfort went with her, leaving him only pain and bitterness.

The courtyard was already full. Ardenis's palms sweat, but Laida looked as calm as ever. They took a position near the back of the crowd. Ardenis looked for Amalia's comforting presence, but she never attended the drawings. Instead, he spotted Bram, who eased his way over, weaving between bodies.

"Good morning, Laida. Ardenis." He stood next to Laida. "Did you enter your name?"

She raised an eyebrow. "Of course."

"And she's already cleaned out her house." Ardenis's weak attempt at a smile became a grimace.

Bram glanced at her. "You're that sure they will draw your name?"

"I've never been surer." There wasn't a hint of humor on her face. Her instincts must have been pushing her very strongly.

She gazed ahead, where her transfer workers deposited the lottery box and opened the record book. The record keeper dipped his quill in fresh ink. Ardenis recognized Idonea beside the box, but didn't know the two others. The lottery box appeared safe and sound. He glanced around for Hector, but he wasn't amongst the throng. Then, as the first name was drawn and people shuffled forward, Ardenis saw him. Hector stood on the other side of the crowd, near the council hall. He was alone, staring at the lottery box. Hector could sulk if he wanted, so long as he did it from over there.

They passed the first name to Idonea. Ardenis held his breath.

"Sarafina."

His heart hammered.

Idonea passed the paper to the record keeper, then turned to receive the next name drawn from the box.

Ardenis's palms became sweaty.

"Marcus."

"Bram."

What? Had he heard right? His gaze snapped to his friend. "Bram?" Ardenis gaped.

Laida smiled fondly.

"I wasn't sure my name would be drawn, so I didn't say anything." He met their eyes, and the smiling eyes of those around him.

Laida clapped him on the shoulder. "I'm happy for you, my friend."

Ardenis couldn't believe it. "Why?"

Bram glanced at him. "It's as good a time as any to be born. If I can't be the elf, my birth can still be important. Maybe I'll be able to help the elf in some way."

A weight constricted Ardenis's chest. What would he do without his friend? Bram had always been there, a constant he could rely on, faithful and true. So much change in such little time.

"Of course it will," Ardenis said, recovering. "I'm happy for you." Ardenis grabbed Bram's shoulder and squeezed.

Bram grinned.

"Shhh. They're still drawing names." Laida focused her attention up front again.

"Felix."

"Vira."

"Citrine."

"Phaddius."

And on and on. Idonea's voice could hardly be heard over the pounding in his ears. Laida gripped his arm, staring at the lottery box as if she could will her name to be called. Ardenis stared in hope her name would stay inside.

The record keeper looked up and shook his head at Idonea. "Okay, that's all," she said. "We've met the quota. Good journey to all those who travel to Thera today."

"What?" Ardenis cried out. "How can that be?" Laida wanted this so badly. She just had to be picked.

Laida glanced up at him. "It's okay, Ardenis. It wasn't in the Fates' design." She gave a tight smile and then walked away.

Ardenis and Bram glanced at each other and followed her. He worried, but nothing about her posture said she was upset.

He didn't know what to think. Laida had been so sure today was her day, she had him believing it too. What did that mean? Would she try again tomorrow? Or choose to stay after all? He shoved any excitement about that possibility away with both hands.

Despite Laida's calm steps, disappointment radiated from her lack of words, even if she didn't recognize it for what it was.

They followed her all the way to the transfers, where Bram took his place at the back of a long line. All around them friends said goodbye to one another, while the line steadily moved ahead.

Ardenis shook Bram's hand, clapping him on the shoulder. "Travel well, my friend." He'd never meant the words more than he did now.

Bram smiled. "You as well, Ardenis, when your time comes."

Laida gave him a hug. "Maybe we'll meet again on Thera." They smiled at each other.

Ardenis frowned, his hopes for Laida to remain in Acantha dashed.

They waved goodbye to Bram, Ardenis lingering longer than what was normal. His heart ached anew for another friend leaving him behind. He finally followed behind Laida past the line of people and friends, and into the transfers.

"Laida," he said, catching up to her. "What are you doing?" He placed a hand on her arm until she stopped.

"Since I'm not going to be born today, I'm going to do my duty, Arden," she said, matter-of-factly, and then walked away.

"Laida," someone called out.

Laida turned, looking for whoever had called her name.

"Laida," Idonea said again as she rounded a corner into sight. "I was hoping you'd be here."

"Is something wrong, Idonea?" Laida raised her eyebrows— almost like concern—glancing around the transfers and the borns in progress.

"No." She grinned. "Someone changed their mind about being born today. They said it wasn't their time yet."

Laida nodded.

"We had to draw a new name." Idonea held up the strip of paper.

Laida

. . .

Laida gasped. Ardenis snatched the paper from Idonea, reading it again and again. Laida was right.

She was destined to be born today.

Blood rushed to his head. The room spun. He grabbed the wall, nearly stumbling under the weight of this cataclysmic revelation.

"I knew it," she breathed.

"I'll take you to the front of the line." Idonea smiled. "Good journey, my friend."

What?

This wasn't happening.

"Thank you, Idonea," Laida said, hugging her.

Laida faced him. It was his turn to give the customary farewell. He couldn't breathe, couldn't find the words. He stood there, crushing the small piece of paper in his clenched fist.

"Arden?"

He stepped closer, forcing his burning eyes to her. This was the last time he'd ever see her. He brought the back of his hand up to stroke her cheek, but pulled her in for a hug instead. He wrapped his arms around her lean frame and breathed her in, a scent sweeter than roses. Her golden hair tickled his nose as she leaned her head against his shoulder. She pulled away decades before he was ready, but he let her go. His heart tore in two.

He forced a wavering smile. "Travel well." *My love.*

She smiled in return, a friendly everyday smile, like they weren't parting for eternity, never to see each other again. "Watch over Thera for me."

He averted his eyes and nodded, once. If he opened his mouth, he knew he'd start begging, pleading for her not to leave him alone. He'd spend every waking second combing the kingdoms of Thera down to the last person until he found her. There would be no other choice.

Laida turned and walked away. Ardenis clenched his robe in tight fists. It was all he could do not to pull her back into his arms. He could scream for her to stay, and it would do no good. This was her path. He was a fool for thinking he could defy the Fates.

The heartache was too much to bear. How did Amalia do it? How did she ever move on from such a loss? Maybe she hadn't. He knew he never would.

Idonea placed Laida at the front of the transfer line, just outside the building. Ardenis stood inside the entrance, watching her take the final steps toward her fate.

The worker who was recording the people in line recognized her.

"Laida Transfer Leader," he said. "Journey well." He marked something in his book, then motioned for her to pass into the building. Ardenis bit his lip against a plea for her to stay outside.

She smiled. "Thank you, Rayman." She walked past him and toward the line indicated by another transfer worker.

And just like that, only five more people stood between her and forever.

Inside, he was screaming.

Someone ahead of Laida stepped into the gateway, then disappeared.

Four people left in front of her.

Ardenis stepped up to the railing between him and Laida. He clenched the beams, and the wood groaned beneath his hands.

Three people.

He couldn't breathe. Grief crushed his chest.

She walked forward in line. Two people.

The room swayed.

"Laida," he breathed. She turned and smiled at him. *Please stay with me. Don't go, please.*

One person.

Laida stepped up to the gateway. She was next. This was it. Ardenis's mouth parted, but the words he longed to say didn't come. Laida glanced back at him, still smiling, still sure of her decision. She looked excited to go.

The last person before her disappeared.

"Your turn, Laida," the transfer worker said.

Laida nodded. She stepped into the gateway, then turned and faced back toward Ardenis. He reached out to her, trying to touch her through the distance between them. She smiled a friendly smile back to him and waited in the gateway.

Then her smiled faltered, and her eyes became unfocused. Her lips parted. She gasped, and her gaze snapped up to his outstretched arm. Her eyes filled with pain, creasing under furrowed brows, then transformed into something Ardenis thought he'd never see. She looked at him as if he was her world, like nothing existed but the two of them, like Eva once looked at Damian.

Laida looked at him like she loved him.

"Arden." Her voice reflected sadness and longing. That one word unmade him. "I... I didn't know." The pain in her admission made it sound like an apology—as if she was sorry for all the unsaid words and wasted time. As if she was sorry for leaving him now.

"I'll find you," he said to her. His voice rang with pain. "I'll crawl on hands and knees to the Hereafter if that's what it takes. I will see you again."

The first tear ever shed in Acantha rolled down her cheek. He hurdled over the railing, ignoring the cry of surprise from the transfer worker. Laida stretched her hand out to him. He rushed the last few feet to where she stood.

She disappeared, their fingertips mere inches away.

He stopped just short of the gateway, breathing hard. His hands shook as he wiped at his face. He glanced at the drop without seeing it—the second tear ever shed in Acantha.

Laida was gone. Thera had removed the emotional veil and opened her eyes to the truth of her heart.

Damn him for not being born with her this day.

CHAPTER
TWENTY-FOUR

Countless moments ticked by as Ardenis stood there, replaying Laida's face in his mind. He didn't care how many people filed past him, all hoping, like Laida, for their chance to be born the elf. The transfer workers ignored him, never noticing he was nothing but an empty shell. Laida had taken his heart with her.

It wasn't until he smelled the smoke that he snapped back to reality.

His instincts triggered an internal alarm that sent his heart racing. He scanned the oil lamps lighting the interior, but they were fine, of course. Then smoke drifted through the air. He grabbed the nearest transfer worker by his robe.

"There's a fire somewhere in the building."

The transfer worker politely pulled his robe out of Ardenis's hands. "Yes, there's one right there." He pointed to the lamp and walked away.

Ardenis gritted his teeth and followed the smoke. It grew thicker towards the side of the building. It leaked out in thin, billowing waves from under the door to the record storage room—the door he'd followed Hector through the other night.

"Fire!" he yelled.

Several people glanced at him, then at the smoke. No one moved. What did they know of fire? The fire from their lamps and candles didn't burn, only created needed light. They'd read bulletins of the devastation it could cause, but it wasn't the same in this premortal world. This world had never seen such things.

Ardenis spotted Bram in line. It was almost his turn for the gateway. "Bram!" he called out. "There's a fire!"

Bram looked past him at the smoke, and his mouth opened. He said something back and pointed, but Ardenis couldn't make it out. He was too far away. Concerned murmurs arose from those closest to the storage room as the acrid air wafted further.

The smoke intensified, and flames licked the edges of the door.

Ardenis reeled. What could he do? This shouldn't be happening. The Fates, Acantha itself, should put a stop to this.

The door went ablaze, and heat slammed into the transfer hall. Ardenis stumbled backward, tripping over someone. Just as fast, the door crumbled, flames springing through. Everyone crowded closer, curious to see the new spectacle. They'd seen the lottery box ruined by fire, but never the mass destruction of a fire this size.

"Get out!" Ardenis yelled. "Everyone, run!"

Some of them left, filing out with agonizing slowness. He wanted to shove them. They didn't know the danger. Neither did Ardenis. What would happen if they touched the flames?

Those near the transfer gateways stood their ground, still waiting to enter the gateway. Others stared at the fire with gaping mouths as people knocked into them, fascinated. It was like watching the lottery box smolder and being helpless to stop it.

Ardenis shot one last look at Bram, barely visible through the smoke near the gateways, then he pushed the lingering crowd, herding them out of the transfer hall. When he broke free of the building, he looked back. His eyes widened in horror. Thick black smoke rolled out the windows of the left side of the building. No one was trying to put the fire out. The crowd watched and pointed as Acanthian's poured into the courtyard. If they didn't get the fire out, he didn't know what would happen to those still inside. And there'd be no gateways left to supply souls to Thera. Something had to be done.

Ardenis was a watcher. He'd seen thousands of fires in his time.

"Acanthians! Form up! We need two lines from here to the fountain." He shouted it twice before conversations ceased. The courtyard plunged into silence except for the noise within the building and the shuffle of those still coming out the doors.

"We must work together to put out the fire. Form two lines from the fountain to the transfers." He pointed forcefully.

The watchers in the crowd were the first to react. They knew what to do. Next the enforcers began directing people. Without question, everyone filed into hastily made lines, shoulder to shoulder.

Ardenis spotted Idonea and ran over to her. She stood with her hand covering her mouth, gazing at the flames now burning through to the outside of the building.

"We need buckets, as many as you can find," he said.

Idonea dropped her hand and looked at him. She nodded and grabbed the nearest person—Rayman the record keeper. Together they ran towards dining hall.

It didn't take long to form a Theran bucket brigade, running water up one line of people and moving empty buckets down the other to the fountain. Ardenis didn't care he was introducing a foreign Theran concept into Acantha without council approval. He only hoped Bram had made it to Thera, and they could get the fire out quickly. If the gateways were destroyed, there'd be no way to continue borns.

Several enforcers spread out around the courtyard, keeping curious bystanders from getting too close and interfering with the brigade.

"Faster!" Ardenis shouted from just outside the building. He motioned with his arms, directing the buckets as people dumped them on the roaring flames.

The fountain seemed to never empty.

The fire had spread far in the short time it took to organize the brigade. The flames roared high off the side of the two-story building. The searing heat blasted his face, though it didn't seem to cause him pain the way he'd it seen it on Thera. For this reason, he cautioned many Acanthians back when they got too close. They didn't have pain as a warning. Who knew what would happen if they touched the flames?

Soon, the brigaders had to step through smoldering ruins to reach the fire.

"Watch out!"

A burning piece of wood broke from the ceiling. Ardenis yanked back a woman by her robe just as it nearly crushed her.

She started to thank him, but he cut her off.

"Please, stay safe. Don't get too close." He left her gaping and moved on.

Too many things competed for his attention; the fire's progress, the brigade, the Acanthians edging too close to the flames because they were mesmerized by the horror before them. Any minute their cloth robes could catch fire from a stray ember, but somehow they didn't.

They tossed bucket after bucket over the flames. A second brigade had formed under the direction of another watcher, Wes. Slowly, the fire was being quenched. They worked tirelessly into the afternoon. Their faces were blank masks covered in ash, but they worked together.

As fire retreated, Ardenis searched for people who may have been trapped, miraculously finding no one. The building didn't collapse. Bram had made it to Thera after all.

When the last bucket was thrown, dousing the last of the flames, everyone cheered. Ardenis panted and wiped sweat from his brow, surveying the damage. Over half the transfer hall had been destroyed. He'd no doubt it would all be in ruin if it weren't for the efforts of the brigade. Surely, this could not have been in the Fates' design. What was the point of such an atrocity? If the food can replenish itself, and the flowers remain in bloom, why was this destruction allowed to occur?

Was the balance between Thera and Acantha tipping?

The triumph of putting out the fire gave way to ominous silence. People wiped soot from their faces with filthy robes. Friends checked each other's welfare. Hector stood on the outskirts of the damage staring at the destruction with wide eyes, not a hint of ash on him.

Gharum seethed beside him, his stance rigid.

Ardenis gaped. Council members didn't leave the council building. Ever. But there he was, and displaying Theran emotions.

Gharum turned and strode away, not stopping to check on the people or the transfers. Hector followed. Ardenis narrowed his eyes.

He took one final look at the damage, then jogged through charred wood and weary bodies to catch up. He spotted them just up the road, speaking to one another, though he couldn't make out the words. They gestured with quick, agitated movements.

Ardenis took a chance and darted off the road, passing behind a row of houses, then turning back once he thought he'd be in line with Hector and Gharum. He crept forward along the edge of a house—Laida's house, he realized—placing one foot in front of the other with care.

"—supposed to start the fire earlier. Before the lottery. What happened?" Gharum, their *head councilman*, practically spit with rage. Ardenis didn't breathe. He stayed hidden around the corner of Laida's house.

"I apologize, Head Councilman." Hector's words came fast, sounding nervous, vulnerable. "You said to follow Ardenis and Laida if they ever went somewhere alone. I hoped to find evidence you could use."

Followed? What had Hector seen? Did they find his drawings?

"That was presumptuous of you, Hector. The transfers are the priority. We are *human* souls born to live out *human* lives. The elf cannot be allowed to be conceived in Thera. You failed and the transfers still stand."

"The fire should have spread." Hector sounded perplexed, his stern demeanor gone. "It was Ardenis. He brought Theran ways into Acantha and used the fountain to put out the fire."

"All the more reason you should have brought him to me sooner. Made up something if you had to."

"He loves her," Hector said quickly.

Ardenis's eyes went wide.

"And can you prove it?" Gharum sounded skeptically hopeful.

Hector hesitated. "No."

"Have you checked his journals?"

Ardenis reeled. Amalia had warned him, but he thought no one would actually read them.

"I have. There's nothing. What few entries there are have been... careful."

"Then it's irrelevant," Gharum snapped. "And Laida's gone now, also thanks to you, so it's doubly irrelevant. Get out of my sight and get to work on the next step. Forget Ardenis. If you fail again, I'll banish you to another region. The borns cannot continue or it could be the end of our existence."

What?

There was a pause, then footsteps sounded as they walked away. Ardenis leaned against Laida's house, heart pounding. They knew about him and Laida. The head councilman of the northeastern region had conspired to set fire to the transfers, destroying them, and prevent the fated born.

Acantha was badly out of balance. Ardenis pushed off the house, hands slick. He had to inform the High Council.

CHAPTER
TWENTY-FIVE

Ardenis ran up the road, back to the transfer hall, adrenaline thrumming.

"Idonea!" he shouted. "Idonea!" Faces turned toward him, but no one said anything. The time was long past to care about maintaining his emotionless farce. "Where's Idonea?"

She stepped out of the smoking remains of the building, covered in ash. "Ardenis?"

"Idonea." He grasped her by the shoulders, and she gaped at him. "You must keep the transfers going."

"But the fire destroyed—"

"You must! Use what is left and keep going. Don't stop for anything." He glanced around, then leaned closer, whispering, "Someone is trying to defy the Fates and we can't let them. Thera needs us to keep going. Laida needs us. We can't send her to the mortal world alone." He squeezed her shoulders once, then released her. She stood in front of him with wide eyes. "Go!"

Idonea blinked, then ran off toward the remainder of the transfers. "Rayman! Get the record book. We're going to continue."

Ardenis nodded to himself, then sprinted away. He had to reach the High Council before Gharum and Hector did whatever they had planned.

A thought struck him, and he skidded to a halt. He had to warn someone in case he didn't make it, or in case the High Council didn't believe him. He pivoted and ran hard toward the tower. Arriving breathless, he pushed through the wooden door. The silence of the watch room slammed into him.

Amalia's wide eyes stopped him short. Her gaze flicked to his usual chair, and it wasn't empty. Hector sat in it, his back to Ardenis. He turned, slowly swinging toward Ardenis. He smiled a friendly smile and straightened his robe back to perfection.

Had he been watching Thera? No, of course not. He couldn't see through the window without the council's blessing.

Behind Hector, Amalia shook her head minutely, eyes still wide with an emotion Ardenis couldn't identify. He didn't know what she was trying to tell him. The other watchers—some viewing Thera, some not—remained oblivious to the charged exchange.

"Well met, Ardenis," Hector said.

"Hector." Ardenis clipped.

"What is that you're covered in? You're not dressed appropriately to enter the tower." Hector's smile turned calculating.

"You know very well what this is. You were there, after all. Watching as the transfers almost burned to the ground. Watching and not helping." Amalia let out a small gasp, but Ardenis stared hard at Hector. "I assume you're here, instead of investigating the cause of the destruction, because you already know who started it."

Hector gritted his teeth. "That's correct, Ardenis. Did you see that in the Fates as well? I do know who started the fire." He rose from Ardenis's chair and shook his head in mock sadness. "You should have come to the council for help before your emotions were affected beyond repair. It's too bad your love for Laida blinded you into starting the fire to prevent her from being born."

Amalia's mouth popped open. Shock.

"What?" Ardenis shouted, mouth agape. "You're insane! You set that fire, under the direction of Gharum." He focused on Amalia, speaking fast in desperation. "I came to warn you. I heard them talking, and they have another plan in place to destroy the rest of the transfers. They don't want the elf to be born."

Amalia said nothing.

"Gharum Head Councilman?" Hector said. "You're accusing him of going against every Acanthian rule there is. And me as well? An enforcer with a reputation of always following the rules." He smiled and clasped his hands behind his back. "It sounds like you're the insane one, Ardenis. Don't worry. It's understandable, when you've worked so closely with Thera for as long as you have. I've seen it before."

Ardenis clenched his fists, holding himself back from punching Hector senseless. Hector should know nothing of insanity, or lies, yet he did.

Ardenis stepped forward, pleading eyes on Amalia. "You have to believe me. They've read my journals. They said themselves they found no proof."

Hector pivoted to face her. He stared, waiting for her to speak and watching her every move. The way he leaned toward her, he almost looked possessive, daring her to defy him.

Amalia's eyes darted back and forth between them, then turned sad. She shook her head in disappointment. "I apologize, Ardenis. I don't believe you. The council would never do something like this. A watcher, though..."

Hector turned slowly back to him, a grin on his face. "You see? No one will believe you over the council."

Ardenis shook with fury. Not even in Thera had he seen such corruption.

"The council has convened a special session to oversee your judgment. You're to accompany me there at once." Hector watched him with trepidation.

"Amalia," Ardenis said. "This must be part of their next step. I am the only one able to believe an Acanthian could be capable of something this treacherous." He snarled the last word in Hector's direction, then looked into Amalia's face, willing her to trust him. "While I am gone, do what must be done to stop the transfers from being destroyed completely." He paused. "It's what you're here to do."

Amalia said nothing, merely stared at him.

Ardenis hung his head. "All right, Hector. Let's go."

"Wait," Amalia said. Ardenis turned toward her, and she rushed over to him and gave him a quick hug. Hector's eyes blazed. She pulled back and looked up into his eyes. "Journey well, my friend."

Ardenis searched her face in disbelief. She truly didn't believe him. She'd wished him well, as if she knew they would force him to be born. But they wouldn't just send him to Thera. No. For something of this magnitude, it'd be the black gate. No Thera, no mortal existence, only the Dark Unknown.

Hector smirked and gestured Ardenis ahead of him. With a backward glance at Amalia's vacant expression, he walked down the short hall to the door. As soon as he was outside, he ran in a full-on sprint.

"Hey! Stop!" Hector growled, chasing after him.

Hector never played sports. He didn't have the stamina to outrun Ardenis, and his legs were shorter. Soon he fell too far behind to catch up. Ardenis looked over his shoulder to see Hector doubled over, panting, hands on his knees. Ardenis kept running.

Even if Amalia didn't believe him, and even at the risk of another attempt by Hector to destroy the transfers, he had to inform the High Council.

TWENTY-SIX

A rdenis ran past the museum, crossed the boundary of his home territory, and continued down the path. The sun set, and the darkened trees haunted his hurried steps. He jumped at every movement, half expecting Hector or another enforcer to catch up to him. Intermittent lampposts broke up the long shadows. Eventually, he tired, but did not stop to rest.

Why couldn't the High Council be closer? Beautiful countryside separated each individual region, but he'd never stopped to wonder why before now. It wasn't a rule not to visit other regions, but the thought had never even occurred to him before. The desire didn't exist.

Curiosity—another gift granted to him from watching Eva and Damian's love.

Maybe the absence of curiosity was to prevent the spread of regional information. Or maybe it was to contain emotionally altered souls. Like him. To keep any potential tears in the emotional veil from ripping further.

He stumbled, but pressed on, the trees' shadows following him.

Occasionally, a light breeze blew over him, carrying the scent of roses, reminding him of Laida. Acantha had come undone since she'd gone. Thank the Fates she'd left safely and wasn't here to see it. He had to make it right.

As he drew closer to the High Council, he tilted his ear to the wind. Music. This region of Acantha was having a concert, unaware of the horrors next door. The song was one he'd never heard, less a sweeping melody of violins and more staccato with woodwinds. Pretty, but odd.

This part of Acantha managed the northwestern hemisphere, though the council hall housed the High Council. Based on what he'd seen in the Thera Museum, he knew these Therans were less developed than the people he watched in his region. Instead of kingdoms, they operated in tribes.

He'd never visited this region before. How would he find the way? He jogged past the pavilion, which looked the same as his, and down the lane by the houses. In fact, everything looked the same. Not just the pavilion, but where it was in relation to the surrounding buildings. He headed straight to the council building at a fast walk. The few people wandering the pathways didn't look his way.

The courtyard was quiet, with flickering lamplight, chirping night insects, and no one around. An orange glow from the torches lit the stone pathway straight to the council hall doors. Columns surrounded the building, a perfect match to his own region's. It was almost as if he'd never left and instead ran all that time in a circle to end right back where he'd started.

Barely resisting the urge to read their bulletin, he jogged the rest of the way to the council doors. The carving on them caught his attention. It was similar to the one in his region, but instead of the northeastern hemisphere, it featured a globe, still with the gavel poised above it.

He pushed the door open, and his heart thumped. He should have spent the journey planning what to say. Regardless, the council had to believe him.

The room appeared just the same as the council foyer he was

accustomed to, with its dark wood walls and big oak desk. A woman with thin, straight hair sat behind it, scrawling in the record book. Her workspace, with its splattered ink and scattered papers, was a sharp contrast to Hector's.

Ardenis cleared his throat. She glanced up, smiled, then furrowed her brow.

"I don't recognize you." She placed her quill on the desk. "Can I help you?"

"I am Ardenis Watcher Fater, and I've come to see the High Council." He inclined his head slightly.

Her smile resumed. "Ardenis. Well met. I am Nora Enforcer. We've heard much about your abilities here."

He stood straight and stiff. "I would be appreciative if I could discuss a matter with the High Council. It is very important."

Nora nodded. "Yes. You've come so far." She rose from the desk. "They are in a session now, but I will see if they can meet with you."

She disappeared into council room. Moments later, she held the door open.

"The High Council will see you now."

"Thank you." He walked past her.

"Gharum Head Councilman seemed most pleased to hear you'd arrived." The door closed behind her.

Ardenis froze in the short entryway. Gharum was here? He backed up, reaching for the handle behind him.

"Ardenis," he heard Gharum say, "Please join us in the council room."

Damn it to the Hereafter.

He took a deep breath and straightened his shoulders. There was nowhere to go but forward. His steps were sure—at least he hoped they appeared that way—as he strode to the podium. A group of men and woman sat assembled before him, each with the Theran globe and gavel embroidered in silver on their blue robes. Gharum sat next to a woman in a tall-backed chair.

Though everyone in Acantha was the same age, this woman

looked older somehow. She gazed upon Ardenis with a coolness in her wise eyes. Her black hair was wrapped in a tight bun on top of her head, a proper form of the trend Laida had begun. If not for the circumstances, he would have smiled at the irony. She could only be the head high councilwoman, leader of Acantha.

Ardenis stood behind the podium, hands stiff at his sides. Gharum whispered something in the councilwoman's ear. She nodded and faced Ardenis.

"Ardenis Watcher Fater, I am Rhea Head High Councilwoman. Allegations have been brought against you that are heinous indeed. Do you know of which I speak?"

"I do." His voice echoed soundly through the room. He had truth on his side. He raised his face, drawing himself up. Even if he went down as the most corrupt soul in Acantha, at least he'd tried. At least had done the honest thing.

"I will have Gharum Head Councilman report his findings." Rhea turned to Gharum who stood and smiled politely at the assembly.

"I apologize for the necessity of involving the High Council in this matter," Gharum said. "You've all heard the facts, so I think you can understand why I felt the need." He nodded to Ardenis. "And I thank you, Watcher Fater, for arriving with haste after Hector Enforcer advised you to come."

Ardenis clenched his fists, digging his nails into his palms. Hector had meant to bring him here all along.

Gharum took a deep breath. "Ardenis, Hector kept watch over you when he noticed you becoming emotionally influenced, and you did not report it to the council."

"Please clarify, Gharum Head Councilman," Rhea said.

"Ardenis exhibited signs of aggression and anger, far beyond what an Acanthian should be capable of. He's not the first watcher to succumb to the emotional influence of Thera. He's to be commended for lasting as long as he did. He began spending more time than usual with Laida, former leader of the transfer hall. He grew close to her. Then, it was witnessed that Ardenis entered the transfer hall in our region this morning, the morning Laida was to be born. It is our belief Ardenis tried to stop the transfers from operating by starting a fire, in order to keep the object of his interest here in Acantha. As a result, we've lost half our born capabilities, and the rest have been necessarily halted."

Gharum nodded and took his seat. Rhea's mouth formed in a tight line, and she turned to Ardenis.

His heart stuttered.

"One more thing I almost forgot," Gharum said, standing back up. He smiled at Ardenis and there was amusement behind the malice in his eyes. "We discovered a box of unapproved drawings beneath his bed. We are unsure what their purpose holds."

"Is that all, Gharum Head Councilman?" Rhea asked.

"That is all," he said, taking his seat.

It was enough. Ardenis's shoulders drooped. How could his Fating of him in the future come true now? If he could convince them of even some of the truth, maybe he could still go to Thera and be with Laida. When he thought of it, he didn't know which outcome to hope for.

Behind Rhea's back, Gharum flashed Ardenis an ominous smile.

"Ardenis, as this is a session of the High Council, we will have your side as well. I invite you to share what you know. This will be the only chance you're allowed."

Ardenis swallowed and breathed once... twice. "Rhea Head High Councilwoman, I must deny the allegations brought against me." Murmurs circulated the council members. "To explain myself, I will start back two months ago, when I first had the Fating of the elf being born on Thera. Hector Enforcer came into my house, uninvited, and accused me of lying about my Fating." He paused to let the thought settle, though no one reacted. "Why would he think this if he had not been emotionally influenced? I did not lie, and an Acanthian would not have made such a conclusion."

"In order to operate within the realm of their duties, enforcers will come and go as they please," Rhea said. "Did he specify why he thought you were lying?"

"Yes, he said I must have been lying because there is no way he'd see an elf born in Thera—that it went against the natural order of things."

Rhea's eyes widened slightly. Some of the council members whispered. Gharum glared with loathing.

"Go on."

"As a watcher, I am familiar with the signs of hatred and anger. I recognized these signs in Hector as time passed. Some incidents occurred which I attribute to Hector, though I have no evidence of this. First, the lottery box for the transfer hall went missing. Then the replacement box was set on fire. This morning, I accompanied Laida to the transfers to bid her good journey. We're friends, you see. Our journals could attest to that. I watched her travel to Thera, and that's when I saw smoke. I worked tirelessly beside fellow Acanthians to put out the fire, as evidenced by my robe."

Ardenis stepped around the podium momentarily to emphasize his point, though of course they would have seen the soot stains on his way in. "Idonea Transfer Leader can witness to that. Hector and Gharum were there, but did not help put out the fire. Gharum appeared agitated, so I followed him. I overheard Gharum tell Hector he was supposed to start the fire earlier in order to prevent any borns at all today. That we are a race of human souls, in existence to provide humans for Thera. Then, they said they had to move quickly to implement the next step of the plan to destroy the transfers."

The whispered conversations rose in volume and pitch. Rhea silenced them with an upraised hand. Gharum's face appeared impassive, but his posture was rigid, his breathing fast.

Ardenis went on. "I can only assume I was part of that second plan, because when I arrived at the tower, Hector awaited me, ready to accuse me of starting the fire. I came here to make a report, only to find Gharum has already spoken lies against me."

"And the unauthorized drawings?" Rhea asked.

Ardenis glanced down at the podium. "I am guilty of those." He looked up. "None of them were rejected by the council, I simply have not taken the time to get them approved. And for that, I apologize. It is an oversight I can quickly remedy."

Rhea stepped into the space between the council and Ardenis. She stared at the ground, her hands clasped in front of her. She looked up and turned so she addressed both parties.

"It is troublesome, indeed, to hear such allegations on both sides. It is no small thing to know one of you—an Acanthian—is lying. Lies, deception, intentional destruction of the transfer hall, emotional corruption... we are clearly long past the point in which the High Council should have been informed." She glanced back and forth between Gharum and Ardenis. "The High Council will convene in order to deliberate all that has been revealed today. In the meantime, since one of you can't be trusted, we will quarter you both for the protection of Acantha from further devastation."

It was better than he'd expected. At least they were considering his side.

"Both of us?" sputtered Gharum, standing.

"Yes. Is that a problem?"

Gharum inclined his head. "Of course not."

"Ardenis," Rhea said. "Are you familiar with jails in Thera?"

His heart raced. "I am."

"I would like to be able to trust you both, but since I can't, you'll be held in separate cells until we have come to our conclusion. Nora Enforcer will show you to them." Rhea gestured toward the door, then turned her back on them to her council.

Gharum stomped away. Ardenis remained in place and cleared his throat.

"Rhea Head High Councilwoman, I came here to inform the High Council of Gharum's plans. We have to prevent the destruction of the rest of the transfers. Please, even if you don't trust me, heed my warning and send someone to watch over them. You should know I advised them to continue running, even half gone and with the known risk. The borns must continue."

"Thank you, Ardenis, although that was not your decision to make. We will consider your words carefully. Please follow Nora to your cell."

CHAPTER
TWENTY-SEVEN

Ardenis bowed to the High Council and exited to the foyer, the weight of dozens of eyes on his back. Nora, holding a set of keys that jangled on a big brass ring, smiled and led them toward a side door. Behind her, Gharum didn't blink as he stared daggers through Ardenis's skull. Gone was the mild, impassive council member Ardenis had thought Gharum to be.

They followed Nora down a windowless, lantern-lit hall, then descended a winding staircase. Their sandals flapped against the bare stone. His council hall didn't have this staircase. Realization settled over him, drawing his gaze to every corner. The High Council had seen this type of issue before, enough to have need of cells. What kind of wrongdoings had they dealt with before? Emotional alteration was not a new concept in Acantha, which was why there were such strict rules governing watchers.

His guilt should have weighed him down, but he no longer felt shame for watching Damian and Eva. His love for Laida was worth the sacrifice and more.

At the bottom of the stairs, Nora led them into another long hall. She stopped at a door that looked nothing like the cells Ardenis had seen on Thera. Rather than iron bars, it was polished wood, with carved molding and a golden number. She opened the lock with a key from the brass ring. Gharum edged closer. This was likely the first time he'd ever seen one.

Nora opened the door, smiled at Gharum, and gestured him inside. Gharum glared into the room, but did as requested. Nora followed him in, lighting a lamp. Ardenis glanced back at the empty hall. He could run. Now would be the perfect time... But where would he go? It wouldn't help his case, and it wouldn't help Laida. She needed him to stop Gharum and keep the borns going.

Nora reemerged, locking the door behind her.

"This way, Ardenis." She walked a few paces down the hall, then led him into a room diagonal from Gharum's.

Nora lit a lamp, chasing away the darkness. The inside was just as different from Theran jails as the outside. The room contained a bed with a white down blanket and ample pillows, a desk with a plush chair and a lantern, a shelf of books, and a table with an empty washbasin.

"I apologize for the necessity of this arrangement. Refreshments will be brought to you soon. There are drawing supplies in the desk drawer to help you pass the time. You may journal, if you'd like."

"Thank you," he said slowly. The whole thing seemed bizarre.

Nora smiled and left the room. So much smiling. Is that what the council would have them mimic of mortal life? The click of the lock resounded from the door. He stared at it and sighed. Nothing had gone as he'd imagined. His fate was in the council's hands, and the fate of the transfer hall was in the hands of a madman. Only Amalia stood between Hector and his goal—if she even did as Ardenis had asked—and she didn't even believe him.

He dropped his head into his hands. What a fine mess. Even if the council ruled in his favor, he might still be born because of his involvement and the unauthorized drawings of Thera. Hector—unchecked while the council deliberated—would destroy the transfers. He'd find another way to finish what he'd started. Alysies and its neighboring kingdoms would go childless.

All he could do was wait. Sleep was out of the question. He opened the desk drawer to find fresh drawing paper, charcoal pencils, and small glass bottles of paint, along with a few paint-brushes. He didn't dabble with paints much, as he preferred pencils. After spreading the paper on the desk, he sharpened a pencil with the paring knife, rolling his eyes at the carelessness of the council, then set pencil to paper. He sketched the first thing that came to his mind.

Laida.

Even if he found her on Thera, she wouldn't look the same as she did in Acantha. She wouldn't be the same person anymore. That didn't mean he would care for her any less.

Ardenis started with the outline of her face, the softness of her skin echoed in his smooth lines. He drew her hair up in a loose bun on top of her head, wisps breaking free, chuckling at the memory of her carefree and stubborn attitude.

In the middle of drawing her eyes as they were just before she left for Thera, so full of warmth and understanding, footsteps sounded from the hall. He shoved the drawing in his pocket, crinkling it, and then sketched the rough beginnings of a Theran landscape.

Nora opened the door carrying a platter of meats, cheeses, fruit, bread, and two pitchers of water. Definitely not the fare he'd seen served to Theran prisoners. She set the tray on the table next to the washbasin, filling it with one of the pitchers.

"Is there anything you'd like to make your stay more comfort-able?" she asked.

Definitely not the same. "No, thank you."

She smiled and walked toward the door.

"Wait. Is the council still deliberating?"

She turned, raising an eyebrow. "Yes, they have not reached a decision yet. When they have, you'll be brought before them to receive the verdict."

"Did they send someone to check on the transfers in my region?"

"I'm not sure. Rhea..." She glanced back at the door. "Well, I can't say anymore until your fate is decided. I apologize."

He nodded. "I understand. I am concerned for my friends in my region."

"Get some rest, if you can. There are clothes for sleeping in the armoire and extra blankets if you need them. Also fresh robes if you should like to change out of yours." She glanced at his dirty robe and left the room, closing and locking the door behind her.

Ardenis changed his robe and then used the washbasin to clean the soot from his hands and face. The water turned murky grey. He made a sandwich out of the food on the tray, taking large bites in between sips of cold water and nibbles of fruit. He finished sketching his Theran landscape and groaned. He'd drawn Eva and Isaac's castle in Pavora. He huffed in irritation, brushing crumbs off the fresh new robe.

An empty feeling of helplessness welled up inside. Worse than anything was that Amalia didn't believe him. He'd harbored a secret hope he had at least one friend in all of Acantha on his side. He slumped in his chair. If she thought him capable of committing such violent acts, Hector and Gharum had already won.

Ardenis slammed his fist on the desk, shocking himself and sending pencils flying. He belonged in Acantha. He was supposed to wait until the future to be born. His instincts screamed it to him. It was the only reason he could remain here and let Laida go, the last thing he had to hold on to.

Ardenis glanced at the door. If only it was unlocked, he could probably walk right out of the council building without being stopped, unless the enforcers saw him. If he was caught, they might send him to the transfer hall in this region. He'd be born to a different part of Thera, oceans away and with no chance of ever finding Laida.

He shook his head. He had to hold on to hope the council might rule in his favor. The weight of everything that hung in the balance crushed him. Laida was gone. Vinia and Bram were gone. Amalia didn't trust him. It was his word against the word of a head councilman and a reputable enforcer. It was over.

⬥

Ardenis stared at the desk, contemplating the purpose of it all—his Fating of the future, his forbidden love, his existence—when the key turned in the door. He pried his head from his hands and stood.

Nora entered, smiling, of course. "The council has reached a decision. Please come with me."

"Nora, I need to know." He didn't mean to sound so desperate, but he was.

Her smile faltered.

"Tell me what they decided."

She looked down the hall. "I can't disclose that information. Please, you'll have to come with me."

He'd get no help from her. He followed her out the room to find Gharum already in the hall. He gazed at Ardenis coolly, all signs of anger gone. When Nora turned her back, Gharum's fury returned. The emotions rolled off him like heat from the flames Ardenis had battled all day. He clenched his fists against the urge to yell at Gharum for all the wrongdoing he'd caused. Neither spoke as they ascended the stairs and followed Nora into the council room.

Rhea watched them enter, as did the rest of the council, which seemed to have increased in number. She nodded at Gharum as he took his place beside her. Ardenis stood behind the podium, while a smug smile spread on Gharum's face. He knew something.

They must not have voted in Ardenis's favor if Gharum remained in the council's good graces. Ardenis felt trapped in a game of Tafl, and they had him cornered.

Rhea faced him. "I apologize for the necessity of detaining you. We've reached a decision."

She gave a nod of her head, and two enforcers stepped from the side of the room.

"Ardenis Watcher Fater," she began.

The enforcers moved forward, walking directly toward him, shoulders tense.

"For the sin of becoming emotionally influenced during your course of duty as a watcher—"

Ardenis's palms went slick. He took an involuntary step back from the podium.

"And for the atrocious act of starting a fire at the transfer hall—"

The enforcers split up, walking to stand on either side of the podium.

"We of the High Council find you guilty." She shook her head, almost as if she were sorry, or disappointed.

"No!" Ardenis jumped back and raised his arm in protest. They couldn't do this.

The enforcers flanked him, grabbing him with rough hands. Ardenis heaved away from them, but they only held tighter.

"It is useless to fight, Ardenis," Rhea said in a calm voice. Her stern eyes softened infinitesimally. "You're not the first Watcher this has happened to." She straightened her shoulders. "The punishment for your sins is your immediate departure to the transfer hall where you will bypass all existence and be sent to the Dark Unknown." She cast her eyes to the ground. "Journey well."

Ardenis's heart dropped into his stomach. The Dark Unknown? He'd never see Laida again, not even in the Hereafter. His limbs trembled uncontrollably.

"I swear on the Fates I did not start the fire! Punish me if you must, but let me be born. Please."

Rhea ignored the wild desperation in his tone and flicked her chin toward the door. The enforcers hauled Ardenis backward. He saw everything, all the faces of the High Council staring with wide eyes at the emotionally altered Watcher Fater. Only Rhea looked away. Gharum sneered at him, reveling in his triumph. His hatred would remain unchecked with none the wiser.

Horrified, Ardenis let go of whatever propriety remained. "Stop! You can't do this. Gharum is emotionally altered. Just look at him. Look! I've seen it throughout history. His is the face of a tyrant." The enforcers yanked so hard they pulled him off his feet and dragged him backward toward the door. "Don't trust him, Rhea."

She looked on with impassivity—a mother outwaiting the tantrum of a child—as the rest of the council stood. They had to all be present in order for the gateway to the Dark Unknown to open, the only time they ever left the confines of their part of Acantha. The enforcers hauled him into the foyer. The council chamber door closed with a loud bang, like a nail hammering into his premortal coffin.

He twisted and yanked, but his captors were strong and capable. They didn't utter a word. Soon they had him out of the council hall, dragging him down the stone steps and hauling him toward the transfer hall. The perfect night mocked him. It carried on with its clear skies and warm breeze, oblivious to his world coming undone.

Before they pulled him out of the courtyard, Rhea stepped from the building, stopping at the top of the stairs with an expression as blank as the rest of the council behind her. Suddenly she glanced sharply away. Ardenis followed her gaze. Amalia had entered the courtyard.

What was she doing?

Amalia's mouth gaped when she spotted Ardenis. The shadow of a second person came behind her just before the enforcers rounded a corner, hauling him out of sight.

His heart hammered. The transfer hall wasn't far away. Once they had him inside the building, it would be too late. His instincts screamed, hammering his soul almost in time with the pulse in his ears, begging him to stay. He had to break free of his captor's unyielding grip.

"Enforcers, please." His voice betrayed fear and desperation. "Let me go. I did not do the things Gharum said." They didn't even look at him, still dragging him backward, the heels of his sandaled feet bumping along the stone pathway.

In that instant, he made up his mind. He hated what he had to do next. Violence was something no Acanthian knew of, but it was all he had left. He'd get away. If he ran fast enough, all he had to do was throw himself into a gateway and it would all be over. He'd find Laida, he was sure of it.

As soon as they took the next turn, he would yank one of them off balance—the one on his right. He was shorter than the other. If lucky, he could wrench the enforcer to the ground. They wouldn't let him escape so easily. He'd have to make sure they couldn't follow him to his home transfer—maybe even hurt them.

Could they die if he did it wrong?

No. He clenched his jaw. *Impossible.*

They rapidly approached the turn to the transfer hall. Not long now. He prayed for the Fates to forgive him. They were to blame for all he suffered now, and all he would suffer if caught after committing his violent plan. Blood rushed through his veins. Instincts screaming. His eyes darted like someone half mad.

He craned to look over his shoulder. They were so close, too close. He breathed in and out, struggling to control his racing heart. Not only would he go down in Acanthian history as the most emotionally corrupt soul ever to exist, but he'd also be an example forever of the consequences of those emotions.

Ardenis tensed for the moment of no return.

The enforcers dragged him around the corner. Ardenis's arms twitched up to knock them to the ground.

What am I doing?

Cold shock washed over him, and he dropped—dead weight in their hands. He couldn't do it. The enforcers didn't spare him a glance as they readjusted their grip and hurried on to the transfer hall. It loomed ahead, a tall and white interruption to the starry sky.

The council crowded the path back in the far distance, Gharum in the lead, slowly making their way. The few Acanthians who weren't already looking at him, stopped to stare at the spectacle of the High Council.

Ardenis blinked and he was through the door.

"Inform Arenna Transfer Leader we are here for a forced born to the Dark Unknown." The enforcer's words pinned Ardenis to the floor, sucking the last of his hope away.

They dragged him past the record keeper, whose eyes trailed him with a blank stare. A dead stare. These people knew nothing of what it meant to live, to be a human soul, destined for greater things.

The enforcers passed all the lines, heading straight for the black gateway in the corner. Its presence pulsed through the room with waves of fear and despair.

This is what he deserved. Let them throw him in.

Ardenis stood on his own two feet, attempting to wrench his arms from his captors. They finally let go as he stepped toward the gateway, all the air sucked from his lungs. He'd done this. He disobeyed the watchers' edict, knowingly. Willingly. And he'd do it again if he could.

Again, and again, and again, and again, for the gift of loving Laida and the brief glimpse of her love in return.

Ardenis took the final step into the gateway. The darkness consumed him, sucking all the light from the air around him. It was cold, so cold. Goosebumps raised on his arms—a first. He turned, knees shaking, to face the outside as the council piled into the room, one by one. As soon as the council members were all present, his existence would be over. He stared down at his hands, clasped to keep them steady.

Laida, I'm sorry. I promised to watch over you and I failed.

TWENTY-EIGHT

"S top!" A commanding voice broke Ardenis's concentration.

He looked up, but the darkness of the gateway was nearly complete, allowing only a sliver of light through the black.

"Ardenis, come forward." It was Rhea's voice, calm with just a hint of urgency.

He stepped out of the gateway, but it pulled at his legs and robe, as if the darkness did not want to give him up so easily. He blinked as the light returned, the torches bright after the black. His body trembled. Warmth crept back in, but his teeth chattered. Fear would not allow hope to rise.

Rhea stepped quickly past the gawking transfer workers. Amalia followed. The rest of the council lingered at the entrance. The enforcers bowed to their leader. Amalia offered him a blank expression and a quick nod.

What did that mean? The blackness loomed at his back, pulling at him, calling to him. He dared not turn around.

"Enforcers, please escort Ardenis back to the council hall." Rhea pivoted and walked away. The council, including a fidgeting Gharum, followed.

Hope finally crept from the shadowy depths of despair. His captors reclaimed his arms. Their viselike grip had lessened, but Ardenis leaned heavily on them. His muscles wouldn't move right; weak and shaking. Did Amalia's presence mean she believed him? Her words denying him still burned. He didn't dare breathe as they left the transfer hall and the dark gateway behind.

Amalia followed Rhea without a word. What if they needed him back to implicate his friend? He wouldn't, even if she didn't trust him.

Ardenis stared at Amalia's back as they walked, ignoring any onlookers as his muscles regained their strength. She didn't turn. He played the perfect prisoner between the compliant enforcers at his side, but they did not let him go. He prayed to the Fates this was his second chance. His Fating of the future bolstered his hope.

Nora Enforcer smiled from her desk when they entered the building. Rhea walked straight into the council room and took her place at the front. Ardenis's captors led him to a chair near the door where they released him. He rubbed his arms while Amalia walked to stand behind the podium. As Gharum and the rest of the council took their seats on the tiered benches, Ardenis scanned the room, and nearly yelled in surprise.

Hector sat in a chair at the front, near Rhea. His wrists were bound with twine, and he wore a deep scowl. Ardenis rubbed his eyes. He willed Amalia to look at him, but she stared straight ahead.

"We have reconvened in light of claims of compelling evidence by Amalia Watcher," Rhea said. "Amalia, please share what you have discovered."

Amalia nodded, placing her hands on the podium. "Thank you for the opportunity to speak." Her voice held no sense of stress or alarm. "When Hector Enforcer told me Ardenis started the fire at the transfer hall, Ardenis denied this and requested I take measures to monitor and safeguard the remainder of the transfers." She took a deep breath. "I know much from watching Thera, and the anger in Hector's behavior gave me pause, so I followed him."

Hector shifted in his chair, as did Gharum on Rhea's other side. Ardenis held his breath, all senses tuned to Amalia's every word.

"I witnessed him attempting to start a fire in the remainder of the transfers using torchlight and oil."

Small gasps echoed around the room. Gharum's hands clenched into fists. Ardenis almost pumped his arm in the air.

Rhea glanced at the presiding council, and they nodded. "We are grateful to Amalia Watcher for preventing another catastrophe." She turned back to Amalia. "What happened when you approached Hector Enforcer?"

"When he saw me, he gave himself up. Nevertheless, I felt the restraints were necessary." Amalia's face remained impassive, but Ardenis swore her eyes twinkled with the hint of a smile.

Why in Acantha would Hector give himself up? Ardenis studied Amalia, but could glean no information from her relaxed posture.

"I'm not sure if I approve of your methods, Amalia Watcher." Rhea turned to Hector. "What compelled you to turn yourself in?"

Hector hesitated, and Amalia spoke up. "He gave me something which may help. I have something in my possession that might change the High Council's decision regarding Ardenis's fate." Amalia faced the council with cool impassivity, a portrait of emotional control. "As I stated upon arrival, I have evidence of Ardenis's innocence which the High Council needs to hear." She locked eyes with Ardenis and gave a slight nod.

He couldn't help but gape.

Amalia pulled an unassuming brown leather-bound book from the pocket of her robe and held it before her. It had no writing on the outside, nothing to indicate what it contained. Except, every Acanthian would recognize it for what it was. A journal. "I bear news of an alarming nature."

Gharum jumped up, eyes wide, pointing. "How did you get that?"

Rhea's eyes dropped to the book, ignoring Gharum. "I doubt

anything could surprise me at this point, Amalia. Please, speak your piece."

"It's Gharum's journal. If you'd allow me, I would like to read a few specific entries. It is most disturbing."

Ardenis thanked Amalia's foresight once again for warning him about his own journal. There was nothing in it to implicate him should the council decide to read it. Gharum must have been too confident in his position to believe he needed the same caution. Or maybe he didn't know of deceit the way a watcher would. Though Gharum was clearly emotionally altered, he wasn't a watcher of Thera. Ardenis saw treachery nearly every time he entered the tower. Gharum had barely dipped his toes into the cold world of lies, and perhaps wouldn't know to hide them.

Rhea's mouth formed a thin line. "First, I would hear from Hector Enforcer. How did you come by this?"

Hector cleared his throat. "Everything I've done was at the request of my superior, Gharum Head Councilman. He assigned me specific duties pertaining to events surrounding the Fating of the elf." His eyes lowered. "Prior to that, I assisted with other tasks as outlined in his journal."

Gharum shook his head violently.

Hector looked up at the podium where Amalia stood with the journal in her hands, his words, soft for once, almost pleading. "When Amalia Watcher found me attempting to start another fire, at Gharum's request, I knew only his journal would absolve me. I took it from his home before Amalia brought me to the High Council."

Rhea put her fingertips to her temples. "Go ahead, Amalia."

Amalia opened the book. "The journal of Gharum Head Councilman." Gharum sank down on the bench.

Ardenis's heart beat with new hope.

"I succeeded in forcing Mevette Councilwoman's born today. I didn't even have to call a formal meeting. I informed her I would tell the High Council she'd defied me if she didn't choose to be born herself. She struggled at first, but no one of consequence saw. The number of council

members who will openly oppose me in a session are dwindling. And with Hector to do my bidding, we'll rid the rest of the opposition to my leadership."

The faces of the council members turned into exclamations of shock. Rhea's head snapped down to look at Gharum. He stared at the floor. Ardenis recalled the councilwoman he'd seen dragged from the council hall. He'd thought nothing of it at the time. Now, the reality washed cold over him.

People with power tended to want more power, but that only applied to mortals, with the emotional capacity to make those kinds of mistakes.

Amalia flipped to another page.

"Laida defied the rules again today. She has no respect for authority. She didn't even blink an eye as I questioned her. She convinced the council her hair was within the realms of the rules. The majority agreed, so I had no choice but to allow it. I must get rid of her and the opposing council members. Then, with the full support of my new council, we will take over the High Council. Only I seem to know what's best for Acantha. What should or should not be allowed. Acantha is at risk until then."

Rhea covered her mouth. Her gaze became unfocused. Ardenis fought to control his fury. Laida was safe from him now. What else had Gharum done to defy the rules of a head councilman? People being forced to be born before their time, but what about withholding information from Acantha? Too many of Ardenis's reports were never posted to the bulletins.

Amalia turned to the middle of the journal. *"I discovered a secret about Hector Enforcer today, one I plan to use to continue my important work. Few share my vision, but I will see it through to the end. I must protect our people from Thera's evil. After all, humans are superior beings. They rule over Thera. Acanthians exist to supply the souls for humans, not some subspecies that Ardenis Watcher Fater claims the Fates revealed. He'll be disgraced and exiled when I'm done."*

Amalia's calm voice grew louder and clipped with heat by the end, betraying her emotions.

Rhea's eyes and mouth opened into a mask of shock. Ardenis was sure he wore the same gaping expression of disbelief.

Amalia closed the journal.

The horror and extent of Gharum's treacherous reach went far beyond what Ardenis could imagine. This was more than simply preventing the first elf from being born. Most likely there were many more journals that spanned the ages. There was no comprehending how far it might have spread. Gharum had been head councilman for centuries.

"Please detain Gharum and Hector," Rhea said, her voice sounding detached. "Ardenis and Amalia, you are dismissed to await our ruling in the council foyer."

Not the cells? Ardenis held his breath, not wanting even a whisper to collapse his fragile hope.

The tall enforcer approached Gharum, whose lip curled in plain hatred. The enforcer took his arm, and Gharum did not resist. He glared at Amalia the entire way out of the room, even turning his head to look back at her. Hector followed the short enforcer without protest, head hung low.

Amalia didn't return Gharum's attention. She stepped down from the podium, and together she and Ardenis accompanied Nora into the council foyer. When the door to the council room closed behind them, Ardenis let loose the breath it seemed he'd been holding since Amalia showed up.

"I thought you didn't believe me," he said.

"I never doubted you, Arden." She lowered her voice to a whisper. "I only said I did."

Nora watched them with raised eyebrows, so he said no more. They took seats on wooden benches along the wall. Only the scribbling of Nora's quill broke the silence. Finally, they were called back into the council room. At Rhea's gesture, Ardenis stood at the podium. Amalia sat in a chair near the door.

"It's been a long night," Rhea said. She sounded weary and overburdened. "Many things have come to light of which the High

Council was unaware. Many more things have yet to be uncovered." She shook her head. "But, we have reached a decision regarding your fate, Ardenis."

She stared straight at him, and his heart picked up speed. He swallowed and glanced at the door. The council knew he was emotionally altered. He'd displayed it perfectly for all to see with his useless struggles and pleas. If they reached the same decision as before, he'd run for it. He wouldn't make the same mistake twice and be sent to the Dark Unknown. He'd go to the very same gateway Laida had used, if it was still there.

"Ardenis Watcher Fater," she said, "in light of the new evidence, the High Council finds you innocent of attempting to destroy the transfers." Ardenis breathed a pent-up sigh of relief. "However, we find you guilty for the unauthorized drawings. Therefore, we have no choice but to take action." He gripped the podium. "Given your efforts, your unique ability as a Fater, and the fact you saved the transfer hall from decimation, you will remain in Acantha within your watcher function. But you shall be demoted to night watch. Also, you will, of course, need to submit your drawings to the council for approval."

His hands fell to his sides. Night watch. He'd been very fortunate. Rhea hadn't even mentioned his emotional state. Shackles of tension lifted off of him.

"You and Amalia may go. We have much bigger issues to contend with." She straightened her shoulders. "Please return to your watcher duties. Thank you for your assistance in this grave matter. We may call on you as our inquiry progresses. I trust you both to keep this to yourselves."

Ardenis opened his eyes wide. Free to go? He glanced at Amalia, and she looked at him. Then they both inclined their heads and moved to leave at the same time. He wouldn't even think of how Rhea had just asked them both to lie by omission.

"One last thing, Ardenis," Rhea said. He looked back at her. "Report to me directly if anything else turns up amiss."

Ardenis considered her words, then nodded. His own council couldn't be trusted, not yet. He turned and followed Amalia out the door before Rhea could change her mind. Nora smiled pleasantly as they left the council hall, wishing them goodnight.

He breathed in the night air, reveling in the perfectness of it. The new moon meant little light aside from the glowing lamps, and the cool air touched upon his heated skin. Ardenis could hardly contain his joy, but they walked in silence until they were out of sight of the council building.

When they passed the residential area, he stopped and turned to Amalia, grinning from ear to ear. "How did you do that?" he asked.

Amalia quirked her mouth into a sly smile. "It wasn't me. It was the Fates' design." She continued down the path.

Ardenis stared at the spot she had vacated, then shook his head and followed her. "No, really. How did you do that? How did you get Gharum's journal? And how did you get Hector to come willingly?"

Amalia stopped. "I'm sorry, Ardenis, for saying I didn't believe you."

He looked away, uncomfortable that she felt the need to apologize after all she'd done for him.

She moved into his line of sight until he was forced to look at her. "I hoped you'd see the truth, despite my words. I see now that wasn't the case. I had to lie, or Hector would have tried to take both of us to the council hall, or invent some lie about me, and I would have been unable to stop him." She took both his hands and squeezed. "I truly am sorry, my friend."

The fear of being forced to be born, then the acceptance of it, and now the joy of the council's verdict of his innocence was almost too much. Through it all, he was accompanied by the sting of Amalia's words and the hurt and betrayal they had instilled in him. But, he was still in Acantha where he belonged, and he had Amalia to thank for it. She'd only done what she'd thought was best.

He pushed aside his leftover bitterness and gave her a hug. She smiled and hugged him back.

"Of course all is forgiven, Amalia. I should have known you'd never betray me. I'm sorry." They broke apart, and she put her hands on her hips and nodded.

Amalia smiled as they continued their trek home. They'd reached the midpoint between regions, with only trees and lantern light for company. The shadows welcomed him as old friends.

"As for Gharum's journals," she said, "you gave me the idea when you mentioned they'd read your journal. Hector led me to them willingly. It seems Gharum's been trying to get rid of me for a long time, though I was careful never to give him a reason."

"Why would Hector help you?"

"He's protecting himself," she said quickly. "He thinks Gharum's journal will absolve him of his treachery."

"Hmm, he may be right." His brow furrowed. "Hector deserves to be punished just as much as Gharum. I hope they see that."

"It's for the council to decide now."

They walked in silence for a bit.

"So Hector helped you on the chance he might not be forced to be born?" He ran his hand through his hair. Why would Hector care about staying in Acantha? It seemed he would stand more of a chance at remaining if he'd continued to deny the truth. Amalia sped up. "What else do you know?" He matched her pace.

Amalia sighed. "I..." She stepped off the stone pathway and stomped over to lean against a thick oak tree.

Ardenis raised his eyebrows at the scowl on her face, made plain by the glow of the nearby lamppost.

Amalia crossed her arms. "I don't want to tell you, Ardenis."

He walked over to her. "Okay. You don't have to tell me. Can I ask why?"

Her cheeks turned red. She was blushing. *Blushing.* He'd never seen Amalia betray that emotion before.

"Look. I'll tell you, but you must promise to keep it to yourself, and I don't want to hear any more about it."

Ardenis nodded slowly. "All right."

"Hector issinluwime," she mumbled and stared at the ground.

"Umm, what?" It was almost humorous seeing Amalia so undone. She was the strong one, the sure one, never letting her vulnerabilities show.

She let out a huff of frustration and started down the path again. He followed. "About a century ago I came under Hector's attention. He must have recognized me as emotionally altered. He never caught me breaking the rules, but he always seemed to be around when I felt particularly sad or upset. So, I nearly punched him when he tried to kiss me."

Ardenis stumbled, nearly falling.

Amalia didn't look at him. "He eventually confessed his feelings for me, though he didn't know to call it love." She paused and Ardenis fumbled around, trying to remember how to do basic things like walk and close his mouth. "He's tried to force me to be born ever since, with Gharum's help it seems."

"Why would he want you gone if he... loves you?" It was hard to apply such an innocent and raw emotion to someone so hateful and corrupt. And how did Hector learn of such emotions? From Gharum?

Amalia sighed. "You know Hector. He likes control. He can't stand the thought of having forbidden emotions he's unable to contain. Emotions that are against the rules and laws of Acantha. He blames me, I'm sure. He has only become more angry and bitter over the years."

Ardenis stared straight ahead. So many things clicked into place —his obsession with the rules, his displays of anger, and the fact he recognized Ardenis's own emotional awareness and love for Laida.

Amalia finally looked at him, wariness in her eyes. "I don't love him."

"I know," he said quickly. "Have you thought about telling the High Council?"

"And let them in on my secret? That I know how to recognize love? No. Besides, it turned out to be convenient leverage in our situation. Hector knew I had caught him, but I convinced him to come willingly to help prove your innocence."

They walked along the path toward their homes in silence while Ardenis tried to comprehend everything he thought he once knew to be true. The dark sky turned into a blue dawn, tinging the white buildings in the distance. It had been a long day. Thanks to Amalia, he'd be able to continue watching, and hopefully find Laida.

He looked over at her. "Thank you, my friend. You took a big risk following Hector and bringing him to the High Council." The small words couldn't convey the depth of his appreciation.

"It's what anyone would have done," she said, shrugging. They both knew that wasn't true. Not in Acantha. "I hope the High Council can finally right some of the wrong that has occurred."

"Have you fulfilled your purpose here, Amalia?" He grinned, though his stomach clenched. He couldn't lose her too. "Are you going to be born now?"

She stared at the path ahead, a smile spreading on her face. "I don't think my time is done in Acantha. Not quite."

Ardenis nodded. "I feel the same, although I have the Fating to confirm it. I think it's what's helping me overcome the..." He didn't want to put words to what he felt in the aftermath of all that had happened. Corruption. Destruction. Deception. None of it existed for him before. Maybe now he could pretend it never had.

Except love. He didn't want to forget love.

He missed Laida fiercely.

She nodded. "The pain. I know it well."

"Yes," he said, grabbing at his chest, wishing for rain. "I didn't know it could feel like this."

"If this is what it's like on Thera, I can wait a little longer to go."

"Something tells me it's just a fraction of what it could be like," he said. "Both the good and the bad."

They exchanged wistful smiles.

CHAPTER
TWENTY-NINE

The sun peaked over the horizon as Ardenis and Amalia reached their homes. Bone tired, he wanted nothing more than to go to bed, but he had something he needed to do first.

Amalia looked at him. "Go find her, Ardenis, if you can."

He smiled and grabbed her hand, squeezing, before taking off down the path to the tower. He breathed a sigh of relief when he entered the familiar room, so white, and crisp, and warm. He was a night watcher now, but no one here would know that yet. Only a few of them remained, and they didn't look up. His chair empty, he sat, focusing on Thera.

He let his instincts take over and was led right to King Isaac and Queen Eva. They slept peacefully in each other's arms in Eva's large, plush bed. It would be another two weeks at least before he'd know if today's lottery yielded a child for Queen Eva. And another eight months after that before the child would be born. Even then, there was no way to be sure the baby was Laida. He'd watch Queen Eva, and every other pregnant woman in Thera, until he found her.

He ended his watch and arose from his chair, stretching. His slow, tired steps took him home. Before he went to sleep, he looked under his bed, where Laida had put the box with his drawings just one day earlier.

He pulled it out and gave a forlorn sigh. Turning them in to the council would hurt—they were one of the last things left that reminded him of Laida. But, he had several centuries of being an Acanthian before he would be born. Until then, he'd have to follow the rules and resist giving in to his acquired emotional impulses.

He gathered the drawings up, and something slipped out and fell to the ground. It was a letter. Ardenis dropped the bundle and snatched the letter off the ground. He unfolded it and read.

Arden,

There is no doubt in my mind I will be born today, and so have brought your drawings back to you. You once told me you would miss me when I am gone, and I did not understand what you meant. I thought it over, and I know now what you were trying to say. Although I won't be truly gone, simply elsewhere, I won't be here in Acantha, for you to see and talk to every day.

We both have our own purposes to fulfill in the Fates' design. Perhaps our paths will cross once again. Until then, I will miss you too, Arden.

Every moment with you, I'll take with me.

Yours truly,

Laida

Ardenis clutched the paper to his chest, breath shaky, eyes stinging. On his knees beside his bed, he read the letter again and again. When his hands stopped shaking and his heartbeat slowed, he placed the letter tenderly back under his bed, along with Laida's favorite drawing of Eva and the crumpled rendering he'd done while at the High Council.

Laida had said she'd miss him too, even before the veil had been lifted from her within the gateway.

He gathered the rest of the drawings and went to the council hall. A different enforcer sat at the front desk in the council foyer. She gave him a pleasant smile, then waved him into the council room.

Already, a new head council member, Averick, presided. The council whispered, pointing at his soot-stained feet, but otherwise didn't betray any emotion. Averick accepted the drawings for review and informed him he would return them if approved. Ardenis knew better than to expect them back.

He wanted to ask about the events of the previous night—both the fire and the High Council—but the council made no mention of it, so neither did he.

Trudging home, Ardenis collapsed in his bed. He'd have to wake up when the time came for the night watch, but he knew he'd rise much sooner. Laida was down there somewhere.

As he expected, curiosity won over sleep. He awoke in the afternoon, hungry, still badly needing a bath, but wanting to check on Eva. A bulletin might be posted by now on the fate of Gharum and Hector. Amalia ought to find out too.

After a quick bath in his pool, he dressed in a fresh robe. He walked to Amalia's, just a few houses down from his, and knocked on the door.

"I'm sleeping, go away," she said from inside.

He smiled and knocked again. "I want you to come with me and read what happened to Hector and Gharum," he shouted back.

She pulled the door open, bleary-eyed, but grinning. "How could I refuse?" She closed the door behind her, tying on her robe, and together they went to the council hall.

When they arrived, there was a clamor of activity. It seemed their entire territory had come. Everyone spoke in tones that bordered on worry, but Ardenis only caught clips of conversation. Gharum and

Hector's names were the main features, as well as the fate of the transfer hall and talk of the fire.

They finally made their way up to the bulletin board to read the notice for themselves. Amalia nudged her way in front of him, blocking his view. She scanned the document.

"They sent Gharum to the Dark Unknown!" Amalia exclaimed as she read.

Ardenis nodded. "I doubt they hesitated in that decision." He moved to peer around her, but she held a hand up, blocking him again.

"Hector remained behind, back here, and..." She read on silently, then gave a burst of laughter. She covered her mouth with her hand, but even that couldn't disguise her joy.

Ardenis stepped around her and scanned the bulletin down to where she left off. He grinned.

They had assigned Hector to dishwasher at the dining hall. It had been publicly announced, so there'd be no confusion he no longer held the position of enforcer.

Only an emotionally altered watcher could find humor in it—washing dishes was just as important as anything else in Acantha—but still, Ardenis's day was complete. He and Amalia walked away, laughing companionably, amidst curious stares. Part of him pitied Hector. He loved someone who didn't love him back, and it had driven him half mad—an emotion all too familiar. Then Ardenis remembered what Hector had done to Laida, and brushed the feelings aside.

"Hector must have done a good job convincing the council he acted under Gharum's direction," Ardenis said.

"I read a lot of Gharum's journal on my way to the High Council. If you'd read it, you'd believe Hector too. Gharum confessed to a lot of things he'd asked Hector to do, though Hector was more than willing to do them."

Maybe Gharum really had been blackmailing Hector, if he'd learned Hector knew how to love.

When they left the council courtyard, Ardenis glanced around to ensure no one stood near. "I can't help but feel like we're responsible for Gharum and Hector's behavior."

Amalia nearly tripped. "What? Why?"

"We let Thera affect us. More than that, we fell in love with people in Acantha. We brought Theran emotions through the emotional veil."

"That's farfetched, Ardenis." She eyed him. "But even if it's true, the objects of our affection are no longer here, so it's not a concern anymore."

Her statement plummeted both of them into contemplative silence. Their heads hung, staring at the path. The only sound was their shuffling footsteps and the melody of chirping birds.

When they came to the rose garden surrounding the tower, a thought occurred to him. "The object of Hector's affection is still in Acantha." He almost smiled, but he'd been warned not to tease her.

"I told you not to mention that." Amalia glared.

"What I mean is, if an emotion as powerful as love threw Acantha out of balance, and Hector still feels that way toward you, how can Acantha ever be righted? Assuming my theory is correct."

Amalia put a hand on her hip. "Are you going to be the one to tell Rhea you know what love is?"

He raised his palms. "But knowing what love is, and being in love are two separate things."

"You wouldn't recognize love if you hadn't watched it, becoming emotionally altered. For example, you never realized Hector had feelings for me back when he was acting on them. Because you didn't know at that time. The knowledge and the emotion are connected. That's why the watchers' edict is so specific. If you tell Rhea, you know what will happen to you."

He did. And that was a consequence he wasn't willing to face, though how could Rhea not already know? Ardenis gave a quick nod, which Amalia answered with a satisfied smile, and they entered the tower.

THIRTY

Ardenis spent the next two weeks watching Eva without falter or deviation. The two-week mark came and went with no sign of pregnancy. He didn't have a hope of figuring out which lucky Theran had conceived Laida this early on, but still he watched.

One evening, as he prepared to leave home for the tower, a knock came at his door.

"I'll be right there." Ardenis tied his robe in place.

He checked himself in the mirror, smoothing back his wet hair. The reflection of his blue eyes gave him pause, reminding him of the pale blue eyes in the Fating of his future self. He didn't go to the public baths anymore—it was difficult enough pretending emotional neutrality at the watchtower.

Another knock sounded, and he shook his head. Leaving his bedroom, he crossed through his living area and opened the door.

"Rhea!" He blinked, trying to make sense of her being there. She stood alone on his threshold, staring at him with her wise eyes. Though they were nearly the same height, her presence towered over him, making him quake.

"Ardenis Watcher Fater, may I come in?" She raised an eyebrow.

"Y-yes, I apologize. Please come in." He stepped aside and waved her into his house. Why had she come here? Had they found something in Gharum's journals? No enforcers accompanied her, but Ardenis hardly took comfort in that.

Rhea sat in one of his wooden chairs surrounding the table where he once played Tafl with his friends. Ardenis remained standing, not knowing what else to do. This could not have been a simple social visit.

Picking up the soldier piece, she gave a slight smile, then placed it back on the board. "My region doesn't play this game. How does it work?" she asked.

"You want to know how to play Tafl?" He could not disguise the confusion in his voice.

She nodded.

"Well... It comes from a time of revolt in Thera, around 300 years ago." He took a seat across from her. "The citizens, tired of oppression, rose up against their leaders. The leaders hired soldiers for defense, but few citizens would employ themselves as soldiers to the tyrannical rulers. The ones who trained as soldiers were outnumbered and hated by the poor citizens." He became more animated as he talked, moving the pieces around the board to show her how it worked. "In Tafl, there is one soldier, and the rest of the pieces are citizens. The citizens try to corner the soldier, while the soldier tries to pick them off one at a time."

He finally glanced up at Rhea, and she wasn't looking at the board. Her penetrating eyes told him she knew exactly what the rules of Tafl were, and could probably best him at it.

She took the soldier from his hand. "Like the way Theran emotions eat at our watchers, Gharum wormed his way into the minds of the council, picking them off one at a time." She sighed. "He forced many innocent souls needlessly ahead of their time, and we've forced many more in the wake of his corruption."

Ardenis nodded. He'd seen a lot of new faces in the council hall over the past two weeks. Many changes had happened in the fallout. Was he next to fall?

He kept his face blank and didn't fidget as she seemed to study him, though he longed to rub his slick palms on his robe.

"I admit Gharum lied about a good many things, but an element of truth rang within it, and that gives me cause for concern." Her lips formed a slight frown. Whatever she had to say next couldn't be pleasant. "I believe you to be emotionally influenced by Thera, Ardenis, though perhaps not to the extent Gharum claimed."

He took a quick intake of breath.

She narrowed her eyes in speculation. "Your reactions in the High Council hall made that apparent. Even now there's something off about you, more so than the typical watcher."

Ardenis could guess where this was leading. He was next on her list of forced borns. He wanted to speak on his behalf, plead for his place in Acantha, but nothing would make a good defense. Rhea didn't seem to know half of how emotionally influenced he'd become, and he wasn't about to offer that information, even though he respected her greatly.

"Under normal circumstances, you'd have been born already, but the Fates gave you a gift—a Fating of the future ensuring your continued presence in Acantha." She placed the soldier in the middle of the board, its starting position. "In the final words of his defense, Gharum stated we've doomed Thera, and Acantha, by allowing the elf to be born. He said his instincts had prepared him to prevent this eventual outcome in order to protect our worlds."

Doomed Thera? Ardenis's Fating and instincts told him otherwise.

Rhea sighed. "My instincts tell me there is more to this puzzle, more to come of which we do not yet understand." She stood and smoothed her robe. "Your fate is tied to the elf's in some way, and so you'll remain. This is your chance for a new beginning."

Relief, which he hoped wasn't premature, washed over him. He inclined his head almost enough to pass as a bow. Guilt heated his face, but he couldn't tell her the entire truth. If she knew he loved Laida, Fating or not, he'd be gone. "Thank you, Rhea."

She gave a small smile. "Don't allow yourself to fall further from Acantha, Ardenis. I won't be able to give you another chance." She crossed the small living area, pausing at the door. "May your gifts serve you well."

"Rhea?" he said, stopping her. He shouldn't ask his burning question, but he had to know. "I know mortal emotions are forbidden, but why?" He held his breath. Would she read more into the question than she should? See his curiosity for what it was?

She studied him, paused at his front door. "It's not for watchers to know such things, but the council has edicts, just as every calling does. Our most important is to keep mortal emotions out of Acantha, specifically love." Her gaze weighed down on him. "Our world survives because of our desire to fulfill our roles and be born, aiding in the cycle of life. I can't imagine what might happen if that cycle were broken, if souls no longer had the desire to leave." She shuddered, and then let herself out without another word.

When the door closed behind her, Ardenis slumped in his chair. Rhea knew about at least some of his emotional state, yet she'd allowed him to stay. Despite everything, she trusted him, and that gave him courage. She wouldn't let him remain if she thought he was a danger to Acantha. Some tension left his shoulders as a great weight lifted from them. He could hold on and stay strong until his time finally came to be born.

THIRTY-ONE

Six weeks to the day from when Laida departed Acantha, Ardenis left the setting sun outside and entered the tower, early for his watch. Amalia smiled and stood, her shift ending.

She winked. "I wouldn't hesitate to look in on Eva if I were you."

Ardenis raised an eyebrow, and she left. He shot to his seat and focused his gaze into Thera and right to Eva. She sat on the edge of the bed, throwing up into her chamber pot.

Her maid, Mary, entered the room and gasped, rushing to the bed. "My queen! Are you all right?" She patted Eva on the back as Eva leaned over the edge of the bed, retching. "Fetch the physician!" she called toward the open door.

Eva leaned back into her pillows. "I'm all right, Mary. I feel better now. I'm just so tired."

Mary patted her hand, and her eyes crinkled in concern. "Can I get you something, my queen?"

"Some water would be nice. And some bread." Eva snuggled under her covers.

"Yes, my queen." Mary bowed and left the room.

Eva watched the door until it closed, then threw off the blanket and cradled her stomach through her white cotton nightgown, smiling.

"I know you're in there, my little secret. I think it's time we tell your father." She pressed her hand into her belly, feeling around. Her eyes twinkled, gaze unfocused, and she smiled.

Someone knocked on her door, and the physician, Romand, entered carrying a bag. Ardenis had watched him take care of the royal family for a long time. He'd lost weight and hair in equal measure in recent years, now bald except for a white mustache and beard.

"Hello, physician. I'm not sick. I think I'm pregnant." She beamed.

Romand's eyes widened. "Do you now?" He set his bag on the table next to the bed.

"I believe so, yes. I haven't bled in eight weeks. I was always regular with the full moon before."

He took a cone shaped tool from his bag, and listened to her heart, then felt her pulse at her wrist. He ran the back of his hand over her forehead. "Do you mind?" He gestured toward her stomach.

She shook her head.

"Lay down for me, my queen."

She did, and he gently poked around on her stomach. She grimaced when he prodded too deep.

"Nausea? Fatigue?" he asked with raised eyebrows.

"Both," she replied smiling.

"Well, my queen, this is indeed happy news." He placed his tools back in his bag and smiled. "You'll need to rest. We can't be too cautious. This child is the heir to the throne."

"What child?" Isaac asked, emerging into the room.

The physician bowed to him. Eva smiled and held out her hand. She truly had learned to love Isaac, but Ardenis had seen her hold her hand out to Damian, and the warmth here paled in comparison.

"The most wonderful news, Isaac. We're going to have a baby."

He took her hand and sunk to his knees at her bedside. He pressed his forehead into her palm, and she kissed the top of his light-brown hair. When he looked up, tears gleamed in his eyes.

"You've made me a happy man, my dear," he said. "Out. Everyone out." He looked around the room, and the lone maid and the physician quickly retreated.

"Isaac?"

He placed a hand on her stomach. "This child, our child, is more important than anything. My family's legacy will continue because of our love." He kissed her belly. "You'll have round the clock care while you remain in bed. You'll not want for anything."

She propped herself up on her elbows. "In bed? I'm not staying in bed for nine months. I'll grow so bored."

His brow creased. "There are not many things you'll find me requesting of you, and even less I will command. But this I must insist upon. You're carrying my son— "

"Or daughter."

"—and the heir to my throne."

Eva laughed. "You're joking. Are you truly not going to allow me out of my room?"

"Out of bed, dear." He placed a finger under her chin, lifting her face to look at him. "No sulking, Eva. I love you, and this is a happy occasion. We'll have a feast tomorrow to celebrate."

"And will I be able to attend?" she asked, face incredulous.

He chuckled. "The servants will bring you all the dishes. You won't miss a thing."

"What if the physician says I'm fine to move about the castle?" Her tone turned soft, as if she already knew his answer.

"I'm sure Romand will agree that your health and the baby's health is better served with you resting."

Ardenis shook his head. Royals often went a little insane when it came to their heirs, but surely Isaac would listen to the physician's advice.

Eva smiled, but it appeared forced. Isaac kissed her stomach again, then left the room. "Queen Eva needs her rest," he said.

Mary bowed from beside him in the hall. Isaac motioned for her to follow, and she set a plate of buttered bread on a table before the door shut behind them.

Eva's smile dropped into a frown, and she sighed. "I worried about that, little one." She leaned back into her pillows and soon fell asleep.

Ardenis shifted his gaze to Isaac. He walked down the hall, its stone floors adorned with sporadic crimson carpets, and candelabras gracing the walls. His steps were quick, and his servants and advisors hurried to keep up.

"Place two guards at her door. Her safety is everything. I want the best care for her. She'll have whatever she desires." He turned a corner to his throne room. "Where's Mary?"

"Here, my king." She bobbed an awkward curtsey while trying to keep up with his breathless pace.

"Eva's not to leave her bed. And do not let her grow bored. Monitor her progress and report directly to me."

Mary's eyes widened. "Yes, my king."

"Hammond!"

"Your Majesty?" A middle-aged gentleman stepped to Isaac's side. He wore an eager to please expression beneath his thick brows and worry lines. Ardenis recognized Hammond as one of Isaac's father's advisors.

Isaac paced up the middle of the throne room toward the dais. Servants who'd been dusting and sweeping rushed to stand invisible at the side of the room. "Announce the happy news to the monarchy. Make sure our neighboring kingdoms hear of it. We'll have a feast tomorrow to celebrate."

Hammond bowed as Isaac took his throne. "Right away, Your Majesty."

Isaac nodded and Hammond rose, leaving the throne room

swiftly with the rest of the servants. Isaac stared straight ahead, a slow smile spreading on his face. Letting out a breath, he clasped his fingers together and pushed them outward, stretching, the proud father-to-be.

CHAPTER

THIRTY-TWO

Ardenis watched Eva's progress over the next few months. He gave up looking elsewhere for Laida. There were too many possibilities of where she could be. Whenever he tried to look, his instincts always led him back here. He put all his hope in the possibility that she was nestled safely inside Eva, even if the entire kingdom claimed she carried a boy.

But what if it was Bram? They left Acantha at nearly the same time. It could very well be Bram that Eva carried and not Laida. The thought riddled him with guilt. He couldn't hope for better for one of them over the other. It was in the hands of the Fates.

Per Isaac's command, Eva remained in bed, and her belly grew steadily. She had a constant stream of visitors, between courtiers, servants, the physician, midwifes, well-wishers, and Isaac, who no longer slept in her bed for some ridiculous fear of harming the baby. People brought her food, and books. They read to her and kept her company. Baby gifts arrived from across the kingdom, ranging from furniture and clothing, to jewels and silver spoons.

Ardenis still watched nights. One good Fating and he'd be able to have his pick of watches, but until then, he remained stuck. Most of

273

what happened during the day came secondhand from Amalia or the bulletin board. Usually, he arrived early and worked past dawn so he could see Eva awake for himself. All of Acantha clamored for news, because, Laida or not, Eva carried the first elf in Thera—the potential for a new race.

Around seven months into the pregnancy, Ardenis watched Eva in her bed, when she woke up. She peered around the dark room, lit only by the light of the moon from the windows. She rolled out of bed, popped her feet into slippers, and then gazed at a sleeping Mary in a small cot across the room. Isaac no longer let Eva sleep by herself. Throwing on her robe, she took one last glance at Mary, who didn't stir under her thick quilt, and tiptoed out the door. Closing it softly behind her, she turned around to the surprised faces of her two door guards.

She jumped, placing her hand against her round stomach.

"Good evening, my queen," A guard said as they both bowed to her. He rose from his bow and glanced at his companion. "Is there something we can do for you?"

"Good evening," Eva said, though her eyes reflected irritation. "I'm off for a little stroll." And she turned down the hall away from them.

The guards exchanged glances, then chased after her. "My queen, we're under orders not to let you leave your room."

"By who?" She didn't glance back and didn't slow.

"Hammond, Your Majesty, and his order came from King Isaac."

"I outrank Hammond. Please return to your post." The guards made no move to do as ordered. Eva stopped and spun to face them. The guards skidded to a halt, their eyes wide. "I've given you an order, guards, and you will obey your queen."

They dropped into deep bows. "Yes, Your Majesty," they said in unison, then trudged back down the hall to their posts, watching her over their shoulders the whole way.

Eva turned and smiled, appearing satisfied. Ardenis watched as she made her through several hallways and downstairs to the kitchen. Countertops lined the large room, with shelves of stacked bowls and pan, herbs hanging upside down in rows, multiple ovens. Many people worked even this late at night, preparing the next day's dishes. All progress halted as Eva entered the room.

Everyone bowed, and Eva sighed. "Please rise, and someone get me some cake." She clambered onto a stool at a table in the middle of the room.

Cooks and kitchen maids scrambled to obey. Pots and plates clanked as arms flew and people bumped into each other. Puffs of powdered sugar clouded the air from several locations.

Five different people carried five different whole cakes on plates sprinkled with sugar, or drizzled with sauce, and presented them to their queen.

The oldest cook bowed. "Which would Your Majesty prefer?" He pointed as he listed them. "We have raspberry truffle, apple tart, chocolate mousse, orange crème, and iced vanilla sorbet with spring berries."

Eva placed her finger to her lips, looking at each plate. She smiled. "I'll have some of each."

The cook didn't hesitate. "Very good, Your Majesty." He nodded to the servants, and they flew into action.

Five smaller plates, each beautifully presented, were set before her. Her eyes widened in delight, and she picked up a fork and dug in. Each piece was but a small segment of the whole, and she ate them all to the last crumb, finishing it with a tall glass of milk.

"That was wonderful!" She dabbed her mouth with a napkin. "My compliments... Oh!" She smiled and put her hands to her belly. Ardenis focused and saw her stomach move as the baby kicked. She laughed. "My son sends his compliments as well."

The servants and cooks beamed. Eva shoved her body from the stool and waddled back toward her rooms. When she neared, approaching candlelight flickered on the wall, casting shadows across the intersecting corridor. Eva slowed, but didn't stop. She rounded the corner, and Isaac stood in front of her, along with Eva's door guards and several servants.

Irritation blazed in Isaac's eyes. "Eva, you're not to leave your bed," he hissed.

"I was hungry." She looked away. "Our son needed cake." She smiled and glanced back up at him.

A smile tried to break through his anger, but he wiped it away with a hand over his face. "Your guards will get whatever you need. This is my decree, Eva. It's for our son's protection. You will not leave your bed again."

She sucked in a breath, narrowing her eyes. "I'm tired of bed, Isaac. I will do as I please."

The servants behind Isaac gasped, glancing at each other. Isaac's gaze flicked behind him and then back toward Eva. "You will not defy your king." He grabbed her wrist, and her eyes widened in shock.

Ardenis slammed his hands on the marble ledge in the watch room. How could Isaac be so heartless to the woman he loves? Someone so innocent and in need of love and comfort after all she's been through.

"Take her to her room." Isaac pulled her toward Mary, then released her.

Eva turned back toward him, one hand on her belly, eyes full of hurt. "You're my king, but you're also my husband. We used to be so close. Don't only now push me aside for your kingly duties. I would never do anything to harm our child."

Isaac's eyes softened. Some of the tension left his shoulders. He looked at their audience, then approached Eva, putting his hand against her cheek. She leaned into his touch, and closed her eyes, clearly craving what she'd been denied for too long.

Isaac's voice was soft, pained. "Do you remember I told you my mother died during childbirth?"

Eva nodded against his palm.

"She went into early labor because she fell, tripped over her gown and tumbled down the stairs." He squeezed his eyes shut. "I won't let anything happen to you."

Ardenis sat back. He'd forgotten about Isaac's mother. Logic often left the mind in the wake of trauma.

Eva gasped. "I didn't know. I never realized. I'm—" Her hands shot to her stomach, and she winced in pain. "Oh!" She cried out, hissing through her teeth. She reached and grabbed onto Isaac's arm.

Isaac's mouth gaped open, and his eyes sought Mary. "What's happening?" he cried in alarm.

Mary pushed through the narrow hall to Eva's side. "My queen?" she asked, darting a look from Isaac to Eva and back again.

Eva shook her head, eyes clinched shut, breathing in short bursts. Tears leaked down her face.

"Get her to her bed, now!" Isaac yelled. "Fetch the physician!"

Mary and the guards surrounded Eva, picking her up. They carried her quickly, but gently the short distance to her bed, setting her down with care. Eva turned to her side, curling into a ball.

Isaac knelt next to her, rubbing his hand over her back. "What can I do?" he asked.

"It's nothing... he's stretching." She placed her hands tighter into her stomach, opening her eyes. "That's better," she breathed. "I'm holding his foot from kicking my ribs."

Isaac's eyes were as big as saucers, and his mouth hung open in horror. Romand burst into the room, wearing his robe and rubbing sleep from his eyes.

"I'm okay," Eva said. "He just rolled into the wrong position. We're okay now." She smiled and sank into her pillows.

Isaac rose unsteadily to his feet, holding a hand to his chest. He moved aside so Romand could take over.

"Never again, Eva," Isaac said between shaking breaths. "You're not to leave your bed again. I'll not risk his health. Or yours." He ran a hand over his paled face and left the room.

Eva stared after him, the physician poking and prodding her belly, and fresh tears ran down her face.

Ardenis let out a slow sigh.

⬦

Isaac stayed away from Eva after that night. Ardenis watched him sit in his throne room, constantly asking about her and the baby, but never visiting. At night, he would look in on her, whether to check on her wellbeing or to ensure she indeed stayed in her room, Ardenis couldn't say. Isaac had a lock installed on the outside of the door, ensuring Eva would enjoy no more late-night strolls.

Eva grew angry and bitter. Ardenis didn't agree with the way Isaac treated her, even if his overprotectiveness was born of deep-rooted fear and pain. At the same time, the baby, who could have been Laida, was safe from the dangers of the castle and outside threats.

"Would you like me to read your favorite book again, Queen Eva?" Mary asked, holding it up, the word *Lyria* printed on the cover. "You've always loved the forbidden romance, even if it's too predictable for my tastes," she added under her breath.

Eva narrowed her eyes. "I'm sick of that book." Mary opened her mouth to speak. "I'm sick of all these books." Eva pushed herself up. "I'm sick of every book in every library in every kingdom in all of Thera." She grabbed handfuls of her blanket. "You know what I need? The story of a young farmhand named Damian and his true love. *That's* a story of forbidden love."

"Yes, Your Majesty. Would you be so kind as to tell me the name of the book? I will get it for you at once."

Eva sighed and fell back into her pillows. She stared at the grey clouds outside the window and a quiet tear slipped down her cheek. "It's called Injustice, but no copies exist anymore. They were destroyed and left out in the rain to ruin."

"I'm sorry, Your Majesty. It sounds like a good story."

"It was," Eva said, sadness ringing in her voice. She cradled her bulging belly. "It was," she whispered.

Ardenis ended his watch in the late morning, head hanging. Eva's melancholy tormented him. Isaac was an idiot. He would have given anything to have Laida's love. Anything. Isaac had the love of a beautiful, compassionate woman, and he squandered it. Mortals could be so dense. He hoped he wasn't that foolish when he became mortal.

He wandered to the dining hall for some breakfast before going home.

"Ardenis," Amalia called, smiling from down the path.

"Good morning, Amalia." He stopped and waited for her to catch up, falling in step beside her.

"Good morning. Anything new in Thera?" she asked.

"Isaac is still ignoring her." He sighed. "He's driving a wedge between them with his controlling foolishness, afraid of history repeating itself."

She echoed his sigh. "I know. I'd give anything to experience reciprocated love. They don't appreciate what they could have. Though I'd say Isaac's love is more obsessive now."

Ardenis smiled. They were very in tune to each other these days. She swept her braided hair behind her. "Do you think it's Laida?" She didn't look at him.

He glanced at her. "I don't know. I hope, but... you know."

She nodded. "Yes, I do. I looked forever for my Maven, but doubt I ever found him."

Amalia stopped abruptly, and Ardenis glanced up at her. She stared straight ahead. He followed her gaze to where Hector had just entered their path, blatant hate smoldering in his eyes.

"I see you two have become friendly." The remorseful tone he'd had at the High Council was completely gone. "I'm still watching you. You'll slip up. When I become enforcer again, I'll make sure to—"

"Hector," Amalia said. "It's never going to happen. Leave us be." She linked arms with Ardenis.

Hector clenched his jaw and pointed at them. "I will be an enforcer again. Or maybe I'll become a watcher."

Amalia rolled her eyes.

Hector growled, grit his teeth, and stormed into the dining hall.

Ardenis's smile wavered at the guilt he felt holding Amalia's arm. He tried to ignore it. No matter the reason, he'd tried to hurt Laida. And Hector still thought he held authority over them.

Amalia pulled her arm from Ardenis, proof she'd done it just to rile Hector. They exchanged grins.

"Come on," she said. "Let's enjoy our meal."

"Sounds grand, my friend."

THIRTY-THREE

I n the final two months of Eva's pregnancy, Ardenis watched as she declined, both in spirit and in health. It was as if her husband's rejection had taken her fighting strength. Ardenis rooted and prayed for her, but each trip to the watch window only worried him more, and she didn't get better.

Word of her infirmity spread, and mages from all the major schools in the continent offered their services. Queen Vatrice even sent Allister to render aid, but, like a fool, Isaac sent them all away after the first mage left Eva crying in fear for her baby's wellbeing. Though mages were mainly renowned for healing injuries and not sickness, any help would have been better than none. Except maybe Allister. Ardenis did not trust him or his queen.

One month before she was due to give birth, Ardenis arrived early for the night watch, but she was already asleep, and still asleep when his watch ended, so he stayed on. The sun rose, but the room remained dim behind the closed curtains. Eva finally roused when Mary came in with a bowl of soup and forced her awake.

"My queen, I'm sorry, but you must eat to keep up your strength." Mary shook Eva's shoulder.

Eva's eyes were crusted shut, but she rubbed at them and they fluttered open. Mary fluffed a pillow behind her head, sitting her up slightly, and then opened the curtains.

Ardenis gasped. Eva's face had drained of all color except a yellowish tint accented by a thin sheet of sweat. Her brown curls were a matted mess. She fumbled feebly at her twisted nightgown—the same one she'd worn the day before.

He shook his head in disbelief. This wasn't depression. It wasn't like Eva to give up. She'd lived through the loss of Damian and persevered. Eva was sick.

Mary turned from the window and clasped a hand over her mouth. She took a shaking breath and pulled a stool next to the bed, picking up the soup. The spoon clinked against the bowl as her hands trembled. Eva ate each bite with a blank expression. After the sixth spoonful, Eva shook her head, refusing more.

Mary set down the soup, then dipped a rag into a bowl of water and mopped Eva's forehead. "What's wrong, my queen? Why won't you eat? Your son needs you to eat."

"I don't feel right, Mary." Eva said listlessly. "Tell Damian I'm sorry."

Mary wrung her hands, glancing at the door. "You have to come out of it, Eva. You have to get better before something happens to you or the baby."

Mary stepped out to the hall and had a guard summon the physician. She rung her hands, eyes creased with worry until he finally arrived.

"What is it, Mary?" Romand asked, glancing toward Eva's door.

"I don't know what to make of it." Her voice shook. "She's out of her mind. She'll barely eat." She leaned in closer and whispered, "She's having visions of story book characters and such."

"Ardenis."

A hand on his shoulder pulled him from Thera. He blinked and glanced up, his blurry vision slowly bringing Amalia's concerned face into focus. She leaned down close.

"Ardenis, my friend, you look pained," she whispered. "Others are beginning to notice. Perhaps it's time you give Thera some distance."

He grabbed her shoulders and pulled her closer. "Eva's not well," he said, voice cracking. "I could be watching her last moments on Thera."

"Use your head, Arden. You've fated her birth of the elf. You know she lives."

Amalia's use of Laida's nickname for him washed over his anguish like cold water, forcing him to his senses. He nodded. She was right. "Watch over her, please. Let me know how she is. I'll be back after dinner."

"Get some rest." She stood back to let him rise.

He took a breath, glancing around and catching a few pairs of eyes. No one else seemed to notice or care about their exchange. He stood and left the tower, heading home.

He managed to squeeze in a few hours of sleep, but awoke before dinner. He tossed the blankets off, threw on a blue robe, and walked with fast steps back to the tower.

Amalia was sitting deep in her watch when Ardenis arrived and took his usual seat. He almost interrupted her to ask about the events of the day, but instead gazed at the white marble pool until it glowed, opening the window into Thera. He quickly took his gaze to Eva.

She lay on her side in bed, dozing fitfully, still in the same grimy nightgown. Taking shallow breaths, she moaned. Mary paced the floor, and it surprised Ardenis to see Isaac. He sat slumped in a chair at Eva's side, head resting in his hand with his fingers shoved through his unkempt hair. His other hand clutched a fistful of Eva's nightgown. When Isaac glanced up, Ardenis saw his splotchy face and swollen eyes.

Ardenis gasped. Had the physician given them bad news? What had he missed?

They sat like that for what seemed like forever—a long time to an

Acanthian. Then Eva twitched, and her eyes slowly opened. Isaac grabbed her hand, stroking it too fast to be comforting.

"Eva, my love. You're awake." He dashed tears from his eyes and gave a forced smile.

"Isaac?" Eva tried to sit up, but lacked the strength. "What are you doing here?"

Isaac's face crumpled. "I'm so sorry, my love." He put his forehead to the back of her hand. "I should never have left you alone. I shouldn't have made that ridiculous rule you had to stay in bed." Tears splattered her hand. "I thought I was protecting you."

"Shhh." Eva rubbed his hair and smiled weakly. "I understand, my king. I've missed you so. It's been lonely without you and only little Isaac to keep me company."

Mary's gaze dropped to the ground. Isaac cried harder, his body shaking with sobs.

"Please don't leave me, Eva."

Eva's half-closed eyes opened up wide. "Leave you? My feelings were hurt, but I'd never leave you, Damian."

Isaac's head snapped up, and his mouth dropped open. His gaze went to Mary.

Ardenis gripped the marble ledge of the watch window. Anguish hit him anew. She was really sick. Her illness had taken her thoughts back to her lost love. Would she be heartbroken when she learned whom she was truly speaking to?

Mary nodded. "There she goes again, Your Majesty, carrying on about some storybook character. The physician said it's the fever talking, but he can't bleed her for fear of harming the baby."

Eva shook her head against the pillow. "What are you two carrying on about?"

Isaac squeezed her hand. "How about some broth, my love? You need to eat."

"Maybe later, Isaac. I'm not hungry at the moment. Though I'm so sleepy." She closed her eyes.

Isaac took a glass of water from Mary. It sloshed in his hand.

"Eva." He shook her. "Drink this. For me." He raised her head and placed it to her lips. She drank a few sips without opening her eyes. Most of it dribbled down her face onto the pillow.

With shaking hands, Isaac set the glass down on a tray. He stood, backing up until he reached the door. "Keep trying to get her to drink, Mary." He fumbled for the handle. "I'll be back later to check on her." Isaac flung open the door and rushed out. It hit the wall and bounced back, closing hard behind him.

Mary jumped. Eva did not stir.

Ardenis left Thera and looked up to find Amalia watching him. Her worried gaze told him she'd seen everything in that sickroom. Their shared fears latched hands across the room.

❦

Ardenis and Amalia watched Eva closely as the following days passed. Having opposite shifts worked to their advantage. Both of them viewed longer than required, so they overlapped, ensuring they had eyes on her at all times. Amalia insisted her instincts didn't pull her elsewhere. They were bound in this.

Two weeks before Eva's due date, in the middle of the day, Ardenis lay in his bed at home, sleeping. A knock on his door woke him up.

"Ardenis," a man called out.

He shot out of bed, tossed on his robe, and tied it with fumbling fingers as he rushed to the door. He flung it open and beheld Wes, a day watcher.

"I apologize for waking you, Ardenis," Wes said with agonizing slowness. "Amalia sent me to retrieve you to the tower. She said it was most important."

Ardenis gasped and rushed by Wes, not bothering to close his door. He ran as hard as he could to the tower until he burst into the watch room. Who cared about keeping up the unemotional pretenses?

285

"Amalia! What's wrong with her?"

Everyone startled out of their watch, including Amalia. Some raised their eyebrows at his outburst. Amalia opened her eyes wide.

"It's time, Arden. You better hurry." Mouth in a tight line, she glanced back to the watch window, her gaze going unfocused.

Ardenis shot to his chair, ignoring the curious looks. He focused into Thera as fast as he ever had. His instincts screamed at him the whole way, until he found her.

Eva lay in her bed, sweat pouring off her, soaking her white gown through. She panted and moaned, weaker than other mothers he'd seen. Eva labored, too frail and lacking the energy to support her body. Pillows stacked behind her propped her up. Maids and midwives surrounded her, preparing towels and blankets, and bowls of water. A midwife attempted to poke a thread through a needle, missed, and tried again. Romand held his fingers to Eva's wrist, checking her pulse. Isaac was nowhere in sight.

The regular furniture had been moved out. In its place, chairs now filled the expansive room, supporting all manner of lords and ladies. They watched Eva labor and waited for the birth of the baby —undeniable legitimacy of the heir to the throne, a practice that had never sickened Ardenis before he'd become emotionally aware. It did now.

Mary mopped Eva's head with a moist cloth, while another maid fanned her. Eva's damp hair stuck to her forehead. Her cheeks were hollow, her sunken eyes closed. Her chest rose and fell with the deep breaths of sleep for a few minutes.

Then she awoke, clutching at her belly and moaning in pain. While she panted through the contraction, servants brought food and drink to the watching courtiers. They mingled and ate, oblivious to the state of their queen, though some watched on with morbid curiosity, waving off the trays of wine and sweetmeats.

The pattern of sleep and waking through the pain continued into the night for some hours. Then, as the sun began to rise, Eva's pain seemed to reach a new intensity. She no longer dozed between contractions, and her moans turned into screams.

"It's time to push, Queen Eva," Romand said. He sat on a stool at the end of her bed. Midwives held both her legs, for she lacked the strength. "I want you to push with the next contraction."

"I can't," she cried weakly through closed eyes, oblivious to her audience. Ardenis doubted she noticed anything at this point. He sent a silent prayer for her to find the strength she needed.

"You can, my queen," Mary called out from beside her. "Your son needs you to be strong now."

Eva took a shuddering breath. She screamed as she pushed. When she'd expended all her air, she collapsed, exhausted, onto the bed.

She did this several more times.

"I can see his hair, Your Majesty!" Mary exclaimed. "Oh, he has thick hair." She smiled and covered her mouth. Behind her, courtiers clinked glasses and scooted to the edge of their seats, leaning for better views. Ardenis looked away, stomach roiling.

After another quarter hour, Ardenis gasped, staring wide-eyed at the familiar scene. His Fating of the first elf had caught up to him.

"That's it, push! He's almost here." Mary said.

With a scream of effort, Eva pushed with all her might. Romand assisted by pulling as she pushed, and the baby came the rest of the way out. Eva sagged back against the pillows, panting and shaking. Mary cut the umbilical cord, and the physician held the infant up for the room to see.

Gasps rang out from wall to wall.

It was a girl. A beautiful baby girl with pointed ears. Ardenis's hands splayed on the edge of the marble pool. His heart sped tenfold.

Moments later, the newborn's first cry filled the room. Filled the world. Filled his soul. The sound pinned him to the floor. Breathing escaped him. It was the most beautiful sound he'd ever heard.

King Isaac burst into the room, smiling from ear to ear.

"A girl," he said. "Eva just knew it was a boy, but I had a feeling it was a girl." He shook hands with the closest courtiers. He went down the line, receiving claps on the back and words of congratulations, even as the lords and ladies glanced uneasily toward the baby. "How's my Eva?"

Eva lay forgotten by the masses, with only Romand tending to her. Isaac left the courtiers and stepped up to the bed. Next to him, Mary bathed the newborn with damp cloths, trading soiled ones for clean as she went. The baby wailed, but quieted as Mary poured warm water over her head.

Isaac paused, eyes going wide. He pointed, mouth agape.

"Her ears!" He glanced around, meeting the eyes of his court. He sidled over to the physician. "What's wrong with her ears?"

Ardenis barely noticed the baby's ears. Mary had finished washing her hair. It was short but shone as gold as the sun.

As gold as Laida's.

Romand's mouth formed a tight line. He shook his head, refusing to answer Isaac and break his concentration from where he still worked on Eva. Isaac's eyes trailed down, and his face washed white with horror. There was so much blood.

"Her cry is magical," Eva said, her voice a whisper. "Give her to me."

Isaac trembled. "Eva, my love?" His words shook. He stepped to her side, placing his hand on her forehead. "She's so pale. What's wrong with her?"

Ardenis tore his gaze from the baby and focused on Eva. Her eyelids were half closed. Blood was everywhere, more than what was normal. Romand's shoulders sagged. Ardenis pulled at his hair.

Mary swaddled the baby and placed her to Eva's chest. The baby quieted down, instinctively snuggling closer. Eva offered her bare breast to the infant who latched on, suckling.

Eva smiled. "Faelyn," she whispered.

She kissed the baby's forehead, and then closed her eyes, never to open them again.

CHAPTER
THIRTY-FOUR

D *ead.*

Ardenis ripped his gaze from the bloody scene. He couldn't watch the fallout of Eva's death. Breath came in strangled gulps. His eyes bore into the white pool. Strange. The water rippled, he noted absently.

Warm hands pulled his grip from the marble, and the rippling stopped. Amalia. His friend. He'd been trembling, shaking the pool.

He couldn't be here, in front of all these witnesses, when the inevitable breakdown hit.

He stood and walked out of the tower. Amalia's steps sounded behind him as he circled around, deeper into the rose garden. He felt outside of himself, like it wasn't his legs that carried him. Dawn's golden hues touched upon the perfect blooms, mocking him. He sat hard on a bench, clutching his middle and rocking back and forth. Amalia put her arm around his shoulder.

"I'm sorry, Arden." She squeezed. "Mortals die. Eva is with Damian in the Hereafter now."

He cleared his throat. He didn't know where to begin. "I can't believe she's dead. She can't be. She had nothing but pain and loneliness her whole life."

"But she had love. Don't let her fate be your undoing here. Be strong for her."

Yes, she had love, and she'd paid for it, as if her time in misery wasn't enough to make up for the true love she'd experienced, so the Fates took her life. "I... I feel so empty, Amalia. Nothing prepared me for this kind of pain." He grabbed at his heart.

First Damian and now Eva. Two innocent souls who'd suffered so much at the hands of love. They'd lived for it, sacrificed for it, bled and died for it. Eva was supposed to be a mother to Faelyn. Her happy innocence had graced Thera and was gone too soon. Was she happy now that she suffered no more? Would she watch over her daughter in death? Had Damian and Eva found each other in the Hereafter?

Yes. He believed that. Just like he believed he'd see Laida again someday.

Ardenis took a deep breath and straightened up. Amalia dropped her arm.

"That's Laida down there. Did you see? The baby girl with the pointed ears and the golden hair. Faelyn. I'm certain of it." His gaze became unfocused. "Laida just lost her mother."

Amalia shook her head. "You can't be sure—"

"Don't tell me I'm wrong." His voice came out harsher than he meant it to, emotions overruling control. "I trust my instincts. It's her, and I promised I'd watch over her. I will watch over her."

Amalia gave a tight smile. "You may be right, Ardenis. Either way, something this important will need the devotion of a dedicated watcher. I don't doubt you could convince the council for it to be you."

He nodded, considering. He'd do it with or without their approval, but with would be best if he wanted to remain discreet during his time in Acantha. Rhea's words about the High Council watching him came back to him.

"Thank you for helping me, Amalia. I can't go back in there right now." He shuddered at the thought of seeing them handle Eva's body. He couldn't watch Isaac's grief knowing it would be everything he wanted to do, but couldn't because he was Acanthian.

"I'll report my findings to the council," he said. "I'll come back for my regular night watch. Perhaps the both of us could observe her, like we did for Eva." His words sounded normal, logical, but his mind had gone numb from the shock of it—Eva's death, Laida's beginning. She was safe. She'd made it to Thera unharmed, despite Gharum and Hector's best efforts.

The only thing keeping him grounded, keeping the tears at bay, was the thought of that baby girl. "I'm never going to see her again, am I?"

Amalia placed a hand on his shoulder. "Remember to do your duty as a watcher, Arden. You'll be all right." She met his eyes. "You never know what the Fates have waiting to surprise you with."

The council posted the report of Eva's death and Faelyn's birth on the bulletin board in the courtyard later that afternoon. Before long, the news traveled to all Acanthians. Ardenis endured, too busy watching and grieving in the days that followed to listen to the bittersweet gossip.

While he mourned for Eva, Amalia remained his steadfast friend. Damian's death had been much harder to bear. He'd been new to it. That experience had been his first to deal with the pain of a mortal death. He'd bore it and was stronger for it, but Eva's life and death mattered too, and the pain wasn't any less. Damian and Eva had been the one to show him love, to show him what it really meant to live and care for someone. Theirs was a precious gift he'd always cherish.

That gift had changed him. He was no longer like any other soul in Acantha. And that was okay.

Only Amalia shared his secret suspicions about Laida being born as Faelyn. As an elf, being unique and unprecedented, her life was bound to be difficult. He would keep his vow to watch over her until the Fates decided otherwise.

More than anything, she was the one who gave him strength and comfort. He found reassurance each time he looked into the watch window onto Thera, and Faelyn. Maybe Fate would help them find each other again. The words in her letter reassured and reminded him he existed for a purpose. This didn't have to be The End.

ACKNOWLEDGMENTS

There are so many people to thank here. Writing a book is a lot like raising children—it takes a village. But first I'd like to thank my husband, Jonathan. From the very first word I wrote back when I knew nothing except the kernel of a dream that had taken root inside me, he supported and encouraged me.

I want to thank my parents for my childhood, from my dad telling me stories with funny voices and silly wigs, to my mom patiently writing down the ideas that came into my head even before I knew how to write.

My daughters, for their support and their never-ending curiosity and questions—one of which sparked this series.

My sister-in-law, Rachel, for being one of my first beta-readers and one of my biggest supporters. She never tired of hearing me vent or letting me run story ideas with her.

My friend Christina, for catching last-minute typos and giving me honest feedback, which mostly consisted of how awesome she thinks the series is.

Author Sally Britton, for taking me under her wing and sharing her wisdom as I navigated the publishing journey.

I'd also like to thank Scribophile, the online writing community that really pushed me to the next level. There are many who shaped me into the writer I am today: John Hamilton, Elizabeth Giambrone, Nancy Fudge, and the Ubergroup, to name a small few. If I hadn't found that website when I did, I wouldn't be where I am today.

And finally, I'd like to thank you, the reader. Thank you for starting this journey with me. Here's to many more adventures together.

ABOUT THE AUTHOR

Kristin L Hamblin was born and raised in Tulsa, Oklahoma, and grew up with a deep desire to own a unicorn. When that didn't pan out, she decided the next best thing was to write about worlds where fantastical things are possible. She reads and writes stories containing magic and love. Kristin lives in Oklahoma with her husband, raising their four daughters and a menagerie of pets, including two wiener dogs, Ruby and Sunny.

Kristin loves her readers and loves getting to know them! Connect with her on social media or say hello and join her newsletter at kristinlhamblin.com

facebook.com/kristinlhamblin

instagram.com/authorkristinlhamblin

tiktok.com/@authorkristinlhamblin

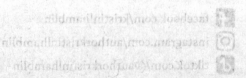